COFFEE SMUGGLER

*An Adventure Based on the
True Story of Gabriel De Clieu
who Brought Coffee
to the Americas in 1723*

Dave Holman

Dedicated to my
Grandpa and Grandma
Alexander and Adele Holman
who encouraged me constantly to
write and publish this story.

www.dave-holman.com

© 2014 Dave Holman. All rights reserved.
ISBN 978-0-9862450-0-8
First Edition. First Printing of 250 copies
November, 2014

Design/editing: Katie Murphy | univoicehistory.com

Printed in Portland, Maine by Walch Printing
on 100% recycled paper.

Front cover image of Gabriel de Clieu used with
permission by Derek Anderson of www.coffeeroad.dk
original work from Michéle Bertiers' Petite Anthologie
du Café.

Back cover image: 1720 Map of the West Indies with
the Adjacent Coasts of North and South America by
Emanuel Bowen (1694-1767)

Publishers

My sincere thanks to 73 backers from 8 countries who supported
Coffee Smuggler's Kickstarter campaign, raising $3,514 towards a goal of $3,100.
This allowed me to hire professional designers, e-book formatters,
create marketing materials, design a better website, and print the first edition
paperback and hardcovers books. These generous people provided me
with more motivation and concrete support than most first-time authors receive
from traditional publishing companies. **To all my backers, thank you!**

❧ Swashbuckler · $500+
John Moore, Nobletree Coffee (nobletreecoffee.com)

❧ Bucanneers · $100+
Andrew Bartels • Oscar Boyson • Jason Carpenter • Eric Fitz
Ari & Heather Guhlers • Luke 'BARTELS!' Hasskamp
Adele & Alex Holman • Mary Jackson • Aaron Leconte
Jason 'J-Lo' Lord • Shy Mukerjee • Susanna Place • Joshua Seely
Shane Squires • Aaron & Susan Shapiro • Amrit Tuladhar

❧ Skippers · $50+
Laura Allred • Matt Hawkins • William P. Fleischmann
Eric 'Heyyyy Brother' Holman • Lewis & Mary Holman
Janet & Rick Parmer • Portland Food Map • Colin Witherill

❧ First Mates · $25+
Evan Allen • Susan Attermeier • Chelsea Holden Baker
Beth • Caitlin Canfield • Kellie Carim • Jennifer Goff • Ben Hahn
Katharina • Beth Kracum • Marmæl • Owen Mcgillicuddy
Joel Osgood • Nick Pascarella • Margaret Porter • Arne Radtke
Claudia Risch • Duncan Scherer • Brian Sprague
Matthew J. Swenson • Mark U. • Mimi Wan

❧ Coffee Smugglers · ‹$25
Becky B • Bernard C. La Borie • Berhardt Coffee (bernhardtcoffee.com)
Ellie Burke • Steve Cook • James Cooney • Holger Durer
Rob Dominick • Erika • Hayly Holman • Jessica Goad • Evan Jensen
Jess • Kirk & Erica Mazuzan • Marie McKinley • Cédryck Mimault
Mark Moskovitz • Caroline Ring • Peter 'Peaches' Robbins
Nathaniel Rosenblum • Christina Schumann • Matt Seaver
Scott Squires • Sue • Hannah Ulbrich

ACKNOWLEDGEMENTS

At six in the morning when I wanted nothing more than the blissful non-existence of sleep, my alarm would go off and I'd hit snooze. My wife Rommy would give me a little push. Half asleep, she'd mumble, "Go rye yer book," and give me a harder push. I'd ooze my way out of the warm bed and into a trance-like state where my only concern was to make coffee before falling down. After some NPR news and caffeine, I'd sit down for my daily (or not-so-daily) hour or two of writing and research before work. Without Rommy this book wouldn't exist. *I love you Ro.*

Also at the top of my thank you list are my four editors. Three of them also happen to be my mom Mary Suter Holman and my grandparents Adele and Alex Holman. Without their loving mix of encouragement and editorial criticism, you'd be holding a very different (worse) book. My fourth editor is a published author who spent dozens of hours coaching me on how to edit my writing. He wishes to remain anonymous and has my heartfelt thanks.

I owe an enormous debt in the writing of this story to the authors and friends who provided me with research and encouragement. I must thank the heroes on the Interlibrary Loan Staff of the University of Southern Maine who somehow tracked down a paper copy of De Clieu's 1774 letter, scanned it, and emailed it to me. Amazing.

Thanks to Tom Standage, author of *A History of the World in Six Glasses,* who initially encouraged me to write this story. A posthumous thanks to William H. Ukers, whose titanic tome *All About Coffee* provided me with many fruitful leads.

Others deserving great thanks for their help and patience include Maureen Stanton for her advice and connections, humorist Roy Blount, my fourth-grade writing teacher Donna Colbeth, intrepid mariner Jenny Goff, Martinique-connoisseur Jean Christophe Moran, madman and motivator Shy Mukerjee, publisher of Islandport Press Dean Lunt, Dan O'Brien, Shane Squires, and Allison Bundy of the Brown University Library.

FACT AND FICTION

Coffee Smuggler mixes the gin of fiction with the tonic of truth and I want to allow you to distinguish in what proportions this drink has been mixed.

For instance, most of the major events and dates are historically accurate and researched, while all the dialogue springs from my imagination. Descriptions of places and events are all based in historic fact while most of De Clieu's daily actions are not. This story recounts every documented fact of De Clieu's life that I could find in four years of research, but when facts were lacking (and this was often!) I wrote what might have been.

This is fitting because historians think De Clieu did some embellishing of his own career in the only known account he published just before he died at the astoundingly old age of 88. With the help of a librarian, I obtained the original French letter he published in the 1774 *L'Annee Litteraire* Vol 6, page 217. This tantalizing document is the source of much that has been written about De Clieu in the past 240 years. I have included the original French letter and a translation in the back of the book along with a list of the sources that provided helpful information and background, most notably Ukers' infamous tome *All About Coffee*.

Also in the back of the book you'll find a list by chapter of fact from fiction. You may want to skip ahead and read that now so that you can chew the savory meal of history whilst pulling out the bones of fiction. Or you may choose to read this afterwards and perhaps be surprised by the fiction that seemed real and the actual events that seemed like fiction. Or you may be like me and not read introductions, synopses, and bibliographies at all and just dive into a story, and enjoy a grand adventure.

Chapter I
Desmarest's Pilorie

Just after sunrise on March 12th, 1719, with mist still clinging to the sugarcane, a muskrat bit me right through my leather boot and dove into the bushes. I hobbled to my plantation to find Pierre.

Pierre frowned, "Sir, I heard Doctor Scie was in Le Carbet attending Colonel Petit's mistress. Perhaps he's back now."

I smiled, "Quite the mistress that Petit has, eh?"

"Yes, sir!"

I pulled down my gray stocking to reveal the wound. Pierre examined it, slapped his thigh and declared, "*Megalomys desmarestii*, Desmarest's Pilorie!"

"*Mon Dieu!* That sounds like a terrible infection. I thought you were a doorman in Paris before you got shipped out here, not a Latin scholar?"

Pierre chuckled, "Did it smell musky?"

"Very musky."

"It looks infected, shall I get the rum?"

"Why not?" I gave my leg half of the bottle and we split the rest. We prepared to head in to Saint-Pierre to call on the doctor, just in case. Pierre walked outside, wet a finger and thrust it towards the flawless blue sky. Fragile wisps of cloud curled along the far eastern horizon like a line of horses' tails.

"If we must depart, let us do so now. It may storm by tomorrow, wind's out of the west. You are stationed in the garrison next week, right? Drilling those new recruits?"

"Ugh, yes. Let me put on my uniform. You gather some food for the coming days, and we'll head down to Saint-Pierre."

Pierre filled a wicker backpack with bananas, mamey apples, cassava and, of course, more rum. Then we drank like cattle from the Rivier du Prêcheur that flowed by my plantation. Squinting in the bright sun, I gazed up towards the towering cone of Mount Pelée, or *Le Volcan Debonaire* as the socialites in Saint-Pierre liked to call her. She was active this week, producing an eggy mountain flatulence.

Along the trail, songbirds gossiped from the swaying coconut trees and foliage. A spectacled thursh swooped and yanked up an earthworm right before my feet, yanking the poor sluggard out of his hole and carrying him aloft. I stumbled backwards as a venomous fer de lance exploded out of the undergrowth, missing the bird as it rose. Fortunately, the reptile snapped across the path and disappeared into the wet bushes as fast as it had emerged.

Vines grew on vines growing on trees that looked like vines. The relentless undergrowth reclaimed fields cleared hardly a month earlier so the slaves never rested. Every footstep on Martinique's mountainous slopes went either up or down, never flat. I rounded a dense stand of house-sized ferns and my leg began to ache again.

Here the trees still grew over two hundred feet tall, because cutting and hauling them from this green hell was not worth the effort. I sat down on a log to rest, puffing and blowing like a baleen whale. A pandemonium of white butterflies scattered from the log and flew up to brilliant orchids and bromeliads dangling from branches above. Pierre moved to speak but I silenced him.

Something was tickling my back. My hand encountered bumps moving on me and I instinctively snatched them off with a jerk. All at once my body lit up with pain from my feet to my shoulders! Regiments of ants sent lightning bolts through my nerves. I screamed like an impaled jaguar and became a whirlwind of swatting, cursing, and stamping.

Pierre dumped an entire bottle of rum down my back and over my head. Apparently, ants can't handle their liquor because the attacking army ordered a retreat. I drew air into my lungs and savored the end of my anguish. Relief lasted only a few moments as one hundred bites began burning.

I scoured the earth, suspicious of every stick and leaf. Pierre brandished a full bottle of rum. I took a long pull that boiled down my throat.

"How does the muskrat bite feel now? All better?"

I cursed Pierre's mother and raised the bottle for another drink. Pierre chuckled and patted me gently on the back. I stiffened and inhaled in pain.

"Look closer at this tree behind you, but don't get too close. Yuku ants. Spaniards call the tree *palo santo*."

The bark was gray with hundreds of holes and a reddish tone that came from ants teeming over every square inch of trunk, branches, and leaves.

"Monsieur Girard ties his slaves to these trees for an hour if they're out of line. Imagine that. That's why that slave Leonce went mad," said Pierre. I muttered something about tying Pierre to it and hoisted myself up to continue towards the Dujon plantation.

CHAPTER 2

CHUMMY

The land was an ocean of undulating sugar cane. The Dujon distillery soiled the pristine sky like an octopus squirting ink. I hailed young Emile Dujon who led four slaves carrying heaps of sugar cane.

Sugar prices had fallen for the past several years due to increased production on Martinique and the Windward Isles. The ill effects of hurricanes, floods, and disease made matters worse. Martinique boasted a coterie of sugar barons like the Dujons, but they didn't like to mingle. Certainly not with soldiers like me. The slaves and common folk called them and their descendants *békés*.

As the paths widened into the tiny cluster of homes that formed the village of Le Prêcheur, I heard the familiar creak of cartwheels. Two old slaves strained to haul a cart heaped high with sugar cane. They churned through deep black mud on the path to Saint-Pierre where the distilleries gobbled up raw cane and spat out refined molasses, rum, and sugar.

Thanks to speculators and politicians back in France, few of the small Martinique planters like me saw much profit from our labor, just enough to keep us in business. The idea of saving was almost unheard of. We bankrupted ourselves on alcohol and prostitutes to the degree that death was not an uncommon result of receiving the monthly salary.

Outside town hundreds of barrels of rum and molasses sat stacked on the beach. At the shore, a man called Chummy stood coiling rope by a fishing boat. Forty years of fish grease lubricated the bottom of the boat better than whale oil. Chummy got up from his filthy seat and extended a leathery hand. I grasped it and bid him good day as Pierre stood back respectfully. Six fat bonitos and a grouper my own size oozed over each other in the bottom of the boat. I presumed them dead until one suddenly twitched and made a gasping noise. Chummy snapped the oar out of the oarlock and swung it over his head and down onto the offending bonito.

He turned and smiled, his teeth reminding me of encrusted coral. "Caught ese big uns here early, hungry they were!" Chummy heaved the mast up into its lock and began threading lines. He then stopped. His eyes narrowed to dark slits under the furnace-like sun. He professed abruptly, "From a young age, I wanted to be a commodities trader."

"What's a commodity trader?" I asked. I had an inkling, but hearing it from Chummy would be dandy.

He gave a crack-toothed smile. "Why, it's like instead of me being a fisherman, I could be a fishmonger. Like that except I don't monger actual fishes, but buy and sell contracts for fishes among other commodity traders."

I paused, "So you want to be a fishmonger?"

"No, sir, fishmongers still have to deal with these slimy monsters."

He kicked the grouper, which flopped and then lay still.

"No, sir, commodities traders buy shares of incoming cargoes on mercantile exchanges and then they sell them to the highest bidder. They never see the actual cargoes or get fish smell on them. They're all fabulously rich, sir, like King Louis hisself."

Chummy summoned up a fearful wad of spit that fell near my feet. I congratulated him on his ambitions and excused myself to go find the doctor.

Dr. Scie squinted at my skin, coming so close that his pipe tickled my ear. He lurched back, brushing his white hair out of his eyes and back under his hat. "Mother of Jesus, these ant bites... I would have sworn you had pox and declared a quarantine... Pele's been pretty grumpy recently, eh? Did you feel that rumble last night?... So, how's your wife? Aurélie is her name, right?"

"Still dead. God rest her soul."

Dr. Scie leaned back and took out his pipe, red faced. "Oh, *merde*, De Clieu, what a fool I am! I knew that. Yellow fever, wasn't it? Such bad airs we have sometimes."

"No, fer de lance got her ankle. There are whole nests of them up where I've cleared in Prêcheur. My Pierre parts them in half in the fields with his cutlass."

"You let your slave have a weapon? Tsk, tsk! Let me tell you how my first wife died. Indian attack!"

He went on, running his hands over my bites and down to my aching leg. "The Caribs didn't leave this island willingly, you know!" I knew. "Oh no, we had to fight for every inch. Did you know that bay you pass on the road is called the Tomb of the Caribs because that's where we won the final battle to kick them off Martinique?" I knew. Everyone knew. Dr. Scie told and retold these old stories in the taverns of Saint-Pierre. He cleaned my wound with cotton swabs and a bucket of near-boiling seawater as I clenched my teeth. He rambled on as he worked and tied the final bandage. "Hurt much?"

"Indeed it does, Doctor."

"Good. You haven't lost feeling, then. Should heal within a week. If it doesn't, just come back and we'll amputate. No liquor for a fortnight." I winced. "Good luck training those new recruits. I heard they were from Nantes...Make sure they don't drink from their powderhorns and set fire to their water flasks."

Chapter 3
A Coffee Trader's Tale

The *Cheval Marin* docked on May 14th of 1719 with the glad news that she had sunk a Dutch merchant ship as they rounded Barbuda. From the *Cheval's* gangplank walked none other than my old shipmate Percy Boulanger!

I had not seen him since the Battle of Vigo Bay. There he was, thirty pounds heavier and sporting a garish silk eyepatch. His long brownish grey hair flowed out from under his cap and he was wrapped in merchants' clothing. As we embraced, the particular perfume one acquires from four months of wearing the same clothes without bathing assaulted my nostrils.

"Well, blast my eyes if it isn't little cabin boy De Clieu! And lo, an infantry captain's stripes you wear!"

I escorted him to the Martinvalet Raphael, a seaside collection of shacks serving a blistering spiced rum *poulet boucanier*. Their *boucanier* was served fresh off the Arawak-style wooden buccan.

After our third salvo of halved coconuts awash in rum, Percy finished narrating his Atlantic crossing from the Levant and Persia. He complained about dockside scandals over damaged goods and bragged about the astronomical profits he earned. He now represented a trading company and came escorting their consignment of coffee for the governor of New France.

Percy leaned in towards me and began on a waft of rum, "I have been in Constantinople these past two years representing *La Compagnie*," which I took to mean the French East India Company, but dared not open my mouth and prove myself ignorant.

He went on, "We have a vast warehouse there in Constantinople, waiting for ships to come and go. Business is good, but the new company director, John Law, has unsettling plans. Last I heard, they were expanding the colony on the isle of Bourbon off of Madagascar and establishing a trading post at Pondicherry in India."

I knew this area from my navy days and exclaimed, "A foothold right under the noses of the English and Dutch!" I paused to hiccup, "But who is this John Law? Surely that's not his real name." Another hiccup. "It sounds positively British."

Percy heeled to port and spat a viscous wad on the white sand. "He's as English as King George the First…Of course, George hardly speaks English. He's—" now it was Percy's turn to hiccup, "—German, you know."

I nodded, intrigued, as he leaned close again. "The money being made back in Paris makes my head spin. Why, now even commoners like myself are buying into *La Compagnie* and all manner of ventures. It's all so tenuous though; we don't have the naval force to back it up like the English nor the trading posts like the Dutch. Everyone is mad for spices. Pepper is now alarmingly popular. Why, you even see it sometimes offered in restaurants! Pepper! Imagine that! I didn't trade pepper, though,—too valuable. I was in coffee. Of course you know of it?"

"I do," I told him, "but have not tasted it. Not many on the island have it. I've heard the Dujons brew it and that the Le Robert estate received a bag last hurricane season."

Percy shook his head, "The Turks and Abyssinians just chew the beans raw sometimes. But the Mohammedans prefer this drink when the berry is dried, husked, hulled, crushed, baked, *and* boiled."

"That sounds terribly complicated just to produce a drink for these Turks …"

"From London to Constantinople, coffee is spreading like the plague now," Percy chuckled. "Mohammedans are really Puritans when it comes to their diet, though you wouldn't expect it if you judged by how many wives they keep. Living there was alternately delightful and intolerable. One minute feasting, the next fasting. It's the same with coffee—they cannot make up their minds whether it's a blessing from Mohammed or a terrible curse. They've been back and forth from censuring and celebrating it for centuries. My favorite coffee story is this one."

Our fourth rums arrived and I settled in for Percy's tale. "In 1511 there was a governor of Mecca named Kair Bey. Mecca is their holy city, of course, like Jerusalem for us Catholics. Kair Bey is strict and religious. The city blossoms in coffee houses, full of violins, music and dance. The Sultan is in Cairo, far away, so Kair Bey wants to show his power to the people and rule his own little fiefdom. And Mecca! Mecca is where coffee houses first sprung up. They call them *kaveh kanes* and the Dervishes drink coffee there to stay up all night spinning."

I interrupted, "What's a Dervish and how does it spin?"

"De Clieu, Dervishes are like Mohammedan monks or friars. They study, pray, and spin around in circles for hours to achieve a state of religious ecstasy. They quaff coffee out of a big red urn, dipping into it with little bowls to drink."

Percy continued. "Kair Bey walks around Mecca and he sees these vibrant coffee houses with music, dance, and talk bubbling forth. Why, it's like alcohol without the alcohol! The Mohammedans strictly forbid alcohol, and most of God's other gifts...except for women, as I mentioned, whom they sequester like songbirds. Kair Bey leaves the mosque one night and sees a group of men drinking coffee in preparation to pray all night long. He's humiliated that these commoners show more faith than he, and he disperses them angrily. Kair Bey decides to ban all coffee in Mecca and holds a council to decide the matter. He invites all the leading scholars, physicians, and philosophers to his hall and urges them to condemn coffee. He complains that it impels men to play insidious games like chess and mankala, or even tambourines and harps under its influence. He summons two of the best physicians in Mecca, the Hakimani brothers, to pass judgment over the matter."

"All this because he had felt shame leaving the mosque? And how would the medical doctors decide a religious matter?"

"The Hakimanis had just written an anti-coffee book," Percy shrugged, "so of course Bey invited them to speak. They said coffee was evil, and against Muslim law. All the thinkers and citizens assembled saw what was happening but made little protest, for Bey was a brutal ruler and not to be crossed.

"But there was a religious leader in the audience, the Mufti of Aden, a Sharia law scholar and wise man. Coffee first came to Aden, you see, and then spread through the Middle East, so the Mufti was an authority on coffee. He drank six cups of coffee every day to help him stay awake for late prayers. He inhaled coffee's aroma with the rising sun every morning, reverently roasting, grinding, and boiling his coffee beans like an artisan at his craft. He alone had the bravery to point out the obvious; that everyone drank coffee, had done so for generations, and that it was harmless under Muslim law."

I downed more rum and wiped my mouth with the back of my hand, "I bet Bey loved that."

Percy's eyes twinkled. "Kair Bey was not concerned. One of his loyal friends began to speak on coffee's ills. The man swore that the effects of coffee were identical to those of wine. Suddenly the Mufti asked him, 'And how would you know, sir; without having tasted wine yourself?'"

Percy jabbed me accusingly in the chest. "'This blasted sinner has tasted wine, has he not? In violation of the prophet's laws!'" Four whalers with white caps looked up from a neighboring table.

Percy had worked himself up to a frothing pitch, "Kair Bey had to maintain appearances and so he asked his friend if he had indeed drunk wine. The fool grew red-faced and replied that he had. Everyone in the hall knew the punishment for drinking alcohol, and thus Bey had to punish his own dear friend and sentenced him to the *bastinado*!"

I sprayed a mouthful of rum into the air, like a breaching spermaceti whale, "My Heavens! The *bastinado*! They boiled his chestnuts?"

Percy swatted my comments aside like flies, "No, no, no! That's a different torture entirely. *Bastinado* is where they lay you on your back, feet tied to a pole in the air, and whack them with a reed or cane. I saw it several times among the Turks...It looks very silly."

"Oh...I see...*Bastinado*."

"Yes, *bastinado*. Kair Bey *bastinado*-ed his friend and emerged so furious that he ordered all coffee banned, coffee houses shuttered, and coffee warehouses burned. You can imagine the upheaval that ensued. Kair Bey thought to send a messenger to the Sultan informing him of the new anti-coffee law.

"The Sultan was sipping a fine dark brew from Mocha when the messenger blurted out the news. The sultan threw a fit. How dare Kair Bey ban a drink condoned by the Sultan in Cairo? As the last embers of Mecca's immolated coffee warehouses finished smoldering, Kair Bey sheepishly renounced his decree as per the Sultan's orders. You can imagine how the populace reacted. Bey was executed, his brother killed himself, and the Hakimani brothers were also executed. The Mufti of Aden became a hero among coffee-drinking Mohammedans, who respect him to this day. This cycle of indulgence and prohibition has repeated itself among the Turks and Arabians up to the present."

I asked Percy for more stories and he told me the most singular and remarkable tales. The mercantile life seemed to be far more lively than the endless drills, disease, and drinking that was a soldier's life. I declined a fifth rum, remembering Doctor Scie's orders.

Before he departed Martinique, Percy gave me a book as a gift. "No, Percy, this is too much. You can't. An entire book? How much did it cost you?"

"Never mind you the cost. I've read it thrice over. Oh, the ship's cat sharpened his claws on the tenth chapter. You deserve it, De Clieu; it is the least I can do for such a great friend and defender of New France. I've reached my fourth decade and can now afford such luxuries for myself and my friends." I thanked him profusely and tucked the tome away in its leather wrappings.

Percy's *Compagnie* ship continued on to Saint-Domingue on Hispaniola, the richest of all the Caribbean islands, to load more molasses before heading to New Orleans to top it off with beaver pelts.

After Percy's visit, I mingled more with the joint-stock company men called factors in their warehouses by the docks. These merchants saw new shores and immersed themselves alone in foreign cultures where my superiors dared not tread without a full regiment of cavalry. Their dealings earned sums of money in one year that I might be lucky to earn in ten.

CHAPTER 4
THE SAILING DEAD

I strode away from the village of Prêcheur along the beach road. The shacks and shanties at the edges of town faded away to endless sugar fields separated by two ruts from heavy oxcarts. Green parakeets launched themselves into the sky from a lone tree with a chirping chorus. The ever-present sea breeze bore the aroma of flowers. With these perfumes lingering in me, I arrived in Saint-Pierre and entered the drab barracks. There I assembled a troop of men to greet an incoming ship. I found Sargeant Fossieu, a veteran and profane soldier of forty-one years, and ordered that he lead our troop to the docks.

Boys lounging on the pier pointed to her, a black and white spec on an azure sea. As she drew near, her clumsy handling and failure to drop sail properly indicated that she was shorthanded. The *Liberté* reeked of death and disease so profoundly that even the curious dock boys backed off.

The remnants of her crew slowly abandoned the ship, dazed and joyless. We offered these gaunt men water and victuals. They accepted with trembling hands. Dr. Scie leaned on his cane and implored the famished men not to eat too quickly but they paid him no heed and were soon regurgitating.

I encountered the *Liberté's* second mate the next day and heard his story. They had taken on a fabulous haul of three hundred and sixty slaves in Ouidah in exchange for bales of Oriental satins. They sailed easily from the African slave port but were seized by the doldrums five hundred leagues west of Martinique. They languished for three weeks in the scorching sun. When they ran out of water, they collected condensed humidity from sails, open barrels and other sources too wretched to mention.

The captain died of scurvy and so did most of their valuable cargo. They had dumped a steady stream of corpses for the last two weeks and a caravan of tiger sharks nipped at the vessel's wake. One by one, the crew watched their investments plunge into the waves and disappear in a splashing frenzy. What remained was a sorry load of just two dozen half-dead Africans. The customs officials paid the surviving crew their ten-livre bounty per head, and the slaves were quickly auctioned at cut-rate prices. The planters buying these new African arrivals had to educate their new property before they could be productive.

This process consisted of whippings and brutal discipline to prevent any slave revolts such as transpired in 1712 on the British swamp island, New York. Despite the well known British inferiority in all manners including slave management, news of the revolt had a chilling effect on our island. The planters realized that their slaves outnumbered them fifty to one and they clamped down on any expression of free will. Martinique's governor enacted a new, stricter slave code than New York's. The code stipulated that we could no longer socialize with our slaves nor allow them to meet in groups larger than three. Luckily, I only had three.

CHAPTER 5

THE LETTER

On July 11th of 1721, my hands shook as I broke the elegant Naval Authority seal and ravished a new letter from Uncle Joel. He often wrote me of new trends in high fashion, politics, and culture. He considered me deficient in such matters. He was an aspiring aristocrat, constantly attending the most fashionable balls, ballets, and costumed soirées. In his youth, he suffered an affair-related injury that left him with a limp.

I had spent several months training in Paris during my early years in the Navy when I was just an ensign. I had felt trapped and escaped from Paris as if it were the most vile prison. Now, she whispered to me about her high society, wealth and dazzling nightlife. She invited me to hold enlightened conversations in her salons with people who were not smugglers or sweaty soldiers.

After luring me in with such succulent gossip, Joel made his point. He had hundreds of friends, business partners, and mistresses but trusted few of them with his affairs. He had many affairs. I read more of Joel's curling script:

> I beseech you, my nephew, to consider returning to Paris to help me in my business dealings. Your experience in the Indies and blood ties would make you a very suitable partner. I think of you like a son. I humbly ask you to return to Paris to learn my mercantile arts and join me in my ventures. Included here is a Royal order for your indefinite furlough and safe passage to Paris on family grounds should you wish to become my assistant.

I approached my commander, Capitaine de Corvette Francois Augustin Tasse, and showed him my uncle's paperwork. Francois was skinny except for his bloated belly.

"Sir, my commission is up in June. Here is a letter of furlough from the admiralty. While I had planned to re-enlist and would enjoy no greater honor than serving with you once more, familial duty calls me to Paris. I must regretfully leave this post on the next ship."

Francois wiped his mouth and looked up from a worn leather copy of *La Princesse de Clèves.*

"I regret to say that with pirate raids increasing, we need every officer we have, so the royal governor just extended your commission."

Given that Francois was a rat, I had taken the precaution of already calling on the governor. "Sir, there must be some confusion. I called on His Excellency just yesterday and he bid me a very cordial farewell."

Francois squinted at me and hissed, "Avast! Go, then. Hurricane season is coming on us. You're late to make the crossing. I wager your bones will be resting on a reef sooner than in Paris."

I saluted and bowed, "It has been an honor serving you, sir."

Chapter 6
My Second Goodbye

"Pierre, assemble Teetha and Aimee before lunch and I will make the announcement." Pierre stood still and spoke slowly. "Sir, why are you going?"

I could not bear to explain my uncle's letter to Pierre so I lied again. "I have received orders to report back to Paris for a special medal."

Pierre cut me off. "I read your uncle's letter. I had just hoped you wouldn't go."

I ran a hand through my wig. "What have I told you about reading, Pierre? You know the new codes and the position they put me in." Pierre shrugged and we walked behind the house.

Teetha and Aimee ladled soup into halved gourds and distributed slices of bread in the shade of an ancient Guanacaste tree. I stood up and put my gourd down on an old stump that Pierre had carved into a chair. "Attention, everyone. I have some bad news. I've been granted leave. I'm departing Prêcheur and Martinique to attend to my business in France. I'll be placing my lieutenant in charge and I'm afraid that discipline must be brought in line with other plantations. This means no more *looterlu* tournaments, dancing, afternoon teatime, or Friday night *brelan*. Absolutely no reading." I heard their inhaled breaths.

Pierre crossed his arms. "Remember your vow, Gabriel. The Creator is watching. If you betray me, He'll come down with punishment, just as surely as if I didn't hold up my end of the bargain."

I stared into his eyes. "Pierre, I remain grateful for how you warned me about the British ambush on Nevis when we captured you."

"I was thinking about the time I fished you out from drowning."

"Er, yes, that one too. I might have made it to shore on my own...Look, I have had one thousand chances to betray you since

I won you all on Nevis and have I done so yet? Hardly! You live like the King's own Frenchmen up here compared to big plantation slaves. Trust me now and I hope that this journey will benefit us all. In fact, I plan to return, perhaps as a merchant of *le Compagnie* and greatly expand our operation here one day."

Pierre nodded, contemplating his feet and squeezing his hands. "In Paris you should stay away from the Pigalle district at night, sir. I learned that when I served there as a boy."

CHAPTER 7
VIGO BAY

My slaves went back to work and I sat alone under the Guanacaste tree pondering the trajectory of my life. After my birth on June 30, 1687, I spent my childhood by the ocean in Angléqueville-sur-Saane catching frogs and communicable diseases. I always loved the sea. I swam, splashed, and carved toy boats. I borrowed fishermen's dinghies and dove for mussels, scooping great heaps into the bottom of rowboats. Yet, here I was a infantryman and dirt farmer sitting under a tree instead of under sails.

My family was minor nobility but we had a rich uncle, Joel, who would occasionally bestow upon us sufficient funds to maintain appearances. My mother served in a small tea salon that attracted the local elite with her fine blends and dainty cups. My father was a well-respected drinker and thirteen-time Angléqueville drinking champion. He went on to dominate the wine drinking competitions in the Seine-Inférieure and Normandy regions. He didn't want me to follow his profession, largely because he lacked one. My mother saved for years to pay my commission to join *La Royale*, King Louis XIV's invincible navy.

On my fifteenth birthday in 1702, I put on sailor's britches as a lowly cabin boy on the *Esperance*. She was a seventy-two gunship of the line. I adapted to the seafaring life and learned the ropes from flinty and grizzled mariners. There were over three hundred ropes to learn and that didn't include the hawsers nor the extra ropes stored in the hold.

The so-called War of the Spanish Succession had broken out in 1701, pitting France and some Spanish allies against a host of repugnant upstarts like Holland and England. We were ordered to protect the Spanish treasure fleet, laden with silver and other riches from the New World. The English and Dutch attacked us in Vigo Bay, and our formerly invincible fleet was massacred. Cannon balls pierced our hull and grapeshot tore men asunder. Blood drenched the decks.

The captain bellowed the words that recur in the nightmares of all sailors—*"Abandon ship!"* I dove into the sea and swam to shore on a rising tide. I turned back to see burning pieces of our beloved *Esperance* sinking into the bay. Every gasping breath smelled like French ships burning. I emerged like a water rat, and joined the bedraggled French and Spanish forces regrouping.

My next commission sent me to New France. The Caribbean sun faded the dark tragedy of Europe from my memory. Sugarcane outnumbered slaves a thousand to one, slaves outnumbered French one hundred to one, and men outnumbered women twenty to one. Luckily, all of the above produced plenty of rum.

In 1706, shortly after I arrived, none other than Pierre Le Moyne D'Iberville appeared with a twelve-ship flotilla and almost two thousand troops. It was as if King Louis himself had descended on our island. Saint-Pierre sizzled with talk of D'Iberville's raids along the English underbelly from Pemaquid to the Virginia Colony.

My commander, the Comte de Chavagnac, had ordered a raid on Saint Christopher in hopes of impressing D'Iberville upon his arrival. When D'Iberville learned of the raid, he cocked his head to one side like a bird, his wig flopping luxuriantly.

I will never forget his public upbraiding of Chavagnac. "You ignorant buffoon! I have sailed all the way from France to launch a surprise attack on Jamaica and you ruin our initiative for the pleasure of turning a few English colonists out of their thatch huts on an island the size of my arse! What plunder have you brought for me? Crabs? Coconuts?"

D'Iberville relieved Chavagnac of command and planned a raid on one of the largest and richest British sugar islands, Nevis. I attached my powderhorn, a satchel of musket balls, strapped on my brace of pistols, and buckled my sword. They were hardly needed, so utterly did we overwhelm the panicked fort at Charleston. Indeed, the most dangerous part of the raid was rounding the reef by St. Kitts.

Nevis was a veritable bank of sugary wealth in the form of green sugarcane and glistening black slaves. The British, despite their natural inferiorities, were industrious slave traders and planters. Never had I seen so much of one commodity planted in one place. After we won, I ordered our blue and white Capetian *fleur-de-lis* run up the flagpole. D'Iberville decorated me and other soldiers who were not off looting.

I tried to stop some of the buccaneers in our forces from raping and pillaging, but it was of little use until D'Iberville ordered two of them shot. Sadly, D'Iberville took ill with an intestinal tempest and fled to Havana to recover. There, the man who made the British colonies tremble was slain by a murderous diarrhea.

I returned to Martinique with a new scar and more experience. It was then that I bought my small plantation in Prêcheur and married Aurélie, who had arrived with a supply shipment to escape religious persecution. I partook in military forays in the subsequent years that added to my thirst for adventure. Were it not for Aurélie awaiting me at home, I would have transferred back to a ship of the line to chase enemy vessels, surprise Dutch trading posts, and seize British goods.

Her death in 1717 set me adrift on a sea of sorrow for many dark months. After a love affair with spiced rum almost killed me, I plunged back into my duty. I grew reckless in our encounters but was blessed with a good fortune that made me a popular leader among the men. We repulsed several attacks on the island. All the while, Martinique vessels traded illegally with the very same ruffians who fought us.

Many planters and merchants grew rich while I remained only modestly well-to-do with my military and planting income. For my years of service and unswerving Catholicism, the governor of Martinique inducted me as a knight, a Chevalier of Saint Louis, in 1718. He pinned the medal and its red ribbon to my chest and I wore it every day for the rest of my life. I was promoted again to a *capitaine de campagnie* of the Martinique infantry garrison in 1720. The governor ripped the anchor insignia and its two horizontal gold bars off my uniform and ordered his personal tailor to sew on the three vertical gold bars of an infantry captain and give me the corresponding hat with extra feathers.

At first, I basked in these overdue honors, but I soon chafed at the paperwork that comes with rank. I did less commanding and more bookkeeping. I had Pierre secretly transcribe my paperwork. His script was nicer than mine due to his many years as a Parisian footman before an infraction had him sold to the New World. Time wore on and most of my military companions died of tropical disease, drinking, or combat.

After the most dangerous decade a man can live, I packed two trunks, including gifts for those back in France. I made a contract with a second-year infantryman named Marcel to manage my slaves and plantation that we had signed before Judge Adaire. I wanted someone junior enough to be afraid of me and senior enough to not die promptly from alcoholism or disease. I said many goodbyes across the island. At last, on a clear day when the air was thick with a floral perfume, Pierre loaded my trunks onto a highly advanced two-masted schooner, the *Mangeur de Chien*.

CHAPTER 8

A SWIFT AFFAIR

I asked her captain, a hirsute Marseilleis man named Therron, why his vessel had such a preposterous name. He told of how he had captured the ship privateering. They took it from a British colonial crew out of Gloucester, in the Massachusetts Colony, and forced the captain to eat his ship's dog. The story smacked of a lie, but it was well told.

The hold was filled with oak barrels of rum and sugar. I had heard from a foreman on the Plissoneau estate that her captain had bribed customs to leave this journey unregistered. I made no quarrel about the smuggling—I was off duty. She had that reassuring new ship smell of fresh oak and cedar, new lines, and sails which embodied the very aroma of fortune.

I moved into steerage with my trunks, strung up my Carib hammock. I heard heavy boots tramping above me and shouting. I tumbled out of the hammock and emerged on deck to find Francois teetering, visibly drunk. He shouted at Therron to give up his captain's quarters to me, who was twice the man he was. Francois made an outrageous stink, told several fallacious stories of my assistance to the great D'Iberville, and swore at anything that moved. It was an uncomfortable scene as most interactions with Francois were, drunk or sober. I asked him repeatedly to be silent and this only led him to denigrate the captain's mother, who Francois had it on good authority was a Dutch whore.

Finally, Therron relented and agreed that I would have the second mate's cabin, a nicely appointed little room with a porthole view. Francois then took a triumphant piss off the bowsprit, much of which ended up in a yellow pool on the foredeck.

He clapped me too hard on the back and slurred some incoherent words of wisdom to me. Glaring at Therron, he stormed off, leaving the crew chortling like piglets. We cast off the hawsers from the barnacle-encrusted pilings. I doffed my hat to Marcel, Fossieu,

Pierre, Teetha, Aimee, Dr. Scie and all my friends who gathered on the dock to see me off.

Our hull glided over the clear waters as our pilot steered the *Mangeur* through the maze of reefs guarding the harbor. We came within a few yards of one but tacked back as I braced for the white plumes of coral to explode into the crystal waters. Saint-Pierre's narrow streets and stately buildings receded as we swung south by Fort de France. The jagged *Pitons du Carbets* rose sharply over the little town. I had no sea legs, so I took to my newly requisitioned cabin and slept.

The bubbles emerging from the wake of this nimble schooner freed my heart from the soil of Martinique. The tangy salt air cleansed me. The only things that marred my bliss were surly and stinking seamen shouting around me. Therron tolerated a level of complaining that would have made my whipping arm sore. He was more the men's wet nurse than their captain, obliging every care and complaint with an obsequious "Aye, 'tis true."

At first I delighted in my lack of duties aboard the schooner, but I soon grew restless. I pawed through my greasy canvas satchel and pulled out the smooth, leatherbound book from Percy. It felt warm and alive in my hands. I read the gilt lettering along the spine: *Voyage de l'Arabie Heureuse.* I read this *Voyage to Arabia the Happy* propped against the side of a longboat. My imaginary voyage to happy Arabia transported me and I studied every word like an Arab studying his Quran.

Rather than swaying on choppy seas, I rode humpbacked camels with Jean La Roque to visit the King of Yemen. Instead of grog, I sipped imaginary coffee in Bedouin tents with a little kissing sound. I wore flowing silk robes and joined La Roque as he surveyed the king's magnificent garden. The king boasted fine coffee bushes in lieu of the exotic plants popular among royalty. When La Roque asked the King why he preferred coffee, the monarch replied that he loved the bean for its commonality throughout his kingdom, and for tending it with his own hands.

I pondered if my own King might bestow a coffee bush on me. If I could just get a seedling to bring back to plant on Martinique, the conditions would be just like Yemen. I could bypass the entire chain of Mocha middlemen, the Dutch, and their Java plantations to supply France directly. With coffee taking hold among Europe's nobility, I could become so rich that even my slaves might have slaves.

The *Mangeur de Chien* flew over the waves, winning us two hundred miles per day. Therron brusquely informed me that since we were so far ahead of schedule, he would make for Marseille through the Straits of Gibraltar to get a better price for his goods. I responded about as positively as if he had tried to amputate one of my toes. He shrugged. "Sorry, Monsieur De Clieu, I know that you want to get to Paris and all but—"

I cut him off, "I am not a monsieur. You may address me as capitaine, just like yourself."

I yearned to pummel him senseless and wondered if the crew would mind. After a bitter argument, I resigned myself to finding another ship from Marseille to Paris. Soon we passed between Barcelona and the Isle of Palma near the southern coast of France. Lantern lights blinked from a town ashore. We did not proceed to land but instead made our way further east. We anchored for the night near a salt marsh only four leagues from Marseille. A steady flotilla of fishing boats ferried much of our cargo away into the darkness.

CHAPTER 9
DUST AND BONES

Marseille! How fondly I remembered this fine city from my early naval days, always bustling with burly stevedores, and cunning prostitutes. Therron ordered that we sail onwards by night. We entered the harbor well after midnight, coasting on a light breeze. Clouds embraced the heavens, shutting out all moonlight. We slid past the dark battlements of Fort Saint-Jean and Fort Saint-Nicholas. I shivered as we passed the brooding iron cannons that loomed like holes in the night.

I recognized a few Caribbean privateering vessels, no doubt returned to France to invest their buccaneering wages in the most trustworthy banks and brothels that Marseille had to offer. We docked by the *Grand-Saint-Antoine,* an Ottoman trading ship, and cast our ropes around the bollards. The *Grand-Saint-Antoine*'s many flags drooped in the night breeze and we took no notice of them as we unloaded our remaining cargo.

I employed the only two stevedores up at this hour. They unloaded my trunks into a small wagon and began hauling them to a boardinghouse run by Madame Dushon. She was the mother of a friend of mine, Paul-Henri, who had swum ashore with me in the disaster of Vigo Bay and one of the few people I knew in Marseille.

I asked the men casual questions as they strained in the darkness. No response. I found this silence odd, as dockside workers are some of the most gossip-prone creatures that walk on two legs. Indeed, the average stevedore might convey more local gossip in one day than a whole class of schoolgirls in a fortnight.

The streets of Marseille exuded a worrisome emptiness; not one drunk or prostitute in sight. An old woman ran from one house to another, and screamed.

"What the hell is going on here?" I demanded of my stevedores.

They refused to speak, looking down and pushing the cart up the last hill before Madam Dushon's. At the crest of the hill a pile of corpses blocked our way. Their stench assaulted my senses. A dozen vultures peered up at us from their breakfast. Flies swarmed over limbs frozen at every angle. None bore the wounds of combat.

A nameless terror coiled in my gut. My carters heaved around this gruesome obstacle as I stared, dumbfounded. Dogs tore at the meat without looking up. This sacrilege snapped me out of my daze and I chased them off. I shouted at my stevedores, demanding an explanation, but they remained mute.

I caught up to the cart loaded with my belongings which had arrived at Madam Dushon's a block and a half from the pile. Boards barred the door and windows as if braced for a hurricane. My heart sank and I knew not where to look for hospitality. My stevedores unloaded my trunks and spoke for the first time, "That will be thirty livres, sir."

"Thirty livres! *Merde* in my cups! Would you rob me?"

They shrugged off my outburst. "Things 'as changed, sir, thirty livres it is." They stood waiting payment. I paid them this princely sum, desperate and confused. They slunk off like coyotes. I turned and banged futilely on the barricaded door. Nobody answered. I cursed the name of Paul Henri and did not spare his mother. After a powerful tirade, a shuttered window above me opened a crack. To my wonderment, Madam Dushon's raspy voice hissed at me, "Is that Gabriel Mathieu De Clieu? Get in here this instant and hold your crooked tongue!"

I replied, "Open the door, woman!"

"I cannot, it's too well sealed. You must climb up," she countered.

"But my trunks!" I had in them everything I needed for a year in Paris.

"There's nobody to take them. We'll bring them in soon enough." I climbed up a small tree by her window. Madam Dushon hauled me through the window and then nailed it shut, clenching the iron spikes in her rotten teeth.

"Madam, what has happened to dear Marseille?"

She stared at me for a while, as if convincing herself that this was really happening and the fates were not playing some trick on her. "How can you possibly not know? God has sent the Black Death to punish us. We've been under curfew for weeks. Honestly, De Clieu, I never thought you a scholar, but even the animals know what's afoot." She wiped her nose on her sleeve. "Of all the ports in France why did you come to this accursed city? Did your captain not hear the news? Did you see the quarantine flags? That diabolical Ottoman ship on the pier carried the pestilence and spread it through the city. Thousands are dead and we will be joining them soon, I reckon."

Her voice faded out and I felt trapped. I had always imagined dying gloriously in battle. I swallowed, wondering suddenly if her son had died. "And what of Paul-Henri?"

She paused, "He signed on with Olivier 'The Buzzard' Levasseur's crew. More money in buccaneering, better insurance than the navy." She shook her head. "I haven't heard from my boy in two years. Last he wrote, he was headed for Ouidah in Africa. I don't know whether he's alive or dead." The insurance part was true; usually the loss of each body part was compensated at triple the navy rate.

Deep booms of cannon rang outside. A cat jumped up on Madam Duchon's lap and I leapt away in fear. "Christ, Madame! Don't you know that cats carry the plague?"

She sneered at me, "The plague is sent from God to punish sinners, so let those fall who shall fall. I've prayed enough to wear through my rosary beads...But if anyone tries to hurt my Whiskers, so help me Jesus, I'll cut them." I swallowed, my throat sore. The cat meow'ed.

"Madame, I must return to my ship at once and set sail." More percussions resonated like rolling thunder.

"You won't get far, De Clieu. The King has ordered the navy to sink any escaping vessels from this whole coast. Fort Saint-Jean sank three ships this week."

"We stand a chance, Madame. I'm on a fast new kind of ship called a schooner." She sighed and stroked the feline. "A what? What a ridiculous name for a ship. Well, go then, De Clieu, on this spooner. I know my son loves you like a brother, so you have my best wishes.

If you see him, please tell him that I died in the plague."

Madame Duchon pried the nails back out of the wood across the window and opened it. Dawn was now rising pink over the harbor. I gazed out to see the transom of the *Mangeur de Chien* riding low in water.

Fire raged on her foredecks; men leapt off her sides like grasshoppers.

Madame Duchon stepped on tiptoes and squinted out the window. "Was that your spooner, De Clieu?"

I slumped down against the wall to the floor, weeping despondently. I wished upon Christ that I was back with Pierre, home in Prêcheur. I felt feverish already. I tried to swallow but my throat was too dry. After a long a despondent silence I managed to speak. "Madame you've been most kind to me in this desperate hour, but I must travel to Paris overland."

Madame Duchon winced. "People fled the city in panic like the Biblical exodus three weeks ago when the plague arose. The parliament in Aix ordered the army to cordon off the entire Marseille region and kill anyone trying to escape. They say troops fire on entire families and leaving the bodies to rot. When I went out for water yesterday, a neighbor told me they're building a wall. Imagine, a plague wall! I don't know...maybe where you're in the military they'll let you through. I noticed the infantry insignia on your breast...I thought you were in the Navy with my Paul-Henri?"

"Err, yes, I served with D'Iberville and was promoted...A glorious hero struck down in his prime by disease." I got up from where I had slumped. "Madame, I must escape overland. Will you come with me?"

Madame Duchon assessed the empty boardinghouse. She muttered, "All dust and bones...Dust and bones...I'm an old woman now, De Clieu. I turned forty-one last year. You know, my daughter Claudette and granddaughter are in the pile at the bottom of the street, beneath the others." She looked me in the eye Tears trailed down her dirty cheeks and she slumped to the floor next to me. Exhausted and confounded, I drifted to sleep.

Chapter 10
Nightmares in Marseilles

I awoke thinking I was on board the *Mangeur de Chien* and that I had just experienced a ghoulish nightmare. But why was I not rocking back and forth with the waves? Where was I now? I rolled over in bed, failing to comprehend reality itself.

The nightmare was real! I bolted up, yesterday's events playing back before my eyes. I dressed, pinned on my medal, and found Madame Duchon staring at a wall.

I was hungrier than an orphan and explored Madame Duchon's larder. In the cool cellar I found sacks of onions, garlic, wheels of cheese encased in wax, and apples. Madame Duchon's cats followed me around stealthily, hunting for rats. The apples were slightly soft. I also discovered sacks of that preposterous looking New World tuber, the potato, all dents and sprouts. I chuckled, and ate one raw.

I crossed the courtyard and found a wagon with a canvas covering on the back. Seeing a real chance for escape, I returned to Madame Duchon. She sat hunched in a dim antechamber, her eyes following an ant traversing her plaster wall.

"Madame, with your permission, I shall take your cart and make a break for the interior." Silence.

"Madame, may I begin loading the cart? I'll just need to borrow two weeks' food." She waved her hand dismissively.

I set about loading the cart with foodstores, leaving Madame Duchon the vast majority. Indeed, her larder was such that I could not have physically carried ten percent. As I hauled a bag apples up from the storeroom to the wagon, Madame Duchon suddenly popped out from an alcove. We both stopped and stared at each other for a moment.

Her chin trembled and she brushed her white hair out of her eyes. "I'm going with you, snail brains, so pack for two! You don't know the countryside and you'll end up back in Marseille after two weeks of circling the fields like a blind mule. Whiskers is coming, though. So are Twinkers and Sheeshee."

We agreed to leave in the dead of night to avoid looters and unwanted attention.

Chapter 11
Outrunning the Plague

We traveled by night and hid by day, fearing what might beset us. Madame Duchon helped me haul the cart out of the doomed port, heaving on the other handle. The old French widow pulled beside me with remarkable strength; we had become a team of oxen. As we neared the edges of the city, fine two-story homes gave way to a snarl of ramshackle huts.

These soon faded to gardens and fields until we hit an overpowering stench that seared our lungs. A giant pit, blacker than the night itself, yawned open on the west side of the road. Hundreds of twisted, slumped, decaying corpses tumbled over each other in a mass grave. I retched every single crumb that I consumed in my entire life. Madame Duchon regurgitated with me. The smell was so powerful as to be a physical force, squeezing every inch of my skin with putrid fingernails. We fled from the pit like fish from a shark, awash in vomit and fear.

We made slow progress with our heavy cart and night travel. The horror of Marseille gave way to the fertile countryside. We saw no signs of the plague except for weedy fields and overgrown pastures. We passed through unlit hamlets and met other people only once, a silent family with a wagon like ours. Madame Duchon astounded me with her tenacious strength. When I asked, she attributed her vigor to eating four cloves of garlic each day. I also attributed her pungent aroma to this diet.

On our second night, we deviated down a narrow path to camp while the birds still slept. Madame Duchon believed us to be nearing the plague wall, but without contact with other locals we could only guess. As we bumped along the lane looking for a flat and protected spot to lie down and rest, we heard a shout. I whirled to see a small fire twinkling through the trees. I readied my sword and pistol as two figures emerged from a thicket.

"Who goes there? is there plague among you?" queried a fearful voice with a strong Venetian accent.

I retorted, "We are two plagueless travelers! And yourselves, who are you and have you plague amongst you?"

I kept my weapons visible at my sides and the figures cautiously approached until Sheeshee hissed and arched her back.

"We are just travelers like yourselves...Actually, we're Roma... my name is Alessandro...What is that? It isn't a cat, is it?"

Madame Duchon began to speak but I covered her mouth with my palm and responded, "No, of course not! Cats carry plague, but we do possess three miniature Persian hunting tigers."

A dirty woodsman emerged from the gloom and two more lurked behind him. He peered at us and Sheeshee. "It looks like a cat to me," he said doubtfully.

Madame Duchon brushed my hand aside and before I could restrain her.

"Of course it's a—"

I stoppered her again and continued, "Yes, the anatomy bears resemblance, but these are hunting tigers gifted to me by a Persian princess who I yearned to marry. See how this one perches on my companion's shoulder? No cat can be thus trained. Only small tigers can do that."

The second gypsy emerged. "Well, what happened? he begged. "Why didn't you marry her? How did she train the miniature tigers?" The two invited us into their camp and their children played cheerfully with our small hunting tigers.

Several hours later, after feasting on a succulent deer leg that the Roma roasted on a spit, we learned the plague wall's location. We had inadvertently walked to within five hundred yards of this freshly erected palisade. The Roma explained that soldiers patrolled the wall day and night. An army of conscripted peasants was building the wall higher to keep out anyone fleeing Marseille. Alessandro explained how they were digging a tunnel that sank from a thicket about fifty feet before the wall to an abandoned barn just beyond it. A skinny man in a red cloak with a thin mustache said, "We're is not gonna escape via di tunnel, we is charging a hundred livre per persona for the viage." The accent seemed forced.

Knowing a thing or two of siege warfare and tunneling, I spotted some flaws with their claim, such as an absence of digging tools. I asked a string of geological questions relating to tunnel construction, complementing their plan at length. They changed the subject and began swapping stories about wine. Then four heavily armed men came into camp and sat behind Alessandro with a clank of scimitars. A cold, trapped feeling arose in my guts, bordering on panic.

I popped to my feet and picked up two cats by the scruff of their necks. "A thousand thanks to you for your hospitality toward this King's soldier in such terrible times but I'm afraid we must be going. It's now dusk and we must launch our plan to evade the palisade. *Au revoir!*"

A swarthy man took out a crooked sword to cut another strip of venison. "Oh, but you can't go so soon—you're our guests. You must stay longer."

Alessandro said, "You know, the venison isn't free—that will cost you fifty livres." Fifty livres indeed! I might purchase a herd of deer for such a sum!

Another greasy man removed a flintlock from under his cloak and idly polished it. The children moved outside the firelight. A fellow close to the campfire licked his lips. So did Whiskers. Madam Duchon remained silent and looked from me to the ruffians.

A dramatic overture was needed. "As a token of our gratitude we shall bestow upon you one of our rare Persian hunting tigers, which each live one hundred years, and protect against the plague."

Alessandro squinted at me. "We don't want your goddamn cat. We're dog people."

The children broke the silence, rushing back into the camp, gasping with excitement. "Papa," one implored, "we want the tiger! Give us a tiger!"

Another hauled on Alessandro's sleeve. "Papa, it's a good deal! Take the tiger!"

Sheeshee looked at me quizzically from where she'd been picking at a deer jawbone. Madame Duchon stiffened. Three little imps tugged at Alessandro's trousers, begging him to accept my gift. He muttered something and closed in to whisper in my ear. In Marseille-accented French he said, "Take your cart and go to the wall. One word of our location to the soldiers and you'll wish the plague had taken you. Leave us two cats and all your coins. We'll escort you to the wall where the soldiers will shoot you and we'll get your cart and belongings, anyway."

I profusely thanked Alessandro for all his help, plopping a heavy pouch of worthless copper coins into his hand.

I saluted the little gremlins. "Hark, children, how would you like not one, but two miniature Persian hunting tigers?"

A cheer went up from the lusty little trolls. Madame Duchon held herself in check. Perhaps she realized that the cats might enjoy the brigand life, children's attention, and venison pickings. Before the shifty ruffians could deny them, the brats rushed forward to take the felines. The brats chose Sheeshee and Twinkers, leaving us the most disagreeable feline and Madame Duchon's favorite, Whiskers. We turned our backs to the menacing crowd and hauled our cart with Alessandro and his pack escorting us.

A slow rain sizzled down through the leaves and inky clouds scudded across the sky. Alessandro led us on a side branch of our path and soon the familiar smell of decaying corpses permeated the air. We hauled the cart up a long, rolling hill, densely forested on both sides. I broke out in a sweat and Madam Duchon wheezed. The smell got worse as we bumped and jolted over roots until we stopped behind a hedgerow. The rain increased to a downpour and thunder rolled in the distance.

Alessandro pointed ahead and sneered, "Welcome to the *Mur de la Peste*. From here it opens up into a field in front of the wall. This is where they'll shoot you. You can smell the others who've tried. We'll be waiting here in case you lose your nerve and prefer us to shoot you. We try not to waste bullets. We let the wall guards use theirs."

35

He broke out in a devilish laugh, and wheeled around on his heel. I had half a mind to shoot him but agreed with his judicious plan to conserve ammunition.

Alessandro disappeared back down the path, leaving us in the drenching rain.

I scowled at Madame Duchon. "I suppose this is the end, Madame...I don't think I can outfight so many bandits or the wall guards. I'm sorry about your cats. I must admit that they weren't bad companions after all."

"Oh, we'll be fine, De Clieu—don't be such a little baby. We've come this far and I'm not turning back. I'm stunned that those ruffians are giving us any chance at all. The wall guards are probably asleep or inside drinking." She had a point. That was certainly what my men on Martinique did for most of their night watch.

"Let us wait to sneak across," Madame Duchon continued. "If this weather keeps up it will be darker than a sailor's arse. If we can't cross, we are coming back to kill that cursed Alessandro and get my cats back. Either way, we'll have to leave the cart here."

"Madame, I have several extra uniforms and you have the semblance of a mustache!"

Duchon snapped, "I was born that way. What of it?"

"On a night such as this, you might pass for an infantry sergeant! If we can get close enough and you can be silent, I think we can bluff our way through."

Duchon spat and scratched herself. "A sergeant? It's about time I had official rank. God knows I've commanded more men at the boarding house than you have in the field. Besides, I'd like to die in a nice uniform."

I opened my big sea chest and found my belongings dry. I donned my best dress uniform and put Madame Duchon into my tightest bandolier and britches. My uniform draped over her and my hat perched precariously on her knotted hair. We firmed our resolve with a sip of Martinique rum and marched into the open pasture.

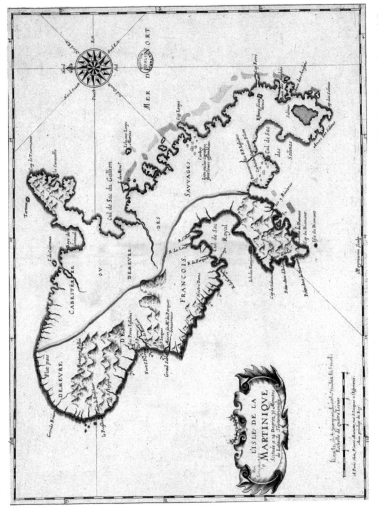

A 1656 map of Martinique showing Prêcheur and Fort Saint-Pierre. The line down the middle indicates "Residence of Savages" where the Caribs maintained control of the east half of the island two years before their final massacre at the hands of the French in 1658. *Source: The Norman B. Leventhal Map Center at the Boston Public Library*

Please note: *All images on these pages are in the public domain or printed with permission.*

Le Prêcheur   Fort de France
        Saint-Pierre

The island of Martinique, from an elegant 1760 map by Houl and Thomas Jefferies. By 1760, millions of coffee trees dominated the island's economy where sugar had once reigned supreme. The village of Le Prêcheur lies about 5.1 miles (8.3 kilometers) from Saint-Pierre. This British maps calls Saint-Pierre Saint Peter, evidence of Martinique changing hands when the British captured it from 1762-1763 in the Seven Years' War. *Source: Houl and Jefferies, 1760.*

This is *Desmaret's Pilorie*, the Martinique giant rice rat that bites De Clieu. *Source: Gervais, Paul, Histoire naturelle des mammiferes..., vol. 1, p. 411, 1855.*

This 1836 image of open sewers and crude thatch huts on a Martinique sugar plantation shows extreme poverty of the Africans enslaved on Martinique. Living conditions and horrific treatment of slaves in De Clieu's time made for short and tortorous lives. *Source: Voyage pittoresque dans les deux Amériques by Alcide D'Orbigny. Via Wellcome Library, London, 1836.*

This 1823 plate by William Clark shows a gang of slaves cutting sugarcane on a plantation in Antigua, just three islands north of Martinique in the Antilles. *British Library, UK*

Sugar refineries on Martinique in the 1700s had boiling rooms where the cane juice was cooked into sugar crystals. Slaves were often burned and even killed in this process. The heat was so intense that slaves had to work short shifts before their limbs began swelling. This image from Antigua one hundred years later shows a scene similar to nearby Martinique. *Source: British Library, UK, 1823*

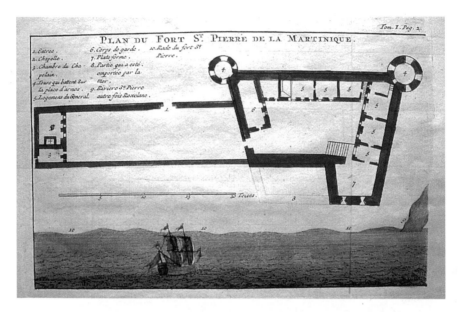

An 1742 copper plate engraving by Jean Baptiste Labat of Fort Saint-Pierre where De Clieu was stationed in 1720. De Clieu knew these rooms like the back of his hand and spent countless hours behind these stone ramparts. *Source: The Maritime Gallery, UK.*

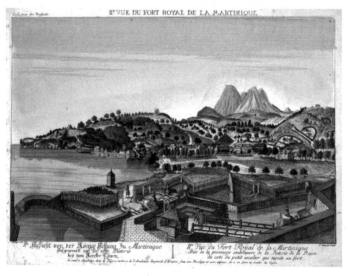

View of Fort de France (then called Fort Royal) in Martinique circa 1750-1760 by François Denis (1732-1817). This was one of several forts on the island that De Clieu eventually commanded. *Source: Archives Anglaises via Wikipedia Commons.*

This etching by Michael Serr shows the city of Marseille in the throes of the Black Plague. The plague killed an estimated 100,000 people and Marseilles took two generations—forty-five years—to recover.

Source: Wellcome Library, London

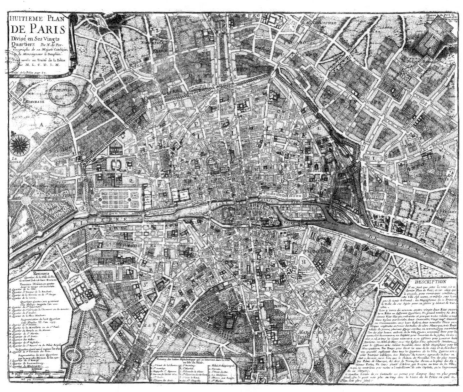

Paris was already a vast urban city in the 1720s when De Clieu returned there from Martinique. This map from 1705 by Nicolas de Fer shows the dense city center clustered around the Seine river. *Source: Collection d'Anville*

44

A 2004 photo of the original 1720 plague wall, or *mur de la peste*. It was built out of stone and reached six feet high, with guardhouses set back from the wall. The plague created panic because it killed between one in four and one in two citizens of the cities it overran, suche as Marseilles and Toulon. Bodies were stacked in the streets and hospitals were overwhelmed. The penalty for communication to or from Marseilles was death. De Clieu would have known about the 1720 plague but almost certainly not in or near Marseilles during the outbreak. *"Mur de la peste" by Psycho Chicken - Own work. Licensed under Creative Commons Attribution-Share Alike 3.0 via Wikimedia Commons - http://commons.wikimedia.org/wiki/File:Mur_de_la_peste. jpg#mediaviewer/File:Mur_de_la_peste.jpg*

Louis XV was crowned in 1715 at the age of only five to succeed his great-grandfather Louis XIV. Power was fully transferred to him in 1723 from Phillipe II, the Duke of Orleans. Louis loved his one and only coffee plant, just as his great-grandfather had, and stubbornly refused to give a cutting to De Clieu. De Clieu was later presented to Louis XV in 1749 and the King honored him for coffee's success. *Source: Bibliothèque nationale de France*

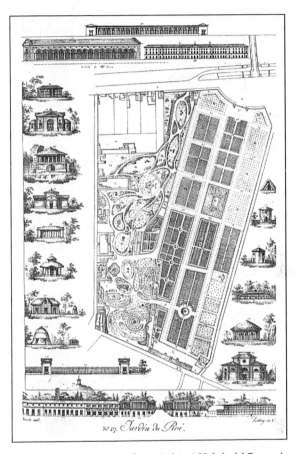

The Jardin des Plantes, founded in 1626, held France's greatest variety of plants—including its only coffee tree—in France's only greenhouse. From here Doctor M. de Chirac took a cutting of King Louis XV's coffee tree for De Clieu. *Source: Jardin des plantes, plate 37, pattern-book Plans raisonnés de toutes les espèces de jardins by Gabriel Thouin, 1820*

Louis Auguste de Bourbon, the Duke of Maine, would have been known to De Clieu and may have been solicited for help in securing a coffee plant from his relative King Louis XV. *Source: Wikimedia Commons*

La Maison appartenant à Madame de Bretonvilliers.

The sumptuous Hotel de Bretonvilliers was built from 1637–1642 for the secretary to the King's counsel, Claude Le Ragois de Bretonvilliers, and was one of many lavish Parisian mansions. *Source: Wikimedia Commons*

PHILIP.HECQUET D.REG.ET ANCIEN DOIEN DE LA FAC.
DE MED.DE PARIS.
Né a Abbeville le 11.Fev.1661.et Mort a Paris le 11 Avril 1737.

Dans son art il n'oublia rien
Pour sonder a fond la nature ;
Mais la Science du chrestien
Lui parut touyours la plus sure.
A ces deux traits, Lecteur, augure
Qu'il fut grand Medecin mais plus homme de bien.

Le Belle pinx.   J.Daullé Sculp.

This engraving by J. Daullé shows Phillippe Hecquet (1661–1737), a royal doctor to King Louis XV. He was a contemporary of the famous Doctor M. de Chirac who treated many nobles as well as the king. Hecquet might have known about Chirac's theft of the coffee cutting from King Louis XV. *Source: Wellcome Library, London*

This Dutch political cartoon from 1720 skewers Scottish speculator John Law who 1716 established the Banque Générale in France, a private bank that was effectively France's first central bank. Law promoted the idea of paper money instead of coins and sold shares to his newly-acquired joint stock Mississippi Company through a marketing program that saw demand multiply exponentially though 1719. His speculations came crashing down when the "Mississippi Bubble" burst in 1720 and he was dismissed from his post as France's Controller General of Finances. *Source: Original 1720 source Het Groote Tafereel der Dwaasheid; scan from Harper's New Monthly Magazine, No. 301, June, 1875.*

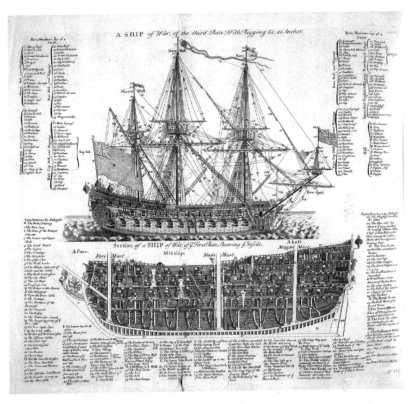

This cross section of a 1728 British warship shows the complexity of 1700s ships of the line which De Clieu sailed on and later captained. *Source: Cyclopaedia of 1728 by Ephraim Chambers*

Barbary pirates (also known as corsairs) attack a French vessel in this painting from 1615, over one hundred years before the very same fate befell De Clieu and *Le Dromedaire*. Barbary pirate attacks captured an estimated 800,000 to 1.25 million people as slaves and made large swaths of the Spanish and Italian coasts uninhabitable until they were finally suppressed by multi-national naval actions from 1815-1830. *Source: UK National Maritime Museum*

Le Dromedaire in a storm might have looked like this 1809 aquatint by Edward Burt of the *HMS Theseus* in a West Indies Hurricane in 1804. *Source: Royal Museums Greenwich*

This undated engraving shows De Clieu sharing his water ration with his coffee plant when *Le Dromedaire* is becalmed. *Source: Wikimedia Commons*

This Mexican coffee plant likely descended from those that De Clieu brought to Martinique. Within forty years of his adventure, Martinique hosted about 18 million coffee trees. Today, a significant (but unknown) percentage of all Arabica coffee is genetically linked to the plant De Clieu smuggled from France to Martinique. *Source: Appleton's Guide to Mexico 1884*

This is an Order of Saint Louis medal like the one De Clieu received and wore every day thereafter for his many years of gallant service, staunch Catholicism, and loyalty to France. The medal was a rare honor among troops during De Clieu's time (though it became more routine later in the 18th century) and was a predecessor of the Legion of Honor. *Source: Wikimedia Commons*

I couldn't resist including this 2013 photo of the tugboat *Gabriel de Clieu* in Dieppe, France, near where De Clieu was born. A ship that helps others is a fitting tribute to De Clieu. *Source: Photo by Alf van Beem generously placed in universal public domain.*

CHAPTER 12
MUR DE LA PESTE

We hauled the cart a little way into the field in the slanting rain and total darkness, hoping to make it harder for Alessandro to recover. Whiskers followed us through the wet grass as we struggled uphill, seeing no signs of humanity.

Suddenly, a flash of lightning lit our surroundings like high noon. A long palisade of sharpened stakes bristled one hundred paces in front of us. This wooden porcupine stretched away to either side of the horizon. Behind it, the beginnings of a stone wall thrust upward at irregular heights and angles. Not a soul moved. A long rumble of thunder groaned in the distance.

About thirty yards from the palisade, I spied a dark guard house. Madame Duchon tripped on something and fell face first into the muddy grass. I peered over in the gloom and recoiled at the body of a peasant lying stricken in the weeds. Madame Duchon launched into her customary string of curses she had learned from the sailors who boarded with her and struggled out of death's grip. From there we crawled on all fours, keeping low in the high grass and feeling our way towards the stakes.

When we reached them, we had to work several loose to squeeze through. It was shoddy construction, and would not have passed muster in my unit. The half-finished stone wall was only three feet high here and Madame Duchon jumped over to the north side. She kicked at the wall spitefully, toppling the poorly balanced rocks until I succeeded in stopping her.

"Who goes there?" yelled a voice from down the line.

I yelled back, "Get your ass over here, private, you sack of donkey dung, it's Capitaine De Clieu!"

A poorly clothed soldier emerged from the darkness clutching a musket in one hand and his bayonet in the other. He was a mere boy of perhaps fourteen years old. I thanked God with all my heart upon seeing the hapless lad.

"Put your hat on straight, you nincompoop, and chest your weapon. This is a field inspection and it won't be pleasant!"

The boy straightened his hat and slapped the musket to his chest, fumbling and almost dropping his rusty bayonet.

"Now, salute! Now turn around, and fix your bayonet! Six, seven, eight! Now, salute again and tell me why in the blazes I shouldn't have you whipped for sleeping on the job? About face! Four, five, six! Now, tell me why you've derelicted your duty? A small army of plague-infested vagabonds could have crossed due to your inattention!"

The boy jumped around obeying my orders like a marionette, alternately saluting and frantically adjusting his kit. I couldn't tell if he was crying or if it was rain. "Now, where are the others, you rascal?"

"Sleeping, sir, over in the—" Madame Duchon stepped forward and slapped the private across the cheek.

"Sleeping, my codpiece!" she belted. "Get them up at once!" I was taken aback but could ill afford to have a discussion with her now.

"Sir, yes, sir!" he squeaked and flew off towards the dark guardhouse.

I glared at Madame Duchon, mouthing a curse for her to stay quiet. A frenzy of shouts echoed from inside the guardhouse. Bumps and clanks sounded until nine privates and a petty officer tumbled into the pouring rain in disarray. They moved like peasant conscripts and did not know this drill.

I strode before them. "Form up! Make a line straighter than a snake shit! Where the deuce are your weapons?"

A red-haired sergeant spoke. "Sir, we only have three muskets and two are broken, and the crossbow strings don't work well in the rain, and Lieutenant Lefarbe told us one man on watch was—"

Madame Duchon's palm cracked across his cheek and the man crumpled onto the grass, his wet hair whirling in an arc. The boy on his right helped him up.

"Never mind what Lefarbe said, you puddle of fish feces!" she barked into his petrified face. "You answer to Capitaine De Clieu—and Sergeant Duchon!"

I began to pity these hapless conscripts, and marvel at Duchon's abilities. I spoke up, "Yes! Never mind Lefarbe; I have strict orders from Paris to test your readiness and execute anyone found lax!"

The shivering men stood straight as ramrods. Not a word was uttered.

"This post isn't lax, is it?"

A chorus went up, "No, sir!"

Their officer wiped his brow. "We've shot almost twenty people just this week, sir, trying to cross."

My eyes bulged. I paced up and down their line four times and on the fifth whirled to face them, removing my plumed hat. "If you are so attentive, how in God's holy name was I able to ride a horse cart through your line?"

I jumped up and down, pointing at the hole we made in their palisade and the stones strewn around from Madame Duchon's kicking. The officer's voice trembled with fear. "Sir, we were merely—" The back of Madame Duchon's hand cracked across the officer's acne-scarred cheek and down he went. I pointed at the silhouette of our cart some distance across the field. "I am a fair man, so I will give you sorry louts one last chance. If my cart and belongings aren't back inside the Mur de la Peste in one turn of my hourglass I'll shoot one in every three of you and whip the rest." They stared at me, confused.

Madame Duchon raised her fist above her head, "You heard the Capitaine! Move, move, move like the devil was after you or you'll wish he was instead of me! Fetch our cart!"

The men shot through the gap like frightened deer. Madame Duchon got a running start and kicked the last one in the buttocks forcefully. He lurched forward and stumbled before bounding over the wall. In short order the men had our cart secured in a nearby hay barn and built a roaring fire inside the guardhouse.

I complemented their efficiency and assured them that there was a good chance I would not execute any of them. Sargeant Duchon pulled up her collar and rested in a corner. I sent two men out to patrol and lectured the rest at length on the importance of setting proper night watches before I let them rest. An hour before daylight, I wrote them a brief note, commending them on passing the readiness test and ordering a thorough armed search of the Alessandro's camp area. We commandeered their mule and left with the cart as they snored.

CHAPTER 13
TREASURE HUNTING IN PARIS

We made much better time with the mule, although he was a surly beast and nipped my coattails. We passed swaying fields of early wheat, hops, and budding vineyards. At several of these we stopped for the night and enjoyed hearty meals with their ruddy-faced owners who shivered at the idea of plague once again stalking the lands. We neglected to mention that we came from Marseilles.

Just outside Paris in a village called Juvisy-Sur-Ogre, Madam Duchon bid me *adieu* at a cottage on the banks of the Seine.

"Well, De Clieu, my niece Juliette lives here with her family and this is where I shall remain. I would have enjoyed the military life had I been born with balls like you. You've treated me well and I wish you the best of fortune. If you see my Paul-Henri, tell him to come here and visit; I miss him terribly." Whiskers jumped onto my lap and I sneezed.

I pressed my lips together, surveying my stalwart companion. "Madame Duchon, you've performed with strength and courage exceeding all expectations under circumstances where many soldiers under my command might break and run. It is within my power to officially conscript you into the King's Royal Infantry and confer on you the rank of sergeant that you have so skillfully impersonated for the past week."

Sergeant Duchon's eyes twinkled, and she brushed the crumbs off the rumpled uniform that she still wore. I unloaded Sergeant Duchon's belongings as she rapped on the door. A pretty young woman with a baby in her arms flung the door open.

On seeing the disheveled and menacing sergeant Duchon, she shrieked, "Run, Laurence, the Army's here to conscript you!"

The woman tried to slam the door shut but Duchon grabbed it.

"Juliette, cease your shrieking. It's me, your aunt Paula Duchon from Marseilles!"

Juliette peered closer at the weathered sergeant and then her face brightened. "Why…why, Auntie…my God, what has happened to you?"

Whiskers meowed at the door and Sergeant Duchon waved to me as I coaxed the mule into a trot north to Paris.

I carted north along a widening road through the outskirts of Paris. An increasing flow of carts, wagons, horses, and people on foot joined me. I passed iron-shod wagons carrying oak barrels of wine and small peasant carts full of fresh greens and pretty flowers, perhaps destined for the court at Versailles.

The gate guards examined my crumpled papers from Martinique. Like sharks circling a wounded whale calf, they sensed I had the wherewithal to pay a fine and that they had cause to levy one. I pre-empted them by insisting I honor their hard work with a silver *écu* for each man on post and mentioned off-handedly the names of the few officers I knew in Paris.

One of these two tactics struck a chord because their approbation at my outdated papers dissolved into gossip about the great D'Iberville. The guards let me through only on my solemn promise to immediately go to the War Ministry to process my papers and receive renewal stamps. I heartily promised, took my leave, and then made for my uncle's residence.

I trotted the mule along the imposing stone walls and battlements into the pulsating heart of Paris, passing innumerable shops and street vendors. The tired sun cast everything in a bold yellow light and traffic lessened as the day grew old. After much circling and consternation, I finally arrived at my uncle's chateau on Rue Du Coca near the imposing Chateau de Louvre. I removed Joel's letter from my breast pocket and compared the address to my location.

Two African servants in fine livery stood by a red oak door that corresponded with the address in his letter. They monitored me and my battered cart suspiciously. I called out to them, asking if

Joel De Clieu lived here. "*Oui,* Monsieur. On whose behalf dost thou inquire?"

I straightened up and gave them my full title, adding a few extra surnames. "'Tis I, Gabriel Mathieu de Clieu, Capitaine du Compagnie, Hero of Nevis, Commander of Martinique, Confidant of D'Iberville…Esquire." The two men furrowed their brows and cocked their heads.

One replied hesitantly. "My apologies. Who are you, then?"

"His nephew Gabriel—tell him it's his nephew Gabriel!"

They whispered to each other and bid me wait a moment as one hopped inside. Many voices echoed from the rear of this stately home. Joel appeared at the front door and squinted at me. I hardly recognized him for his massive girth and long curly wig, but he recognized me at once.

"How is it that my nephew Gabriel, the war hero, arrives a month late in a mule cart covered in filth? Get his things inside forthwith!" he ordered the servants. "Treat him as you would John the Baptist returned from heaven!"

Joel drew me to his bosom, kissing me on the lips like a lover. A servant led me inside and another took my mule to the stable.

Joel embraced me again in his splendid foyer and, after more cheek kissing, apologized "You must excuse me, Gabriel, I expected your arrival over a month prior. Whatever became of you? No matter. I must excuse myself, for I have the Minister of Finance's uncle Gerard upstairs, two shipping brokers, and company I must entertain. By thunder, you must be tired! Our maids will help you and we'll meet once you are refreshed."

Joel rushed back upstairs and left me at the mercy of a small army of maids and manservants. A fussing team of maids whisked me to a lavishly tiled bathing room. They whirled me around, stripped me, and immersed me in a steaming tub. I could not get a word in edgewise and their Parisian French came out faster than I could follow.

My first urge was to flirt with these pretty ladies assaulting me with soaps and sponges, as I had hardly seen a lady in months. Though never a more loyal companion did I have, I would never accuse Sergeant Duchon of being ladylike. The girls took to me with long-handled brushes, the kind used on horses, I think. They exfoliated me so mercilessly that their beauty was no incentive for this abuse to continue. I was plucked out of the hot bath and dunked in a cold one. My heart raced and I bit my lip from the shock. They giggled.

Then the maids came at my throat with a bright, shining blade. I made to parry their thrusts but they gently pressed my arms down and shaved me. Before I could inquire as to their names and marital status, they had me dressed like a doll in a fine blue suit that constricted me like a swamp snake. They laced my hair tighter than my boots and pinned a fancy wig to my skull.

The ladies spat me out of the bath complex and onto my uncle's patio where he puffed on cigars from Saint-Domingue with five older gentlemen. The old men chuckled at intervals and drank cognac from fluted tulip crystal glasses.

Joel welcomed me. "Ah Gabriel! What took you so long?" I blinked.

He motioned me over, "Here he is, here is my nephew Gabriel, D'Iberville's right hand man!"

"Well, I was just a—"

White-whiskered men in flowing wigs silenced my protests. They pumped my hand, introduced themselves and their ancestors back to the Crusades. Their smoky, powdered lips kissed my cheeks more passionately than had my late wife. The old men doted on me, eager for soldiering stories, like mothers fawning over a newborn.

The oldest of the lot, a tipsy fellow named Comte Nicot, took his turn with me. Mustaches and beards were not in vogue in Versailles but somehow my uncle had attracted a collection of Paris' hairiest nobility. Nicot wasted no time shouting at me that he was indeed of that very same line of Nicots who had introduced tobacco to Catherine D'Medici in the French court over one hundred years ago. He winked as he puffed on his tightly-rolled cigar.

Nicot slapped me on the back and said, "Welcome home, my boy! These are heady times, the War of the Quadruple Alliance concluded, Spain held in her place, and the English on our side... The English! Ha! Now there's a laugh. How long will it last, De Clieu? Eh? Why, not longer than it takes to unbutton Mrs. De Clieu's petticoats, I dare say!" Joel's red face exploded in laughter and a rousing chorus boomed into the night.

Nicot carried on, "And my beloved Mississippi Company is so profitable that I have to build new banks just to hold all the coin and specie arriving from investors!"

Nicot forgot about me and complained that carrying too many gold coins had worn a hole in his favorite jacket's pocket to the point where they had exploded out onto the floor at the opera.

A deep-voiced gentleman in a resplendent wig piped up, "Yes, joint stock companies, my boy, that is where the future is. No barriers to trade, you see, just one global marketplace."

"Indeed," piped another, "indeed, indeed. Why, even the commoners want sugar in their tea now. No more profitable lands exist than where you were, my boy—Martinique, Guadaloupe, Saint-Domingue." All agreed, harrumphed, and nodded.

"Except British India!" a skinny fellow chimed in, leaning against a statuette of a horse. All agreed, producing deep throated *oui!*s like a pond of bullfrogs.

"And the Dutch East Indies. Those should be valued thrice over all of New France!" chimed in a badger-like fellow who had introduced himself as Écuyer Baptiste.

The bullfrogs ribbeted another round of *oui!*s and Joel exclaimed, "Well of course, my dear Baptiste, that goes without saying. It was understood! We can leave the dirty Dutch entirely out of this affair! Why, their coffee plantations on Java alone dwarf our tobacco estates in all the Windward Isles."

An older man who had not spoken swirled his drink and furrowed his brow. He glowered at me out from underneath eyebrows that reminded me of lichen dangling from a mountain stone. Nicot burned a finger on his cigar, yelped, and tossed the cigar away in pain. It streaked like a meteorite past the silent old man's face.

"Hell brimmeth over!" the old lichen roared. "Dangerous matter, burning these tobacco leaves in a man's mouth. Why, Nicot, you'll burn Paris down! Next time we'll have a pipe-smoking party at my drawing room."

I explained to Nicot how the Caribs rolled and smoked such cigars, extinguishing them before they burned low. The crowd paid me rapt attention.

Nicot finished licking his finger and piped up, "Fascinating, your account of these things, Capitaine. Errm, you know, we need a good man we can trust to handle daily affairs here, a man who knows these sugar plantations and new colonies firsthand."

Another gurgled on his cognac. "Yes, a man like you! We're in business with your uncle, you see. Joel told us you'd be helping him."

After more gossip was traded about improvements in the sugar refining process I found a moment to pull Joel aside and ask him the question that had been consuming my heart for many months now.

"Uncle, I come to Paris with an idea to amass a fortune greater than sugar and tobacco combined. We can plant coffee on Matinique sell it back to France, and cut out the Dutch and Arabs entirely. What say you?"

Joel expelled air and widened his eyes, "By thunder...now, that's interesting...but it's been tried and failed. Bad air, they say. The few thousand pounds now coming from our colony on the Île de Bourbon are worth more than gold. Are you sure the climate is suitable?"

"I believe it is. The soil is so fertile that anything grows there. My question to you is—how we can procure a seeds or plants?"

"How indeed. Let us ask my friends here. They are wise men, long-time business partners, and can be trusted."

Joel turned back to the group and cleared his throat. "Gentleman, my nephew Capitaine De Clieu has just put to me a most fascinating idea. He means to establish a coffee plantation in the New World. Do one of you cantankerous old bats know how we might procure the seeds of this plant or seedlings?"

Ecuyer Baptiste spoke. "Impossible. Or very difficult, at least. The Arabs sterilize all their seeds and the plants don't seem to travel well. Starting on Île de Bourbon took years and I don't think there's a single plant in all Europe."

A glass of cognac was inserted into my newly-gloved hand. Comte Nicot grunted, "Baptiste has proven himself the oldest bat among us! Those of us close to *Le Grands* in Versailles all know that Louis XV has one single coffee tree. It's so big that it produces fertile seeds that he roasts for his personal coffee. It's the only one in France, located in the hothouse at the *Jardin des Plantes*. I've seen it. Very waxy dark green leaves and big red berries. Why don't you petition our King for some seeds or a seedling?"

This sent my heart racing. I could scarcely believe it. Baptiste inhaled through his nose. "My dear Nicot here is practically a gardener at Versailles. I dine with the royals and talk of more sophisticated matters like art and philosophy. Come with me tomorrow, dear Gabriel, and I'll present you to the Regent, the Duke of Orléans himself!"

Nicot chuckled. "Yes, Gabriel, go with Baptiste here and the best you'll get of old Phillipe II is a peepshow from outside his window on a ladder at midnight. In turn, I actually know many of the nobles who have the boy-king's ear. That's how we'll get you your coffee plant."

Nicot climbed an imaginary ladder with his drink in one hand. He clapped his arm around Baptiste who made a pouty face and then the two burst into laughter. I sensed the peepshow comment had some greater meaning between them.

CHAPTER 14
THE FIRST CUP

The next day I awoke to sun flooding into a broad set of windows. The curtains fluttered on a breeze. A heavenly smell permeated the gentle air. The bed was softer than anything I'd slept on, including seaweed. I rolled over and beheld a silver breakfast platter awaiting me on a slender cherry side table.

An Austrian *kipferl* bread perched next to a small pitcher of warm chocolate sauce for dipping. Two thick pieces of toast accompanied a glass of yellow whipped butter. In the center of the tray sat a china cup of hot chocolate, steam still rising from its murky surface. A saucer of frothy cream was next to the hot chocolate. No more joyous sight could I have beheld after the woes of Marseille and the long sea voyage from Martinique. I dove into this treasure trove and took a long, deep drink from the hot chocolate cup decorated with Chinese dragons in blue enamel.

It sizzled through my guts and tasted like poison. I spat its contents all over the feather bed. The liquid was devilishly hot, un-repentantly foul, and certainly not the Mexican chocolate I had tried in the Windward Isles!

A handsome black manservant in my uncle's livery rushed in and asked fearfully if I was ill. I tried to respond, but was racked with coughing.

The servant gasped and shouted for help. I lurched out of bed and snatched the vile cup, spilling it on my arm and screeching like a banshee. It burned my hair to the follicles. A sludge of little granules oozed on the bottom of the cup, no doubt arsenic or nightshade. I flung the cup aside and it smashed against a wall.

A portly cook in a tall, white hat barreled into my room. He found me dry heaving on the floor, gasping for breath as I felt the poison sealing off my lungs.

"Monsieuer, what is the matter? Was the coffee too hot?"

I stopped and looked up at him from all fours. "The...what?"

The cook trembled like a leaf in an October squall, "Co– co–coffee, sir, fresh from Île de Bourbon, grown just last year! Imported by a partner of Monsieur Joel's firm, green beans roasted until dark and oily. I prepare it the same every day. Master Joel drank from the same pitcher and suffered no ill effects, sir! Perhaps it was the cream. They say some men have a weak stomach for cream."

I picked myself up, waves of relief washing over me. I surveyed my coffee-spackled room. A bed sheet hung from a ceiling lamp, two chairs were overturned, and an oil painting hung at a rakish angle.

"It just went down the wrong pipe, that's all. My fault entirely."

The cook moaned, "Oh dear, I must have made it too hot for you. Monsieur Joel told me to brew it hot, I swear to you, sir, very hot and strong, said he!"

I felt terrible and gripped the man by the shoulders, "Nonono. It was the best coffee I've ever had in all my life…you know, I like my drinks hot, the hotter the better. We don't get coffee in the Army, just old tea and rum punch."

The cook's feverish breathing slowed and he supported himself on the servant, "Well…I see…Just a misunderstanding by this idiotic African slave. He should have warned you it was hot."

I brushed myself off. "I'm terribly sorry for this incident. It was a delicious breakfast—wonderful—many thanks to you both." The cook and servant exchanged glances.

At this moment, the door flew open and my aunt Madame Sofia de Clieu strode in wearing a low-cut yellow gown, exposing her expansive and withered bosoms. She stopped still upon seeing the maelstrom of my quarters.

"My goodness, what has happened? Oh, my dear nephew Gabrielllllle, what is the matter?"

The cook and servant were speechless, waiting for their sentences to be meted out. I glanced from the cook to my aunt and back.

"The coffee, Auntie dear…the coffee was…the most remarkable thing I've ever tasted! I gulped it too quickly and it went down the wrong pipe, that's all. Please forgive the fuss and disorder."

The cook's knees stopped wobbling and he exhaled. Sophia flowed forward and crushed me to her bodice.

"Oh, my poor dear boy! The coffee is from Île de Bourbon. We just got a box of it last week. Straight from our factor át the Compagnie. It's so expensive…my word, one hundred and six livres for just a small box. So—you liked it?"

She released me from her embrace as I replied, "Oh yes, Auntie, it was full of flavor like a—"

She cut me off. "Oh yes, delicate hints of vanilla, touches of orange, and a gentle caress of honey."

"Yes, It was all of those! Who did this come from?"

She swelled with pride. "Oh, from a factor, a representative of the French East India Company who is personal friend of Joel's."

She licked her lips and motioned the cook back to the kitchen, and looked at the servant with a twinkle in her eye. "Omri, help my nephew dress. I've put his uniform in the dressing room. And then clean up this mess straight away. I'll see you before you go, Gabriele; your uncle's waiting for you at the Admiralty." She touched Omri's shoulder and swept out of the room, the doors clicking behind her.

After a nice shave, I squeezed into the most majestic dress uniform I've ever worn, with a dashing tri-corner hat. I adjusted my new black wig. Black always looked good on me. I looked at myself in the gilded mirror and gasped. In place of a dirty plague refugee, I beheld an imposing infantry captain standing before me.

I met Sofia in the foyer and she pointed to a white and gold Comtoise clock that showed it was just after noon, "My goodness, you slept late Gabriel! You are late, you know. I'm sorry I didn't see you when you arrived last night. I was at a ball with my duchess friends. Furthermore, Joel's old rapscallions were here and I can't stand their cigar smoke and chortling."

"Please do not worry, Auntie dear, it's wonderful to see you."

She bestowed on me a hand-colored map of downtown Paris. "Here, take this map just in case you get lost. Paris has changed so much since you were here. Construction everywhere, new streets, new bridges on the Seine. Your uncle has big plans for you, Gabriel. But I have much bigger plans for you. Why, now that your poor wife has passed on, you can't just be lingering alone. A proud, handsome soldier like you has his choice of all the pretty virgins in Paris. Oh dear, your wig is crooked, but I like the black curls on you." She adjusted my mane. "I've already booked you to attend four balls, two of which are masquerade; so you'll need costume... five nights at the opera, three plays, and an actual jousting match!"

"I didn't know people still—"

She carried on, "Oh yes, and how they do joust! It's a very important social event. You must be seen in the right company, Gabriel. Oh, and I've taken the liberty of setting you up on a date tonight with your third cousin Raquel and then tomorrow with a widowed duchess! Tremendous bosoms, and keeps the right company, widowed at seventeen just last May. Her ex-husband scheduled three duels to settle various scores in one day. He won them all and went out gallivanting on a rainy night. Then he caught whooping cough. Can you imagine? Whooping cough! He whooped for weeks before expiring."

I recalled that I can only endure Aunt Sofia in short bursts.

"You mentioned I'm late for a meeting at the admiralty?" I asked politely.

She furrowed her brow, "Oh yes, so you are! Rudely late. You must make haste. Don't be seen talking to poor people in the city. *Bon voyage!*"

CHAPTER 15
SMOKE AND CIGARS

I left and gave a gleeful greeting to every mendicant, madman, and scoundrel I passed on my way.

The streets teemed with life, carriages wheeling to and fro. Shops and markets displayed wares from all of Europe and beyond. I strolled by smoked cod from the colonies, dried salmon from Finland, barrels of Bavarian beer from the Wittelsbach breweries, and one hundred round cheeses. City guards in smart uniforms saluted me as I passed. I bobbed my sumptuous hat to them, then turned right onto Rue Royal, saluting soldiers on my left and "Hi-ho-ing" a frothing drunkard.

My leather city shoes clicked on the flat granite cobblestones laid in perfect order. I passed men in even more luxuriant wigs than my own. Men with tight white stockings and gold canes clustered in little groups, some passing in and out of broad columned buildings flanking both sides of the Rue Royal. Blue and white *fleur-de-lis* flags flapped everywhere, imitating the distant ocean.

I strode up the broad steps of the admiralty and saluted the guards at the top.

"I am Capitaine De Clieu of King Louis XIV's infantry. Err, no, wait. I'm also Sub-Lieutenant De Clieu of Louis XV's navy...that's the one I have paperwork for...you see, I was promoted on Martinique but I'm not certain that it was properly registered here in the—"

The guard pointed up a staircase. "Your uncle wants you."

The place bustled with officers and officials sending ships over all the world's oceans. I stepped lightly up the curving marble staircase to the second floor. The walls were filled with oil paintings of French ships of the line in smoking naval battles.

I saw a door with actual smoke coming out from under the sill and read my uncle's name engraved on a plaque in silver letters. I knocked and heard excited voices inside, but no reply. A wave of smoke engulfed me as I stepped onto the threshold.

Disconnected voices spoke from the gloom, "*Merde!* What do you mean, there's not enough money?"

Another unfamiliar voice hissed, "John Law has it all under control, don't worry."

My uncle's voice burst in, "Go tell him to stop selling new shares—it's out of control! Wait 'til we get more beaver pelts, for Christ's sake!"

Joel's voice came from the smoke. "Gabriel, is that you?" I navigated around plush leather chairs and desks piled high with papers until I saw a flame flickering ahead. I coughed convulsively and emerged to find four men leaning in armchairs by a fireplace.

"Here he is, gentlemen: Capitaine De Clieu, D'Iberville's right-hand man!"

"Uncle, is the flue open in your chimney?" A round of coughing ensued before Joel's response.

"The what? I don't know. My usual servants were called away today."

I pulled an iron rod on the side of the brick chimney and heard a clank from inside the shaft. Immediately, the smoke began clearing from the room and funneling up the chimney.

A jolly voice with a Dutch accent applauded me, "*Klootzak!* Juust the sort of goo-getter we need aroond here!"

As the smoke cleared, a big grey mustache emerged from the miasma. Attached to the mustache was the face of Comte Nicot of the Mississippi Company who held a cigar in one hand and a silver pipe in the other. Joel's partners explained the nature of their businesses in Paris, their investments in joint stock companies, and how I was to help them in these operations.

"Now, we're importing coffee from the Île de Bourbon, and we need a broker on the Seine every Thursday to handle contracts. Our man Etienne will show you tomorrow."

Joel introduced Pieter de Raad, a Dutch aristocrat and lumber baron. De Raad smiled and chimed in, "Then we'll meet to discuss warehousing and coin flows. Mr. Law's inflating everything with these stupid paper notes, so we're converting those hush-hush in the Jewish sector."

Raad's Dutch accent itched my ears worse than fleas. I could not stand it. "Uncle, with all due respect, how is it that you're working with a Dutchman?" The men stopped and winced as if I had flatulated.

Joel cautioned, "Gabriel, tut tut. Please be civil. You must understand that these wars come and go. Now, if we can prosper by working with fine financial minds like the good de Raad here, then we'll all be better off. Why, old Raady's been with us since '04 and Lord Mills here since '08, even at the height of the war."

I peered at an angular man in his fifties with an improbably grandiose wig which cascaded to his knees.

"'Ello, Gabriel, how do you do?"

This all seemed so wrong to be consorting with the very people whose cannons tore through our hulls.

Nicot wheezed and patted me on the back, "Now Gabriel, my lad, you must release the soldiering mindset here and see reality. How on earth could we import the volumes of coffee we plan to without working with the Dutch East India Company? Or cinnamon without the British East India Company? Our ships need protection, and we pay top prices."

Raad hiccupped and interjected, "Hardly!" to a round of laughter.

Joel wiped his eyes and continued, "Well, it's true; we often barter our colonial sugar and rum with old Millsy. He drinks most of it before it sees the market. Gabriel, you really must lose these pretensions to be successful in international affairs, we all speak the same language here. Do we not, gentlemen?" I could not help but be intrigued by this bizarre cabal.

"Is what you do legal?" This provoked peals of giggling from all four.

Joel calmed down at last. "Legal? You must not be so naive, Gabriel. Surely you saw how affairs were conducted in the Indies. Was anything happening there legal? Did a single fully *legal* ship set sail from Saint-Pierre? Most of the worst sins a man can commit are *legal*. Of course we do everything *legally!* Why, the law practically bends over backwards to aid us!"

73

De Raad broke in, waving his arms. "Not that we agree with this, of course!"

Joel settled down and explained, "We are servants of our investors, you see. Keepers of their trust and their fortunes. We must be conservative in our bearings, prudent in our endeavors, and unusually legal in our affairs. Our investors are men of considerable merit and include some royalty."

Mills took over. "Young King Louis's protector, Philippe d'Orléans: he's one of our biggest investors. Why, there isn't a pie in Europe that his fingers aren't in! Who do you think lets John Law, that crazy Scot, set up new banks and print these ridiculous paper bank notes?"

The fellows grumbled and hurrumphed. Joel complained, "This Law has quarreled so bitterly with King George of England that we find him on our shores, and the Versailles nobility all infatuated with his financial bird droppings. Coins made of paper? Paper coins? Honestly! The people see Law's friends getting rich and think he's a genius. The masses adopt his paper coins like straw men adopting torches as the latest fashion! It will be the ruin of all France, mark my words!"

The men reproached Joel, pointing out that paper has its place in finance through cheques, bills of lading, stock certificates, deeds, and all manner of other instruments and contracts which I little understood.

After pointing out that Joel himself had a fortune in Law's banking scheme, Joel muttered, "Always hedge my bets," and gave way. He ended the argument after making some derisive comments about Scotland's cuisine and animal husbandry practices.

Mills gestured in the air. "Yes, you see, Gabriel, unlike soldiers we financiers and merchants benefit more from peace than war. We're a stabilizing force, really. Our companies cross international boundaries and create harmony between old enemies. Just look at this room and you have your proof: a Dutchman, an Englishman, and a Frenchman working together."

"What does that make me, then?" asked Comte Nicot.

"A regular scoundrel!" roared Joel, spilling his drink in laughter.

I straightened in my chair. "You misjudge my profession, Lord Mills. There is no greater champion of peace than a veteran of many combats such as I. None would weigh more carefully the decisions that lead to war than he who knows its hardships and horrors firsthand. The ambition of joint stock companies is responsible for ten times more ravages than anything we professional soldiers have done. We're just pawns in your game. I see it daily in the Antilles; everything is sugar, rum, gold, and silver." The old men applauded my speech in agreement.

Mills puffed on his cigar. "Quite so, well said. And for this excellence under duress and forbearance towards the ills of war, we seek to employ you in more peaceful ventures. We've worked with your uncle here on some tip-top projects. Who do you think financed that ravishing dame Marquise de Lambert to open her salon in the Hotel de Nevers on Rue de Richelieu? Next month we're opening a salon and coffee house right across the street from the Cafe Le Procope itself! We're calling it Cafe Le Deux Magots, haha!"

Nicot turned to Mills, "Did you secure the property title from Cornelius and deliver copies to the ministry?" At this, the group dove into logistics and percentages just as a cadre of generals would plan a battle.

Mills extinguished his seventh cigar and pushed back his chair. "Oh bollocks, you're right. I'll go talk to Cornelius straight away. Pleasure to meet you, Gabriel. I very much look forward to working with you. Pip pip!"

Lord Mills pumped my hand and took his leave. They debated the various permits needed to run this new coffeehouse, deliveries of Arabian coffee beans from the warehouse, and whether to allow women inside.

At last Nicot looked up at me from underneath his bushy grey eyebrows and smacked his forehead, "Oh, Capitaine! Why, I quite forgot. I was going to present you at Versailles and it's almost high noon! Come, come, we haven't a moment to lose."

Chapter 16

Versailles

Nicot's carriage clattered down the well-paved road as we transitioned from the urban bustle of Paris to the lush gardens surrounding the court at Versailles. We checked with four sets of royal guards. I felt like an intruder, like a foreigner in the heart of my own land. The shrubbery was more elegant than my best suit. After the last checkpoint, we entered the wide palace grounds.

We stepped down from our carriage which was whisked off to the stables. Nicot made his way past long wings of ornate three-story apartments and saluted several acquaintances passing on the paved thoroughfare. We marched closer to the royal apartments and then made our way left to a splendid door guarded by a dour official. He knew Nicot but questioned me before agreeing to let me pass into the grand entry hall.

Here more noble families moved about their business, and a few were gathered talking, their voices echoing off the marble columns. Nicot climbed marble stairs, past a row of mirrors and sumptuous paintings of French warships, and into a gilded hallway. Each door had a number on it that corresponded to the noble occupying that apartment.

Nicot counted to himself and then rapped on the last door in the hallway, closest to the royal palace. A butler answered and gave way to a large man wearing a fleeced robe and rabbit hair slippers.

"Ah, Comte Nicot, what brings you to my door? Come in, we're just about to have our midday meal. Oh, and who is this? I see you've brought a guest."

"My dear friend, may I present to you one of the great D'Iberville's most loyal soldiers, *capitaine de compagnie* of the Martinique infantry and nephew of my friend Joel de Clieu, Gabriel Mathieu de Clieu. *Capitaine*, it is my abundant honor to present to you the Duc du Maine, son of His Royal Majesty Louis XIV and member of the Council of Regents, the extremely honorable and excellent Louis-Auguste de Bourbon."

I met six members of the duke's family inside and we dined on a fourteen-course luncheon. After lunch, we gossiped over a round of fine coffee served in ornate demitasse china. The duke ignored me and I chatted with his family about the varieties of snakes and spiders I had encountered. After coffee, Nicot brought me before the duke and bid me speak my mind.

I gripped my belt buckle and explained how wonderfully productive and fertile the Antilles were. I told him how I had the means at my disposal to begin a very profitable coffee plantation for the benefit of all France if I would just be entrusted with coffee seeds to sow on my return to Martinique.

The duke was kind but brief. "It sounds like an excellent and profitable plan. I know very little of botany and less about coffee, so you must excuse me on that account. I can tell you that my grand-nephew, the King, has but one coffee tree that bears fruit and he has it roasted for his family consmption as did my father. You drank it today. We all guard this tree quite closely, but perhaps I can entreat him to bestow upon you its seeds. His Royal Highness is busy through the end of the week, but I shall write to you through the Comte here. It has been quite a pleasure meeting you, sir."

I thanked the Duke as profusely as possible without reciting poetry and bid him *adieu*. As we left Versallies, for some reason Chummy's words about being a fish monger ran through my head and I could smell his fishy hands.

CHAPTER 17

ENTREATIES

After two weeks of contract trading, barter, losses, and gains I grew restless for a response from the Duc de Maine. I began calling on Comte Nicot to buy one sort of cigar or other. By the third week I had him teaching me how to whittle pipes in his drawing room. Just after his wife put a stop to that, a messenger came to Nicot's residence.

The Comte's footman passed him the letter and Nicot exclaimed, "Why, De Clieu, it's from the Duke! Let's have a look, shall we?"

My heart thudded in my chest and I felt close to regurgitation. Nicot's gloved hands unrolled the ornate message from the Duke and broke his elegant seal. Nicot mumbled as he read it and I peered over his shoulder. After several paragraphs of formalities and thanks for our visit, my great service and so on, he came to the point:

Regarding the capitaine's very noble desire to enrich our monarchy through this new mercantile and agricultural venture, the King bids you know that his coffee plant is sacrosanct and untouchable. It belonged to his grandfather, the great and illustrious Louis XIV. Every seed, twig, and leaf is meant only for royal consumption of the king and his most favored nobles.

My heart sank to the bottom of the English Channel. How could they chose their own selfish coffee roasting pleasures over the profit of all France? I swallowed. Nicot rolled the message back up.

"Take heart, my man. Surely there are one hundred other ventures by which a similar profit might be made. Why not join me in some tobacco trading? Eh? I have a ship departing for Saint-Domingue just next week that needs someone to oversee provisioning. Perhaps you could help?"

I felt useless. "Surely I shall aid you, my dear Comte, as you have aided me in my search for coffee, but I grieve as if I had lost a friend to whooping cough. I am certain that coffee can become so abundant and successful in the Antilles that it will dwarf even tobacco."

Nicot sniffed. "I understand that you're depressed about this rejection, but don't talk like a madman."

"There must be some other noble who could get us seeds, even just one."

"I don't know, De Clieu, but what I do know is that your next petition cannot be through me since I have already been the vehicle of one royal rejection."

"There must be some other way, then."

Nicot lit another cigar. "Oh, there's always a way. More trading and dealing occurs in Versailles than on the floors of the Les Halles market and at the French West Indies Company combined. Do let me know if I may be of service to you. I like the smell of coffee, you know."

This rejection was my first in a dazzling string of failures. Petitioning other dukes met with similar responses, or none at all. Joel very kindly presented me to the Duke of Orléans, where I was rebuffed in the name of little King Louis' coffee-drinking habit. I turned to God and prayed for a solution. I wrote to Cardinal Andre Hercule de Fleury who lectured me on the sins of greed and implored me to cast off these earthly desires.

When I wrote Charlotte de La Motte Houdancourt, Duchess of Ventadour, she demanded to know what I had told the Duke of Maine about snakes. I wrote her with every serpentine detail and anecdote I knew and I even offered to show her some scars, but I never heard back.

I became so disheartened that Pieter de Raad even helped me write to the Burgomaster of Amsterdam, who possessed the only other coffee tree in Europe. We were not rewarded with even a response after three letters and an offer of 30% profits. I wrote to King Louis himself. There was no response, of course, from coffee-coveting king. I grew angry and frustrated. After serving my country, enduring near-fatal wounds and countless trials, these wig-wearing royals rarely even took the time to reject my entreaties. I began to have dreams of other Frenchmen, connected with the East Indies Company sailing gaily to Martinique with small forests of coffee trees while I stalled and failed in Paris. There had to be another way.

CHAPTER 18
YEARS SLIPPING UNDER THE HULL

Intrigue boiled on every level of society, and each household was a simmering teacup in this cosmos of craftiness. My aunt and uncle juggled affairs, both business and amorous. I longed for the simple military days when right and wrong were clear. Even though most events there were wrong—at least one knew. Everyone in Paris was expected to have at least two ongoing romantic affairs and gossip about them at tea parties and salons. When my new acquaintances were not whispering about their lovers, they turned to a topic far more dear to my heart: piracy.

Society raged at the news of the pirate Bartholomew Roberts' rampage along the coast of Newfoundland. Roberts single-handedly brought the lucrative cod fishing industry to a stop. When word arrived that the same pirate began ravaging my beloved West Indies, I yearned to return home. The rapacious Roberts went so far as to hang the governor of Martinique, a good friend of mine, from the yardarm. Many men sought my opinion on how to stop Roberts. I yearned to strike out and meet this nautical ne'er-do-well on the high seas. Paris became prison. I had a recurring dream of exchanging cannon-fire with old Bart Roberts and running him through with a cutlass. During my waking hours, I was powdering my face and eating pastries in Paris.

I was in the middle of several important business deals for my uncle and could not depart Paris without shaming myself and leaving them half-complete. I learned constantly in my work. It was not unlike commanding soldiers in some regards. I ran from warehouses to ships, dealing with brokers, bankers, counts, and viscounts.

I quarreled with the commodity traders buying furs or selling tea leaves, and then regaled them with snake stories at soirées next door to the Exchange. I began encountering more success in my late night dealings than on the trading floors. Valuable business deals flowed from the docks and mercantile guildhalls into the cafes and ballrooms.

I became friends with a host of officers, minor nobility, philosophers, academics, traders, merchants, ship commanders, stevedores, and dock workers. I learned that wigs not only looked fantastic, but hid the symptoms of syphilis which certain royalty had long ago contracted. Society mimicked the diseased nobles' wig-wearing habits without any persuasion other than the desperate need to be fashionable. I planned to remain a non-syphilitic wig wearer and was quite discriminating in who I drunkenly consorted with in the back rooms of masquerade balls. Paris blazed with secrets and scandals percolating down from the court and Versailles.

CHAPTER 19
THE MISSISSIPPI BUBBLE

Late one night in December of 1720, Joel met with a friend at the Royal Bank and learned a secret. Philippe d'Orléans was going to announce that the Mississippi Company's Royal Bank did not have enough coins to repay its nervous investors. Joel raced home, livid with rage, and begged me to withdraw his substantial deposits that very night with a special letter.

I clattered on horseback to the bank, bribed all sixteen guards, and secured Joel's iron safe in a wagon waiting outside. Panic spread through the financial district in the darkness just like the plague in Marseilles. News of the company's default on its paper notes crackled through Paris like a conflagration, immolating hopes on a bonfire of paper coins.

John Law fled to Belgium and Joel even had to cut back on his daily indulgence in *canard au sang* at the Tour d'Argent. Paris descended into a depression and two men I knew slit their wrists. Bread lines formed as flour became scarce and people fled the cities after losing their savings. Economic catastrophe rippled throughout Europe. British investors vainly tried to exchange their shares in the South Sea Company for gold bullion and this vast joint stock company unraveled. Law's scheme burst the great European economies wide open, like piercing a long neglected blister with a sharp needle. Several of the choicest masquerade balls were cancelled in 1721.

Joel and his partners lost imponderable sums of money as the Mississippi Company collapsed. However, the diversity of their investments helped them survive while those who had invested all their savings in the Royal Bank or in shares of the Mississippi Company found themselves penniless.

Little else transpired that year. Our Pope died and another was instated. The Great Northern War ended in Russian victory. The victor, Peter, proclaimed himself "Peter the Great" but Parisians agreed that he was average for that inferior nation.

The tenure of Philippe d'Orléans grew more tenuous. Parisians stood aghast at the horrors brought on by paper money, vowing never again to dabble in the diabolic stuff. Trade had virtually ground to a halt and I was not needed in Paris, so I visited my dear mother on the coast. Snow swirled around the cart wheels and we ploughed through big drifts to arrive in Anglequeville.

My mother was courting a nice old widower and was more relaxed without my father on hand. My local tavern, La Chaîne Rouillée, had named a drink after my late progenitor. This drink consisted of pouring the dregs of any three wine bottles into an hollowed-out gourd and drinking the concoction while lying on a tabletop. The fellows at La Chaîne Rouillée informed me that my father lived on, for the phrase "drunk as De Clieu" was on the lips of commoners from Calais to La Havre.

After a fond and reflective month with my mother and childhood friends, I contemplated my role in society. The coffee seed was planting itself in my brain again. On the coach journey back to Paris, I longed for the simple life and fair weather of Martinique. Snow drifts became sand dunes and dark trees became field slaves as we slid along.

The year 1722 dawned looking little better than 1721. I spent much of my work time in the Café Le Deux Magot, meeting with investors in seafaring commerce. There, on an oak bench by the bar, I met the drunken botanist.

Chapter 20

The Gabelle

I awaited a Venetian merchant in the Le Deux Magot, but he never came. I thought it odd, because I was there to pay a sizeable debt we owed him. I sat at a table looking over a ship's ledger when a paunchy gentleman in aristocratic garb sidled up to the table across from me. He ordered a coffee and bread roll. He was sweating profusely despite the cool April airs.

He puffed up like a blowfish and wheezed, "*Bonjour*! My name is Sébastien Vaillant, botanist to King Louis, plant master, keeper of biological lore, seer of living organisms: grass, roots, shoots, trees and bees!"

I sipped my cup nonchalantly, wondering if this red-faced fellow had had too much wine.

I extended a hand. "Capitaine Gabriel Mathieu De Clieu at your service, I'm sure...Are you quite all right?"

His hand shook as he ate the roll and drops of his coffee followed the crumbs onto his lap. "Yes, yes, quite all right, just been experimenting with a new herb to cure gout, from the nightshade family, you know, very potent."

"Are those not poisonous?"

"Generally, yes. But take the New World tomato from the nightshade family—delicious! I've found another nightshade that is quite different from the rest. It was brought from Mongolia by an Austrian trader...or so he claims. I don't believe him."

Vaillant launched into a string of botanical adventure stories from collecting pink sea cucumbers in the Nicobar Islands to flesh eating Guatemalan lichens. His shaking decreased and a larger percentage of the coffee fell down his throat than onto his lap.

"Say De Clooo, did you know that the coffee bean isn't really a bean at all? Of course not! It's a seed, comes from trees." He drew a tree in the air, coffee cup in hand, sending an arc of hot liquid onto the bench next to him.

"The coffee tree is like a spice tree. Many captains have lost their lives attempting to cultivate it. The Arabs still control the bulk of the supply. Then you have the Dutch plantations on Java and our new colony on Île de Bourbon. The English have put their hands on some, too, in the Indies. It's very tricky to cultivate, you see. Trees take time, you know, and conditions must be just so."

"As a matter of fact, I am a student of the coffee plant myself," I told him. "I have a plan to—"

Vaillant cut me off, bellowing, "A student, are you? Then I shall teach you! Back in 1616 a Dutch captain, Pieter Van Der Broeke, stole the trees from Mocha and brought them to Java, but he was loose with the native women and died of a ve– a ve– a ven–"

He erupted in a disastrous sneeze that momentarily stopped all conversation in the coffee house and spackled me with a mist of phlegm. "–eeeeariall disease!" He wiped his mouth with the back of his sleeve.

"As the King's botanist, I care for the only coffee tree in all France. There are only two in Europe, you know. The Dutch have the other one. We had a couple before in the Royal Botanical Gardens but they never did well. They died, the poor little things. Shriveled away."

"Monsieur Vaillant, how did King Louis XIV acquire this plant?"

He crossed himself. "In 1714 Louis's negotiations with the Dutch concluded with them sending a five-foot-tall coffee tree from their Amsterdam Botanical Garden. Our clever old Sun King! The Dutch had the only coffee in all Europe, you know. 'Twas smuggled from Mocha one hundred years ago and survived in their glass hothouses. Imagine how angry the Mohameddans were at that! The penalty for tree smuggling was—and still is—beheading. So, now, this mayor, this…Nicolaas Witsen I think…burgomaster!—" he wiped his mouth again and continued "—of Amsterdam sent a little five-foot tree to King Louis' Chateau de Marly. The Marly botanist was really just a gardener and knew nothing of the plant, so he passed the shrub to my colleague Antoine de Jussieu at the Royal Botanical Gardens." He slurped from his cup, his eyes wandering like an iguana. "Guess what *le Roi Soleil* did with his new coffee plant?"

I hissed for Vaillant to lower his voice. Speaking loudly in public of the deceased King was an even less healthy habit than testing new varieties of nightshade. Vaillant leaned towards me like a tree about to fall and whispered, "Guess what Louis did with—"

"I do not know, I am sure!" I cut him off, imploring him to lower his voice. Spies and informants often lounged around. I recognized one in the back, chatting with three other men about prostitutes.

Vaillant swallowed and leaned in, "Louueee, God rest his soul, used to have coffee roasting parties at seventy-five years of age. He invited the choicest girls in court to the Botanical Garden…and it got really hot in there. Did you know that even at seventy-five, Louis could pleasure two girls in a row? Right on my cutting table by the cacti! He'd then move on to his mistress Madam Du Barry in the fern section—"

I grabbed Vaillant's collars with both hands and wrenched his ear to my mouth, "Lower your voice, dear sir."

I released him and he smoothed himself like a cat. Despite adhering to the Parisian custom of gossiping on others' intimate sexual details, he was spitting all over my face whenever he spoke.

I looked up at the door for the late Venetian. Vaillant said, "Who are you looking for?"

I replied absentmindedly, "Oh, this merchant, Don Manno of Venice, I don't think you would—"

This was all Vaillant needed. "Venice! Some say they were the first in Europe to start drinking coffee. They have cafés all over their piazzas, you know. Terrific smugglers, the Venetians—top notch. Like the Dutch first acquiring coffee from the Arabs in Mocha in 1616."

He whispered even lower, "Did you know that the Dutch planted coffee in the Americas in Surinam? Six years ago. 1714, I think. They failed of course, being Dutch. Not so simple as on their tropical plantation of Java. Imagine the wealth that could be generated by this type of venture! Now, to get coffee, we sail around the Cape of Good Hope or march overland from the Levant. Growing coffee in the Americas would make the transport less than half the distance as from Java. Do you know what happened to the Dutch in Surinam?"

I guessed, "They had coffee parties like Louis?"

"No!" he wheezed, "They tried to start a plantation but their slaves revolted and killed them, uprooted the plants, and ran into the jungle to join the Caribs!"

I wiped his spittle out of my eyes. He carried on without noticing his precipitation.

"Do you know about my friend Michel Isambert? He stole a coffee plant from the Dutch on Java and brought it to the Antilles in 1717 where the climate is perfect for cultivation. And guess what happened to him? He drowned! He boarded a ship bound for the British colonies but it went down in a storm. His coffee plants drowned in the sea!" He waved his arms, almost knocking my drink over, pushing Isambert's coffee out to sea.

I tested him. "Verily, I, too, was in the Antilles in 1717 but heard nothing of this Isambert or his coffee plant. I remember a ferocious hurricane that year which severely damaged Martinique where I was stationed. Pray tell, what was the name of Isambert's ship?" I knew of six that went down.

"'Twas the *Orleans* I believe. Or so they told me. The *Orleans* took poor Michel down to the sea cucumbers, cnidaria, and kelps. He was on a secret mission for France. Imagine if the Dutch had found out he had planted their precious crop!"

The *Orleans'* hull had washed up on the reefs by the gale and was smashed asunder by the rocks and surging surf. Vaillant left the statement dangling in the air and gazed at me. Suddenly, his airs of madness were dispersed by his intelligent and piercing eyes that beheld me from beneath his grey, mossy brows.

At this moment an idea struck me like a crossbow bolt and I leaned in close. "Sébastien…hypothetically, can you get me a cutting from Louis' tree? So that I might succeed where your friend Isambert failed?"

He smiled and looked over his shoulder, "I thought you would never ask, De Clieu. It would be very dangerous. I could be executed for such a thing…"

I lowered my voice, "Naturally, your reward would be sizeable."

"How sizeable?"

"Five thousand livres." I waited for his jaw to drop but it held firm.

He moistened his lips and fidgeted with his wig, "Could it be… more sizeable?"

My right hand involuntarily pounded the table. The group in the back looked up. "No, it could not be more sizeable!"

He went on, unperturbed. "I'd prefer more size, Monsieur Capitaine. I know you have backers who put great faith in you. I know of your petitions to the King for the plant; he has consulted me already. I am intrigued, but I advise against it. To get you a healthy cutting, I'd have to bribe the other botanists to swear them to secrecy. We botanists are not bought like girls in Pigalle."

I suspected that, on the contrary, botanists were bought exactly like prostitutes. I replied, "My original offer was too generous. You could buy an estate with such a sum. Consider the offer retracted. Forget that I ever extended to you one livre."

Vaillant smiled like a coyote, his puffy red face agleam. "Very well, I accept your offer of five thousand! But I'll need an advance."

He waited. A vision of orderly coffee trees growing on Martinique captivated my mind's eye. Vaillant's puffy face morphed into Pierre's. Before I knew it, I reached into my inner pockets, pulled out the purse meant for Don Manno and shoved it against Vaillant's bosom.

Joel and the partners were not going to like this. Nor would Don Manno, for that matter. We owed him for helping one of our ships avoid the fierce Mediterranean pirates with whom an honest merchant like Don Manno had absolutely no involvement or collusion.

Vaillant licked his lips and brushed his curly white wig out of his sweaty face. He weighed the bag and stammered, "I'll meet you back here in exactly one month, to the minute. I'll have to start the cutting to make sure it can live outside the hothouse. I'll build a special glass case, you see, with a hinged top for watering. I'll meet you here on the twenty-sixth of May."

Vaillant thanked me and took his leave, leaning heavily on his ivory cane. I finished my coffee and left to tell Joel of my plan. My head whirled with ideas and I paid no heed to the lively traffic on the streets.

I collided head-on with what felt like horse's gut. The gut belonged to none other than an overjoyed Don Manno of Venice on his way to Le Deux Magot, two hours late. The bear-like Venetian was lavishly dressed, with a long, rolling black wig. A whiff of criminality clung to him like cologne.

"De Clieu!" he gasped, the wind knocked out of him.

"Don Manno!" I stammered.

"You walk like a Frenchman, De Clieu, totally out of control and not paying attention!"

"Oh, surely, Don Manno you know that this collision is your fault and that Venetians are the worst walkers in Continental Europe!"

His eyes blazed, "We are also famed for settling any disputes immediately. I challenge you to a duel!"

I wasted not one moment, "I accept. I demand satisfaction this very instant! Nobody besmirches a De Clieus' ambulation and lives to tell of it!"

Don Manno drew a long, thin blade from a jeweled scabbard, took one step back, and bellowed, "This De Clieu is the worst strider in Paris! He lurches like a lobster!"

Bystanders gasped, seeing a duel afoot. I drew my sword as a crowd formed around us.

"At least this lobster will feast on fat Venetian carp! Have at ye!"

The walrus lunged forward and grappled me with his enormous arms. I could not move, my sword pinned at my side.

"Hahaha, how are you, little Gabriel? It's been so long since I've seen you! I thought you'd gone pirating in the Windward Isles!"

I could only nod my head emphatically until he released me from his embrace. The bloodthirsty crowd dispersed, annoyed that a sham-duel had been declared by jocular business partners. These joke-duels were becoming more common among the youth.

He grabbed my left cheek in his big, meaty fist. "You are quite a joker, De Clieu, just like your uncle. *Humph!* I am the best walker in Venezia. You were daydreaming, my boy! You must have been dreaming of some way not to pay me the five thousand you owe! Now. Shall we go settle that affair and attend to our business in the Deux Magot?"

"Well, as a point of fact, I had a sudden encounter and I'm afraid—" Don Manno howled with laughter, tears squeezing out of his squinted eyes. He doubled over and his swordpoint sprang onto my leg, cutting a little slice into my thigh. Blood squirted onto Don Manno's elegant pantaloons and he gasped in surprise and then laughed even harder. Painful though it was, I joined him in laughter.

"Come, my boy, my aunt Lucretia has a fine restaurant in Paris that you really must visit. Sorry about your leg... that's really bleeding. Here's a handkerchief!" I bandaged the cut with Don Manno's kerchief.

Don Manno led me through aristocratic neighborhoods until we came upon a lively outdoor patio with a wooden sign hanging above announcing this as "Lucretia's." A sprawling four-story brick complex rose over a patio and patrons lounged outside at wooden tables sipping cognac and wine. Don Manno stopped for a few minutes at each table to chat with people who looked alternately happy and unhappy to see him. After far too much delay and gossip—even for a Frenchman in Paris like me—he gave his final *"Molto bene! Ciao!"* and led me inside where the small dining room was vacant.

Don Manno opened a closet door and beckoned me to follow him. My suspicions were fully aroused and I gripped the hilt of my sword as I entered Don Manno's closet. The door led to a narrow corridor ending in a stout oak door upon which Don Manno made six steady taps. Several locks were undone and two bolts thrown back until the door was flung open by one of the biggest, strongest, and nude-est African I've ever seen. My head reached only to his belly and he wore nothing except a codpiece. I stepped out from under the slave's shadow into a lobby lit by red oil lamps, lushly appointed orange divans, drapes, curtains, and Romanesque artwork. A large pool lay in the center of the room and a mermaid sat in the aquamarine water sipping a glass of wine.

Some ten other women lounged in this room as carefree and topless as the girl in the mermaid costume, breasts jiggling everywhere I looked. One women wore a transparent silk dress and played a harp in a far back corner. A wigged man massaged her feet as she played.

A young Persian-looking woman arose from a divan, wearing nothing except a black sash around her waist and moved seductively towards me. My mouth went dry as this sinuous black-haired beauty approached. She put both arms around me, the tips of her breasts just touching my chest and brought her moist lips to my ear. She whispered in a honeyed voice, "Your leg is bleeding."

Her tongue tickled my ear. She uncoiled herself from me and sat next to the mermaid on the stone wall of the pool, stealing her grapes. Don Manno watched my astonished face absorbing this seduction and luxury, then motioned me to a curtain in back. We passed an adolescent boy kissing two bare breasted women and pulled back the red curtain to reveal a simple door.

Don Manno knocked once, paused for five seconds and then knocked again. Some muffled speech came from inside and a bolt was thrown back to open the door. The first fully-dressed woman in the place, a hunched old lady, greeted me. *"Buon giorno,"* she cackled.

He addressed her in his Venetian dialect. I think he presented me as "his bad walking friend." I kissed the little old lady on the cheek and she smiled and patted my hand, saying only, "Lucretia."

Don Manno chatted with her briefly in their bird-like tongue; then she excused us. We walked through this simple sitting room and passed down a long corridor with red doors until we came to number nineteen, which Don Manno opened to reveal a luxurious suite with a beautifully-carved wooden bed, bronze bathtub, and two armchairs.

A homely maid dressed in the same antiquated style as Lucretia entered and poured us each a glass of cold white wine. Don Manno pointed to my leg and said a few words to her as she lit the lamps before swishing out and shutting the door. The door opened again, revealing the sweetly curved Persian woman who came forward with a small box. She knelt at my feet, gazing into my eyes and opened the box to reveal an assortment of bandages, salves, and ointments. She poured some ointment onto her hands, rubbed them together and looked up at me. She smiled apologetically and said something in a foreign tongue.

She applied her hands to my sword wound. My leg lit aflame in agony. I opened my mouth to scream but she smiled and pressed one finger to my lips as the pain subsided. She inserted a bandage in through the small cut in my pants and tied it neatly. She arose, her rounded breasts at my eye level. The color of her bosom reminded me of coffee, not unlike the Carib women back in the Antilles.

All I could do was croak, *"Merci."*

"De rien," she replied in clear French, and glided out of the room, the bottom of her bottom emerging from her sash with each step. Don Manno had observed me, swishing his wine all the while.

"So, De Clieu, I see you like my aunt's restaurant."

My instincts put me on edge. "Yes, the food looks delicious."

He gulped down half his glass. "Oh, it's the best gourmet. Many nobles dine here regularly. They always pay their bills. Always prompt and on time."

I adjusted my leg to a more comfortable position; the room felt hot. "Don Manno, no doubt you are anxious to know about the five thousand livres I was to pay you today..."

He pondered the ceiling for a moment, "It had not slipped my mind…Generally, in my line of business, late payment involves disfigurement or the killing of some near relation…But for the nephew of one of my oldest associates I made a temporary exception. I didn't mean to hurt your leg, but it's fitting, given the circumstances."

I knew that my uncle would be anything but happy about today's turn of events. Don Manno glowered, "So, tell me how it is that when I come to pick up my payment I find you scurrying away and no payment offered? It must be a very interesting story."

"You were extremely late…" I decided right then and there to tell him the truth, since such a nefarious fellow would probably ascertain it from some channel anyway. "I invested it!" I blurted out. Don Manno exercised his uncanny ability to raise just one black eyebrow high above the other.

I hurriedly recounted the day's events, "I met the royal botanist Sébastien Vaillant at the Le Deux Magot and he is providing me with a cutting of a coffee plant for five thousand livres. Vaillant is making a special glass box for it so that I can take it back to Maritinique. I shall cultivate it in my fields, then sell coffee back to France and make a fortune. Of course, there's room for more investors. I will need safe passage past the Barbary pirates if I take the southern route."

Don Manno quaffed his wine, and gripped the glass so hard I expected it to shatter. He opened his mouth at the same moment that a woman's feverish moan of pleasure came through one of the walls. The timing was so precise that it seemed as though he had made the sensuous sound. I contorted my face in a desperate effort to stifle the laughter. He put the wine glass down on a small wooden table at his side.

"He asked you for exactly the amount you owed me, eh? Nice story. Very well, De Clieu, you don't have to tell me where my money is. But let me tell you that I positively despise impudent little whelps who lie to my face! Coffee indeed! Get out of here before I slit your throat! If I'm not paid in full three hours from now, I don't care how connected your uncle is. His ships will sail under the waves rather than over them! Get out!"

I barely remember leaving the room and dashing through numerous corridors past men and women in all stages of undress, past calm diners eating their food, and out into the sparkling sunlight. As I made my way to the bank to draw everything out of my account, I noticed that I was still gripping Don Manno's wine glass.

After a Byzantine process at the bank, I withdrew my last four thousand livres that I'd saved in my life's work. I flew to Joel's office and threw open the door. He looked up from a stack of paperwork.

"Uncle, I need a thousand livres this very instant. It's a matter of life and death!"

He peered at me for a moment, looked down and then looked at me again. With his eyes fixed on mine, he slowly opened a drawer in his desk and withdrew a polished mahogany box. He inserted a golden key from a chain around his neck and removed a heavy sack of coins—all the while keeping his eyes on me.

I paused, "You're not going to ask me why...?" He looked at the ceiling and then back and me, shaking his head.

"This is the first time you've asked me for anything and this is a princely sum...But, no, I care not to know what it is for because I am certain that I would not like the answer. My physician recommends avoiding bouts of rage. He says it is bad for my heart. It looks to me as though you're carrying a sizeable bank withdrawal...And a glass from Lucretia's...Not smart to walk the streets with such things...I have affairs to conclude without getting caught up in whatever caper you've stumbled into."

I took Joel's advice and his money. I donned a cape that concealed my valuable baggage. I walked back to Lucretia's, trying to blend in with the commoners on foot. A few tough-looking characters with weathered faces approached but passed me by with little notice. I arrived at Lucretia's moistened by sweat.

I walked through the closet and made six long knocks on the door. The giant African opened it again without a word. I took no notice of the mermaid and half-naked beauties inside. I brushed past a man who I recognized as the royal treasurer's secretary. He raised his eyebrows and winked. I arrived at Lucretia's door in the back and made two knocks. Perhaps it had been more than three hours...Lucretia opened the door with a maternal smile. *"Va bene?"*

I pursed my lips. "Madame, is Don Manno here? I have a gift for him."

She smiled and chirped in her Venetian tongue which I understood no better than the language of sparrows. I replied, "Yes...I didn't understand anything you just said...So I am putting this large bag of gold coins in your custody."

I heaved my savings onto her table. "This is for Don Manno Madame...money...for...Don Manno...from De Clieu." I touched my chest and repeated my name. She smiled quaintly and pointed to an empty chair by her fireplace, *"Grazie, Signiore De Clieu."*

I bowed low, lifted my face in a forced smile, and thanked her again as I slid out the door. A polite voice called, *"Arrivederci."*

My heart pounded in my ears from both fear, relief, and a growing anxiety about this whole impetuous affair. I was in such a rush that I walked headlong into the luscious Persian beauty near the fountain.

She recovered from the collision sooner than I and slid an arm around my neck, "Why in such a hurry, dear sir? Why not stay a while and relax with me?"

This time I found my voice, "Not relaxing here. Me go now!"

I ducked out from under her smooth, brown arm and made a hasty exit beneath the African. I felt like a mole coming out a snakehole. I returned to my uncle's office at the Admiralty, and confessed the day's events. When I mentioned Lucretia's, his brows rose up and he chuckled.

"You know, Gabriel, Lucretia's brothel is just a front business. Did Don Manno take you into the back room?"

"Yes," I boasted, "he did take me past the restaurant. It's quite a splendid brothel hidden back there. He must own half the block. It's enormous."

Joel waved his hands to dissipate my ignorant remark. "No, no, I didn't think he would take you to the back. The brothel is all above board, totally legal. Everyone expects these Venetian restaurants to have something illegal going on in back and his brothel is famous. I mean in back of the brothel, to the warehouse—he didn't take you there, did he?"

"No, I don't think so."

Joel chewed on a piece of dried meat like a squirrel and then gesticulated in the air with it. "Oh, you'd know if he had! His secret warehouse is incredible. I've been there a few times. It's chock full of casks of 'wine' from Chianti!" Joel winked gleefully.

"Wine?"

"That's the beauty of it! They think he's using the restaurant to hide the girls, the girls to hide the wine, when in fact the barrels aren't full of wine—they're full of the most precious white powder on the planet!"

"Oriental opium?" I gasped.

"No, no! Salt, salt! Mountains of it, he's got a whole warehouse full of salt!" Joel waited for some reaction that I didn't make, his meat stick jittering aloft in triumph.

"…Salt?"

Joel poured himself a glass of Burgundy, chuckling at my ignorance. "Alessandro's very picky about which clients he sees. I was on his waiting list for the better part of three years. The prostibulary is just a front for the salt trafficking. He avoids the *gabelle*, the salt tax, by smuggling salt in empty casks of wine through Brittany! Everyone assumes the fake wine is for his fake restaurant, but none realize he has cornered Paris' black market salt trade."

"Why come through Brittany? Wouldn't it be faster from the South?"

Joel blinked in rapid succession, "No, no! It's the arbitrage, you see! There's no salt tax in Brittany, so Don Manno puts it in wine casks and pays rural intendants to turn a blind eye. The salt tax in Paris is outrageous, so he gains in the arbitrage. Anyway, go on with your story. You met him in the street?"

I didn't quite understand the arbitrage part but nodded. I told my story to the end and his brow settled down into a stormy furrow. "Do you know how much money five thousand livres is, Gabriel?"

"Yes, of course I—"

He cut me off, "It's a goddamn *lot,* my nephew, a whole heaping lot."

"Yes, Uncle, I certainly—"

"You could fill an entire house with monkeys, or buy every single pastry in Paris and make a giant statue of Zeus, but you CANNOT give it to strangers for unwritten promises of shrubbery!"

"I see your point, Uncle, but—"

"NO BUTS. You have conducted my business affairs with exceeding craft and diligence up to now. But this plan is worse than trying to milk a bull! I knew I should not have asked you about this. My doctor will be furious with me."

"Uncle, I believe this could—"

"Enough! Now listen. You have two options. Either forcibly persuade this botanist to return our money, or mount this pony and ride it either to glory or ruin. Do you get my meaning?"

Joel took a long sip of brandy in his mouth. I hesitated and he continued.

"Now, just on the off-chance that you don't lose all of our money and actually obtain a live coffee plant... What then? King Louis will be furious when he finds out. He's already denied your petitions for a plant many times. Why, he will destroy you, and may even come after me. The plant would die outside of a hothouse, would it not?"

The rest of our conversation consisted of Joel pondering all the ways this plan could go wrong. That he occasionally referred to my actions as a "plan" did give me some encouragement, though.

CHAPTER 21
THE BOTANISTS' DUEL

Over the next month, I visited every coffee shop and purveyor in the city. I devoured every book and pamphlet on the topic I could find. I learned to discern between this year's crop and the last. With every swish of my mouth I distinguished between beans from Java versus Mocha, Arabica versus Robusta, a dark versus light roast, and so on. One day I drank thirty cups and hallucinated as my heart attempted to liberate itself from my chest and take flight like a hummingbird. I cut down to eight cups per day after that.

One day, a courier delivered a note from Sébastien Vaillant. The botanist's fine script informed me that he would procure what I sought when the time was right, and another note ten days later explained that the time was drawing near. The anticipation felt like the eve of battle—a wonderful feeling despite the strain it brought.

I strode into Joel's office with the details and possibilities of how to get my coffee cutting back to Martinique. I encountered my uncle nestled in an armchair by the window with a copy of the gazette folded over his arm, scribbling a note.

He looked up with a twinkle in his eye as I greeted him, "*Bonjour*, Uncle. To whom are you writing?"

He smiled, "To Madame Vaillant, of course." Joel tossed his copy of the *Mercure Galant* over to me. I caught the fluttering broadside and read the tragic headline.

"Oh *merde*, there's been another Indian attack on the Louisiana Colony. This may harm your sugar interests! Shall I contact Monsiuer Borier to inquire on the—"

Joel twitched, "No, Gabriel. The obituaries."

I began reading aloud in slow horror, "France lost one of its leading botanists yesterday with the passing of Sébastien Vaillant, Royal Botanist of Louis XIV and Louis XV. He died in a duel with another botanist."

Joel could not help himself. "I suppose you won't be riding this pony any further, my boy. It's better this way, a lesson to never do business by instincts; it's all arithmetic and patience. Now I must write to his widow, to express my condolences, the poor thing. She carries such heavy debts, you know. The Vaillants are just halfway through building that new Chalet on Rue Boulanger...Drowning in debts, the poor old lady..."

I glared at Joel, turned to storm out, then doubled back. "Oh, and Uncle: I shall not dismount the pony, dead though she may be. I shall ride her to glory!"

I turned and fled as Joel cackled, "Onwards!"

By June I had reached and surpassed my wit's end. I wrote increasingly despondent letters to King Louis XV, begging a chance to trying planting coffee but I received no response. I was rebuffed in every quarter and scoffed at by every potential investor. I went again to the Royal Botanical Garden with my note from Vaillant and spoke with the new royal botanist, Antoine de Jussieu, promising that I would do all in my power to compensate him as fully as I already had compensated Vaillant. Jussieu listened, but insisted that what I asked was impossible.

I showed him my calculations of how, in five year's time, half of Mount Pelee would be covered in coffee. I offered him a fifty percent stake for his collaboration, but he rebuffed this firmly.

"First of all, my dear man, many thanks to you for your service to our great country. You are no doubt sincere in seeking to help France by this venture but you ask what I cannot give. The young King loves his coffee plant and he roasts its beans regularly. He would be scandalized were I to cut from it and he has told me as much. You are not the only one who has asked for cuttings, you know. True, the plant might thrive in the Windward Isles' atmosphere and your plantation might succeed. But how would you get it there, pray tell?

"Furthermore, coffee, as a member of the *Rubiaceae* family is a small tree and needs ample alkaline soil—it's unsuited to a sea journey. We've tried sending plants to the Caribbean before with Isambert and others, to no avail. The salt water and airs would kill the young plant. How would you protect it? You'd need investors to pay for the plant's care and voyage but you yourself have admitted to losing all your money and being unable to attract such backing."

He waved Vaillant's note in front of me, sneering, "And lastly, you show me this note from that peevish skunk, Vaillant!" Jussieu turned red in the face and switched languages, launching into a tirade of Latin epithets against Vaillant, blaspheming whole genuses and subspecies.

"You say he took your bribe to commit this crime and I believe you because he was a scoundrel and the note is indeed in his hand. He was an insulting old dung beetle and he crossed me for the last time!"

I had paid no heed to the identity of his killer in the obituary, but I now recalled it was indeed Jussieu. This mistake compared unfavorably to that of Dr. Guy Crescent Fagon when he prescribed bleeding for the entire Bourbon family. Fagon thus killed all of the Sun King's heirs, except little Louis XV, whose nanny Madame Ventadour had hidden him in her underwear drawer. Jussieu hardly noticed my sad departure as he switched to Greek after exhausting his Latin profanity.

The next day, I rehashed my encounter with Jussieu over a brew from Mocha. He only rejected my plan for reasons of permission and vendetta. I sat bolt upright. Jussieu might steal my idea and make a cutting for himself! He could already have a partner on some New World plantation!

Alas, I could do nothing but pour my energies into Joel's dealings and question if I would ever succeed in this murky affair. I saw how ill-suited I was to the intrigues of wig-wearing tricksters with their national bank failures and Mississippi Bubbles. I longed for the floral Caribbean airs and the simplicity of life at sea.

By the fourteenth of June, I overcame the malaise of my latest setback. My sorrow gave way to passion. I labored feverishly, feeling enormous pressure to beat Jussieu to an imagined and impending deadline. I never left my room despite pending duties from Joel. I downed dozens of cups of coffee. I paged through books on architecture, botany, and alchemy, scribbling furiously and then crumpling the paper up and beginning again. By the evening I had devised a new invention.

I called it the De Clieu Portable Hothouse. The device consisted of a cedar base with holes bored in the bottom to allow water flow and prevent molding of the roots. Glass plates fastened to the wooden base, and I mounted a hinged glass lid on top for watering. A wrought iron birdcage surrounded the exterior to protect the glass.

I dared not register it with the patent office, lest my plans become known. I imagined another Jussieu sitting behind the patent desk, smiling. The challenge of transporting coffee now largely solved, I just needed a plant.

CHAPTER 22
SEDUCING STATUES

For the rest of 1722 I wrote daily petitions to the King's Council and top aristocrats called *Le Grands*. Though many complimented my plan and my service to France, all claimed to lack the necessary authority or be otherwise indisposed. I could little blame them for the Duc D'Orleans' administration had brought economic ruin to many of them and they were occupied with matters more urgent than a dubious botanical affair.

Phillip of Orleans' regency ended on October 25th, when our twelve-year-old Louis XV was crowned like his ancestors in the cathedral of Notre Dame de Reims. Paris erupted in wild parties and I joined in for lack of a more productive use of my time. The end of 1722 melded into a wine-soaked blur until I found that I was broke and had a nasty cough.

I contacted the Royal Infantry to re-enlist. Through my Parisian connections and decorated service, I was ordered to take command of the Martinique's defenses midway through the next year.

On May 15th of 1723 I attended a ball at the sumptuous Bretonvilliers mansion. Aunt Sofia had been anxiously awaiting this affair for over a month and the public gossip in upper circles swirled like an insipid cloud of gnats over Paris. Sofia helped me pick an appropriate outfit for the occasion and strained to find me a wife before my impending departure. I donned a uniform especially embroidered with our family coat of arms. Despite my growing distaste for the pomp of Paris, I always loved seeing our crest with the eagle, beak open in a battle cry on a field of silver, crowned with three grains of sand.

Parisian gossip bubbled to a climax the day before the event. Stories flew left and right about the fabulous Bretonvilliers mansion on the corner of Saint Louis Island in the middle of the Seine. I had hoped to get a look inside this fabulous place for all my time in Paris.

The grandeur of my hat, perched atop a sumptuous wig, hampered my entrance to the waiting carriage. I knocked it off twice before successfully boarding. I smoothed out the feathers and enjoyed the ride with Joel and Sofia through the cobblestoned streets and across the Pont Marie to Saint Louis Island. The bridge glowed with lantern light on this chilly night. Rumor had it that the Romans had first founded Parissi here and their ghosts wandered these streets at each full moon. Luckily, it was a quarter-moon.

The Hotel de Bretonvilliers loomed higher than the surrounding mansions, its gabled roofs piercing the night. No less than thirty valets in fine livery waited out front to park the carriages, arriving from all over the city. We descended from our ride, fashionably three hours late, and learned from a valet that we were still early, as only sixty other guests had arrived.

We passed under the stone-arched Bretonvilliers entryway where stood an ancient, mustached butler, straight as a ramrod. He asked for our invitation, which we presented with all due formality. He rapped his cane on the stone, held our invitation high and praised our parents and grandparents to all present. The old fellow then complimented my service with D'Iberville which he recited with exaggerations that I left uncorrected.

Once inside, a small army of doormen checked in our overcoats and music drifted across the inner courtyard. The courtyard abounded in statues by renowned sculptors alongside alabaster antiquities, surrounded by flowering plants. We swept through this courtyard and into a vaulted marble ballroom.

Clusters of aristocrats chatted while beautiful girls in white and black gowns passed bearing gold trays of hors d'oeuvres. One offered us fluted glasses of champagne, sharp with bubbles. A line of statues graced the nooks between the marble columns and I went forward to admire the bosom of an Aphrodite statue wearing only a sheet around her midriff. She was exquisitely hewn. The artist had even included the moles on her skin and little arm hairs. I let my eyes travel from her stone toes, up her legs, around her hips, to her rounded bust, and good-natured face.

She looked down at me from her alcove, winked, and whispered seductively, "I'll be free after midnight."

I gave a cry and leapt backwards, spilling my champagne, but amidst the din no one noticed. Aphrodite and her companion statues were expertly painted actors, paid to stand perfectly still. Sofia beckoned me with a long fingernail and pursed lips.

"Don't flirt with the statues, Gabriel, it makes you look terribly colonial. I have to present you to eligible ladies and you can't be looking like a rum-soaked sailor."

So began a long hour of exchanging pleasantries with all manner of pompous personages. I kept hoping to learn of someone with a connection to the Jardin des Plantes or with some other way to acquire a live coffee plant, but none presented themselves. Several of Joel and Sofia's consorts and lovers were in attendance and the two played an intricate dance to keep all parties away from each other.

After meeting a flabby old Count, I excused myself and passed to the imperial *salle de bains*, or the "crapper" as we say in the Navy. Three butlers stood at the marble entry to the *salle* with towels as burgeoning gentlemen relieved themselves in the gilded facilities therein. I adjusted the peacock feathers on my hat and emerged back into the ballroom where an orchestra was tuning up. Sofia presented me to several more dukes and then the music began.

The men formed a line along the center of the ballroom and the women did likewise. We moved back and forth in formal steps until the music guided the two lines back to back and we whirled around. This brought me face to face with none other than Capitaine Luis Claude de Malon's beautiful eighteen-year-old wife Henriette Victoire Collart. I introduced myself into her ear as the first waltz began. She was a graceful dancer, more skilled than I. Her hair kept whisking my face as we twirled, and about halfway through the dance she complimented my hat.

"I hear you're a brave mariner who fought pirates alongside the great Pierre Le Moyne D'Iberville. They say you're the hero of the battle of Fort Charles on Nevis."

I took an immediate liking to this finely-bred young lady, so knowledgeable in history and current affairs. "While I assure you I was just a humble soldier of King Louis, I did serve with D'Iberville and helped beat the British on Nevis. They took Nevis back after we left, of course; that's how things go in the West Indies—always raiding and exchanging exotic territories."

She whispered, "Oh, I do love stories of adventure and exchanging possessions!"

Her breath titillated my ear. "I would give you more tales, m'lady, but won't your husband grow jealous?"

She gracefully led me in a twirl and then pressed closer for a second. "He cannot become more jealous than he already is. But it's all a show. He's had three mistresses since we married and he lost interest in me after my sixteenth birthday. So tell me—what is it you do in Paris?"

"I do business with my uncle Joel De Clieu; he has many joint stock. My uncle is most prudent in business but I am ill-suited to the merchant profession, I must confess. Soon, I will transport a coffee plant back to my home in Martinique so as to cultivate it in the Caribbean for the glory and profit of all France."

She gasped, "How marvelous! How will you do that?"

Luckily, the music ended before I had to admit my failures and inability to advance this quest. Henriette joined her husband in a show of affection as they passionately kissed on the dance floor and his hands drifted low on her back.

A string of portly old ladies and thirteen-year-olds danced with me until the orchestra took a break. During this break Sofia presented me to several military men, including Capitaine Malon. He was a precariously short man with a slight hunch in his shoulders and competitive black eyebrows. He took me aside on the pretense of presenting a suit of armor guarding an alcove. His breath reeked of harder liquor than had been served thus far and he stood uncomfortably close to me. "So," he sneered, "I saw you enjoying your dance with my wife."

This was not what I had been hoping for. "Well, you see, the random nature of these two count Viennese walzes—"

He cut me short, "I am a *capitaine* of the Parisian guard and her boyfriends have a terrible habit of drowning in the Seine. If I see you near her again, your merchant friends won't do you any good…"

I thought him rather like a bad theater actor and could not help but play with him a bit. "Oh, I'm not interested in your wonderful wife. But I'll be sure to wear my swimming outfit next time we meet." In a flash his attitude changed from menace to feigned mirth and he clapped me too hard on the back.

"That's a good one!" Malon pulled me out of the alcove and excused himself with a dangerous smile to go flirt with a Persephone statue.

Aunt Sofia pulled me aside and hissed into my ear, "Nephew, you should not be seen consorting with Lady Malon. Her husband is a snake and it's widely known that she's sick."

"Sick with what? Syphilis?"

"No, it is a strange condition. The experts think it a bad humor of the bile. Or her blood's too thin, or thick, whichever one of those requires leeches and quicksilver. Come on, let us go try some of those snails."

In the next round of dancing, the lines once again paired me with Henriette and I looked around for Malon but couldn't find him. Several Gods had left the pantheon, including the Aphrodite. Henriette whispered in my ear, "How do you like the champagne? It's made by my cousin Francois Gosset in Ay."

"Oh, I was just in Aix."

"Nono, that's quite impossible, it's walled off because of plague. I said Ay, not Aix."

They sounded the same to me but I entertained her. "Ay, Ay, yes, how silly of me. Your cousin is a tremendous grape master; the champagne is superlative."

She had enjoyed more than a few glasses of her cousin's grapes and laughed as she missed a dance step. "You know, I could have you meet Francois. He might be able to teach you about growing grapes so that you can grow your coffee plants in the Antilles."

I enjoyed her youthful cheer but upon mentioning coffee my heart grew heavy again. "Sadly m'lady, I must confess that I am as yet unsuccessful in my attempts to acquire a plant. I wrote many times to the young King and *Le Grands* but none have agreed. I met the famous botanist Sébastien Vaillant and paid him a foolish sum to get me a cutting."

I dipped her down, her bosoms bouncing. She giggled and said, "But, my darling Capitaine, he died, you know. My husband watched the duel. He says that botanists are dreadful at swordplay and Vaillant was the worst!"

The song ended and her hand glided up the back of my leg and squeezed my left buttocks. My eyes wide, she bid me *adieu*, and glided off to a group of ladies.

Midnight had come and nobles began to leave, singing, arm in arm. Joel was thoroughly sauced and Sofia giggled in a cluster of ladies. When the valets pulled up our coach, Joel just squinted at it and declared, "By the rapacious whiskers of King George, that's not my coach! Those aren't my horses! You lying Calvinist dogs give me back my coach!" The valet looked wide eyed at Joel. "But, sir—"

"Give me the ticket!" Joel snatched the ticket and squinted at it. "Joe–elllll…Deee…Clooooo."

He twirled around to face the group of inebriated nobles waiting behind him and roared, "By God, it IS my coach!"

Laughter and good-hearted jokes rippled from the waiting crowd and we piled into the carriage. Joel kissed each valet on the lips and hurled himself into the coach with the force of an angry peasant throwing a cat. The vehicle creaked and bounced on its axles. I sat down and felt a prickle in my back pocket. I pulled out a carefully-folded note tied with a thin pink ribbon.

I opened it and read in breathless silence, "My Capitaine, I can help you in your quest. Meet me at the Opéra, Académie Royale de Musique for the show *Les fêtes de l'Amour et de Bacchus,* box XXIX. Your friend, Henriette."

Joel looked up, "What's this about Bacchus?" I had been reading aloud. I shoved the note in my pocket.

"Nothing!"

Sofia had heard the note in full and understood, "His first real affair! It's not her first, mind you, not even her second or third, but congratulations!"

"Auntie!" I protested.

Joel leaned in, hiccuping. "Never fornicate her at her home and don't write notes because her husband or some other lover may find them."

He over-emphasized "find them," glaring at Sofia. They exchanged barbed looks and then lunged towards each other. I peered out the carriage window as my aunt and uncle kissed and giggled until our arrival.

Chapter 23

Theatrics

Joel sauntered into my chamber as I adjusted my leggings prior to my night at the opera. "This is a splendid first affair for you, Gabriel. And a dangerous one, too. Now you must go tonight in disguise, else many prying eyes will see you and their lips will pass word straight on to Capitaine Malon."

Joel opened a wooden box to reveal his disguise kit, used for eluding jealous spouses and Sofia's confidants. Joel held up a chestnut colored beard and judged it against my face. *"Magnifique barbe!"* He wished me good luck and left me to adjust the beard.

Sofia swooped in unannounced and clipped two big bushy eyebrows over my own. She plopped a black wig on me and disgorged unsolicited romantic advice of the most intimate and audacious nature. I demurred and said Henriette was too young for me, but Sofia insisted, "Gabriel, you need to have a few lusty affairs with younger married women or you'll never get a good wife." I was baffled, but thanked her.

At the opera, a dour old man slid me a ticket through the slot under his window. "Thine is the box of Capitaine Malon." I slipped him a *sou* and met eyes with him, hoping he'd neglect to spread gossip of this.

Something about the lofty heights to which this old fellow's eyebrows raised told me that he had seen through my disguise. Or that he saw disguises frequently. An usher showed me up several flights of marble stairs to box XXIX. The opera had only two exits and held thousands of people on a full night—a veritable firetrap. I had other safety concerns.

A bold carving of a tiger and the Malon family crest graced the door. I tapped quickly and an attractive but unfamiliar redhead with green eyes opened the door. She peered at me. "Excuse me, sir, who are you?"

"Oh, pardon me, wrong box!" She frowned and closed the door. I cruised the upper galleries looking for some other box XXIX, brushing by chattering Parisian elite dressed in their finest. I asked an older usher and he pointed me back to the original door and assured me that there was only one box XXIX. I timidly knocked and was met by the same beautiful red-haired girl. I opened my mouth to speak but her arm whipped out, quick as a fer-de-lance, and stole the beard off my face with a snap. I felt some skin leave with the beard. The girl turned to someone on the other side of the doorway and said, "Madame, I believe it is him. He was wearing this." She then turned back to me, "Are you the capitaine?"

"I am indeed," I said, rubbing my jaw.

She hauled on my arm, "Well, come in, then or you'll be seen in that ridiculous costume!"

Henriette burst with laughter inside. "Oh, forsooth, *mon capitaine!* You look the perfect Don Quijote de la Mancha! So this is how the hero of Fort Charles greets his new friend?"

Upon seeing Henriette laughing with her servant I did feel rather foolish. "I suppose I'm still not accustomed to Parisian society. I was told it was imperative to come in disguise."

Henriette looked stunning. She wore a silky, low-cut red dress that ruffled and hugged in all the right places. A delicate gold chain with a diamond *fleur-de-lis* nestled between her breasts. Her golden hair cascaded over her shoulders and her blue eyes sparkled with enthusiasm. After I removed my disguise, she motioned me over to cushioned seats protected by heavy curtains on either side with an unobstructed view down to the stage below. The opera box was lavishly decorated with Greek amphorae, pretty house plants, and elegant Arabian carpets. Henriette's servant girl sat on a stool next to her and began knitting.

"It's so nice of you to join us for the show tonight, *mon capitaine.* Exciting company is so hard to find here. Most of my husband's friends have never left Paris, let alone traveled the world on ships. Tell me what it is like to sail the seas."

I regaled her with tales of my travels in the Navy and privateering with D'Iberville. I painted her a portrait of my dear little estate on Martinique and my slave Pierre. She told me that she longed to see the world and have adventures in exotic tropical places. I told her of my ambitions to obtain coffee and lack of success. Her maid sighed.

"So you have many slaves on your plantation? I've never seen a slave before. We use only French servants. Isn't it a terribly cruel practice?"

"I have a handful of slaves but I assure you they're the most spoiled, literate, and liberated Africans since the Kings of Carthage. I detest the institution, m'lady, and have received more whippings in the Navy than I've given to my slaves."

"And yet you continue owning slaves?"

"Madame, if I stopped owning them, they would soon be separated, diseased, and their backs shredded worse than a cat's clawing post. Not to mention that without slavery, the sugar for your cakes would quintuple in price. The English, with their vast slave empire, would dominate us. I am a soldier of King Louis and his divine edicts and laws are supreme. What am I to do?"

"I see. It's a terrible position we're in—so unjust, yet impossible to undo," she replied, appearing genuinely distressed.

"All that Man has wrought can, by God's grace, be undone. Nothing is impossible, I tell you…Great achievements require great sacrifices, yet are worth all the more," I replied, and our eyes met.

The night's play began. *Les fêtes de l'Amour et de Bacchus* was a bawdy show with scores of topless actresses cavorting in Greco-Roman scenes. Henriette's soft hand crept over to mine and she moved closer to me, putting her lips next to my ear, "I'm so glad you got my note. You know, my grandfather, the Monsieur Le Ragois de Bretonvilliers, was a great friend of *le Roi Soleil* and also had my condition."

Her talk of medical conditions perplexed me. "Madame, your condition?"

She leaned closer, her lips almost caressing my ear, "He also had bouts of erythematosus, not of the chilblain variety, though. The doctors tried everything to cure him and I've inherited his condition."

Her left hand pressed my thigh. I didn't know what to say except, "I'm so sorry, Henriette. How you must suffer."

Such a long Latin name sounded especially mortal. She giggled and kissed my cheek softly, "Oh, *mon capitaine,* you really are innocent of Parisian society. That means that I can get you your coffee plant." I sat up straight.

Her cleavage brushed my shoulder and all the hairs on my body stood on end. I gulped, "I'm afraid I don't understand. How will your condition get me a coffee plant?"

She smiled and her bosom again caressed my arm, "My dear capitaine, since my family was close to Louis XIV, I have the privilege of consulting the royal doctors."

"Go on," I swallowed.

She smiled at my innocence, excited to teach me something of her world. "Yes. You see, myself and a small group of the *Les Grandes* have access to Louis XV's personal doctors. Those doctors, like your disembowled friend Vaillant, have full access to the Royal Botanical Gardens to administer to the needs of their patients. I actually have two royal doctors for my condition. No other patients have two like me," she smiled proudly.

"I'm visited by the same men who administer to the King: Monsieur de Chirac and Monsieur Philippe Hecquet. Chirac knows me well and would do anything to please me. He can go in and make a cutting of the plant to treat my condition."

I could not help myself. I leaned in to passionately kiss Henriette. She turned her head towards the maid at the last second and my lips brushed a golden braid.

Henriette turned back to me. "Brigitte knows Dr. Chirac intimately as well and could speak with him on this matter. I see

Dr. Hecquet often but he doesn't owe me the kind of favors that Chirac owes." The two covered up smiles.

I had heard of Philippe Hecquet. He was a very popular old physician who ministered the Prince of Conde and treated the young King. He was reputed to be a leech virtuoso and master of bleedings.

I stared at the buxom redheaded maid. "How will Brigitte convince Dr. Chirac to cut the King's only coffee plant to treat you? What if the cutting is discovered? You must forgive me, but you appear to be in the very spring of health and the great man has published many medical books."

Brigitte rose and came to my side opposite Henriette. She leaned in to whisper to me. Her lips tingled my right ear. She described several lurid encounters with the doctor and showed me a gold locket the great physician had given her. I gulped, dry-mouthed, and nodded.

"I see!...That's *most* fascinating...So Chirac may agree make you a cutting of the plant, but what if someone finds out? You both could be culpable of stealing a plant from the Royal Botanical Garden. A crime punishable with death."

Brigitte's hand patted my thigh. Henriette leaned towards us and murmured, "Oh yes, it will be a dangerous adventure, but we want to try. Life at Bretonvilliers is so dreadfully dull. And if Chirac won't do it for Brigitte, I can try with old Hecquet! It's not so dangerous as the story you told about the pirates."

The young women giggled. Brigitte set down her knitting and looked earnestly at Henriette. "We always dream of having adventures. Maybe we could escape with Capitaine De Clieu to Saint-Pierre. They say it's the Paris of the Indies!"

I felt torn in two. "I would be going with the coffee plant aboard a sailing vessel, and it is no place for fine ladies like yourselves. We mariners are very coarse and rough. The journey is very dangerous. You could die of scurvy if we're becalmed or be taken by pirates who do far more unspeakable things to young ladies than what Brigette has just told me of Chirac. A year on a colonial slave island wears on you more than five here in Paris, I cannot subject you to such a life."

Brigitte feigned indignation. Henriette's bosom again brushed past me and her hand moved down to my kneecap. "Oh, but it would be such a wonderful adventure! We could escape from the court life here and live on your estate and plant coffee for all of France to drink. Out in the open air, strolling on the sandy beaches. I like hard work, you know. You should see my rose garden the servants helped me install!"

She gazed into the air. The more these two young ladies became infatuated with the idea, the more certain I was that they would not last one day in the tropics.

"It would be impossible, my ladies. You cannot imagine the risk you would incur in leaving Paris. While I greatly appreciate your aid in acquiring the plant, I must take it alone to Martinique for the sake of secrecy. I would kill myself if anything were to befall you." Henriette leaned back a little, diamonds glittering on her soft skin.

"Why? Aren't we pretty enough for you, Capitaine?"

Brigitte took her mistress's cue and purred to me, "Yes…which one of us do you think is prettier?" Henriette pulled a cord that drew the curtains noiselessly around the box. I whirled around as Brigitte's hand caressed my thigh and began tugging at my waistcoat, her eyes gleaming playfully. I looked at Brigitte's eager face and then heard a rustle from behind me. Henriette's red dress had peeled away seemlessly from her breasts and lay around her waist. She wrapped her arms around my neck, pressing herself close as our lips met. I didn't see any more of *Les fêtes de l'Amour et de Bacchus.*

Chapter 24

Two Children

After Joel, Sophia, and I returned from a tedious Mass in the cathedral on Sunday, a courier arrived at our door. He refused to say who employed him and presented me with an unsigned envelope.

I broke the red wax seal and Henriette's perfume shot up my nose. I swooned for a spell, savoring the aroma as memories of bodies and pleasure washed over me. Joel had crept up behind me and grew impatient. "Well, what's in your envelope? Why have you been staring at the wall and murmuring?"

I withdrew a ticket to the opera for the next Wednesday accompanied by a dried red rose and pretty yellow flower. Joel sensed intrigue like a crab senses dead fish. I flipped the ticket over and on the back was written, "I am bringing your medicine. Make ready."

I understood immediately and broke out joyfully, "Uncle, Henriette is bearing my—"

Joel jumped. "Gabriel! You impregnanted her? I told you how to avoid that! Rule Number Two of affairs—"

"No—Brigitte, her servant, the red-haired servant girl, she has my seedling—"

Joel let out a long "Wheeeew," and ran a hand through his wig. "You had me scared there, Gabriel. 'Tis one thing to have a brief, childless romp with Capitaine de Malon's wife, but quite another if her baby comes out looking like you. Then we're in for a *tempête de merde.*" Joel paced back and forth in the room, waving his hands, "No, no, not to worry about the servant girl. They get pregnant all the time, totally normal, black, white, brown, no problem. Whatever you do, just don't acknowledge the baby!"

I drew a deep breath, "Coffee seedling, Uncle, she is bearing my coffee seedling...Though now that you mention it, I cannot swear that they might not also be pregnant."

Joel stopped cold and stared at me as a man looks at a horse which has just recited Virgil to him. "My God, Gabriel...my God. Coffee? You've done it? How is it that this foolish young woman is bringing you a piece if King Louis's coffee tree that he has so strictly denied you?"

I drew sweet air into my chest. "She is no fool, Uncle. She has a disease. A medical condition. And she has a sizeable endowment of charm for which the royal doctor Philippe Hecquet will try anything. Her maid also seems to have some sway over the doctor too...So I have seduced them to seduce the doctor to cut the plant. I was blind to the idea. She is a very crafty woman, indeed."

Joel's eyes narrowed. "So I suppose you aim to put the plant in that contraption you built?"

"Yes, I'll plant it in the De Clieu Portable Hothouse after she gives it to me at the opera. I don't know how I'll get it back to Martinique. I'm too broke for the passage fare."

Joel leaned back and lit another cigar, pondering cracks in the ceiling molding. "You know how much I lost in the South Sea Bubble, the Mississippi Bubble and how little I have to squander on red herrings like this." He scowled at me and grew silent for a long time.

"You've worked hard for me. Exciting as this news is, I think you'll be re-joining the King's forces in Martinique with a dead plant and some good opera stories. Nonetheless, I'll pay your passage."

I arrived at box XXIX this time in a jaunty suit and leggings. Sofia had taken her turn to concoct my disguise and insisted that I pose as a dancer from Vienna. She grew so excited about the disguise that I had not the heart to refuse her.

I knocked twice at the door but heard no response from within. Something felt wrong in my gut, and my hand instinctively reached for my sword hilt, but I was unarmed. I tried the latch. To my surprise, the door swung open. No one was inside. I closed the door behind me and inspected the elegant opera interior.

On each wall hung a painting of a Greek tragedy in a stone amphitheater. Far below, a small armada of ushers helped a sea of socialites to their seats. I recognized a few in the crowd but dared not shout out. I sat in a chair in the back corner and perused the night's program.

Sémiramis by Prosper Jolyor de Crébillon from Dijon was to be inflicted on the audience that night. Louis XIV had loved Crébillon and all the upper society dutifully parroted this love, despite theater critics reviewing it on par with syphilis. Crébillon was utterly insane—a term which when applied to a playwright, really means something. That only added to his appeal for Parisians, who often look to madmen for rational insight. Crébillon lived in an attic with a bizarre menagerie which only added to his hermetic allure.

My gaze wandered to a graceful Greek amphora standing in one corner with a leafy plant coming from the top. I absent-mindedly admired the plant for a moment and suddenly my heart jumped out of my chest.

"Coffee!" I gasped. At this moment the door to the box burst open and Capitaine Malon charged in.

He looked at the empty seats and spat out, "Where is she now?"

He whirled towards the door and I prayed that he would not notice my presence in the corner. The man exuded malice like Sofia wafted Fragonard perfume. With his hand on the door he stopped and saw me. His eyes widened and he leapt backwards.

"Who the hell are you?" He shrieked. I half drew a non-existent sword and then, realizing I was swordless, swept my arm out and bowed to Malon.

I declared in a ribald accent, "I am the famous thespian Claude Balon, inventor of the great ballet!"

I gave what I imagined was a quick pirouette and lunged in to kiss the startled Malon on both cheeks, positioning myself between him and the amphora.

He stammered, "Balon! Why, I've seen you before on stage! So graceful! Good God, sir, you gave me a shock! But what are you doing in my opera box?"

"Of course you have seen me before, *mon ami!* Everyone in Paris has seen me! Seen *Turcaret? Oedipe? Rhadamiste et Zénobie?* I'm in them all!"

Malon stammered, "Well, yes, of course, but to what do I owe this great honor?"

That was a very good question. He did not deserve any honor.

"… I am checking, you see, checking for the right angles for my dance. I must make sure all you special nobles up here have a good view! I want XXIX to have the best view, eh?"

He looked like a man meeting a supernatural being, "Balon! Uh, I'm looking for my wife. She has golden hair—have you seen her?"

I answered as I imagined the great Balon might. "Golden hair? I wager she is a beautiful lady. Had I seen her, we'd be dancing on the floor!" I thrust lewdly and clapped Malon on the back as hard as he had slapped me at the ball. He jolted forward, almost falling, forcing out a chuckle.

"You know not the half of her beauty, my dear Balon. Yet I fear her beauty betrays her. She must not have come here. I beg your leave, for I seek her urgently. Good luck tonight."

Malon pushed past me, rather rudely I thought, given Balon's great fame. I shadowed him at a safe distance as he stomped back down the stairs to the exit. Such was the press of the crowd that I lost him due to his petite stature. Casting around near the lobby, I found him interrogating several older ladies.

One of them pointed outside the theater and Malon puffed up his cheeks and blew air upwards. I moved closer, trying to blend in as much as the great Claude Balon ever could. From around a column, I saw Malon punch his hat and stalk out of the theater with two bodyguards following him. They climbed into a waiting carriage and the driver flicked the reins. I waited ten minutes, but the carriage did not return.

I raced upstairs to box XXIX, hoping that I could take the plant outside without being questioned. The show was already beginning and the ushers implored me to be quiet. Without knocking, I thrust open the box XXIX door, and stopped dead.

Henriette and Brigitte both lay sideways on the floor, half nude, with their dresses around their waists. Henriette's head pressed against Brigitte's belly and Brigitte's pressed against Henriette's. The curtains were drawn entirely around the booth. Henriette gasped, bolting upright. Brigitte jumped behind her and covered Henriette's breasts. Henriette hissed, "How dare you, sir! Get out of here this instant!"

She snapped at Brigitte, "Why didn't you lock the door so men don't just walk in?"

Then she snarled at me, "Get out, get out, get out!"

Brigette squinted at me. "Wait, Madame, I think it's De Clieu! He's in a different disguise!"

I had forgotten about my disguise. Henriette recognized me, "Oh yes, it is De Clieu! Oh, thank God!"

An usher popped in behind me, begging us to be quiet. I pushed him out the door and latched it shut.

I turned towards the girls and for a few long moments we beheld each other in silence, perplexed.

"What are you two girls doing?"

Henriette giggled and she pushed Brigitte's hands off from where they protected her breasts, "Why, we're listening to see if we can hear each others' babies, *mon capitaine.*"

Brigitte leaned out from behind Henriette. "Yes. Do you want to try?"

"We can't hear anything yet—it's too early," said Henriette.

My old wounds chose this moment to begin aching as if a storm were on the way. This was bad. Very bad. I lost all track of time and place. Little cherubs began clouding my vision, pricking me with their barbed arrows. Henriette's voice brought me back to reality.

"No, no, Capitaine, don't worry, you are not the father."

She giggled. "Oh, look at his shock! Why, he thinks that we women know within a few days if we're with child. No, my dear Capitaine, we knew of this fortnights before you came to the theater. Brigette is now planning to marry Dr. Chirac and mine belongs to either my husband or the Duke of—"

I stopped listening as I was swept away in an ocean of relief. The duties of dual fatherhood, and my probable drowning by Malon lifted off my shoulders.

I regained my voice. "No matter, my lady. Your husband was here looking for you. Don't you fear that he might return?"

Henriette laughed and rose to her feet, her breasts bouncing with her laughter.

"No. I had my friend Madame Béjart tell him that I had come, felt ill, and gone to the late Mass at church instead. We hid in the lady's dressing room until Madame Béjart gave us the sign. He's probably gone off to the widow Thibault's or Lecretia's. I am sure he won't return to bother us tonight, dear Capitaine." Henriette's arms snaked around my neck and her lips united with mine.

After a very pleasurable show, the three of us stood straightening our garments and passing around Henriette's silver hand mirror to fix our respective gowns and disguises.

I wrapped my arms around the amphora and heaved it into the air. I grunted under the weight, "How shall I take the coffee plant down the stairs, ladies?"

Henriette laughed and put her hand on my arm, "Oh, Monsiuer De Clieu, that is just an ornamental bush. It's always here. The opera maintains it. It's not the coffee plant."

My heart sank and I plopped the amphora down. "But yes," she assured me, "we called on Dr. Chirac and he agreed to our plan."

Brigitte adjusted her bodice with an impish grin. "*Oui,* he didn't want to do it, but I convinced him. He fears for his career and won't give you the plant directly. He has sent a cutting to his trusted friend, the commissary Monsieur Bégon at Rochefort in Nantes, to hold it until your departure."

Henriette slid her arms around my neck and her lips touched my ear, "I hope that will work for you, *mon capitaine*. The Doctor insisted on this method. He fears for his life. And though we're loath to stay here, after much thought, I'm afraid we cannot undertake the adventure back to Martinique with you while we're with child."

I returned home with my feet hardly hitting the ground. I felt pulled by two ropes, one held by Henriette, the other by coffee. A ball of fear grew in my gut as I pondered the risks of my upcoming journey to smuggle France's only coffee cutting to Martinique.

CHAPTER 25

LA PAULETTE

W hen I told Joel of my success, he passed wind and digressed into hypothetical situations of how my plan might fail. He produced a bottle of expensive Madeira wine from a liquor stash hidden inside a footrest. "Sofia doesn't know about this one," he chuckled, swinging the top of the padded footrest closed.

She did know about it and had complained of it to me but I couldn't spoil his pride. Whenever she found one of his liquor troves, she would lord the information over him to use in an argument.

Joel complained that perhaps coffee was just a passing fad, his investment in Le Deux Magots not withstanding. He pointed to my father as the perfect example of a typical commoner who rarely let a non-alcoholic beverage besmirch his trachea. I retorted with how England, a nation more industrially advanced than our own, was addicted to coffee.

"Gabriel, remember when chocolate came back from Mexico? No, of course you don't because it was two hundred years ago. I don't, either. But it was a sensation among kings and queens, let me tell you! In my youth everybody aspired to be chocolate mongers, chocolatiers, and start their own chocolate factories. And what has it come to, I ask you?" He pounded his desk.

"Hogwash, Uncle! Chocolate grows more popular every year. It was reserved for royalty and now it's served to commoners because thousands of Spanish colonists and slaves cultivate and export it. The same will be true of coffee if only we can grow it in our own colonies rather than buy it from the Arabs and Dutch. One shipload of my coffee will compensate for all your losses with John Law." I knew how to convince Joel.

Joel scowled, "I concede that point, Gabriel, but can you deliver? Martinique produces more sugar and rum for Paris than all the

East Indies, so why risk a good thing? How will you convince the colonial planters and sugar barons to devote their slaves to coffee instead of rum?"

"I am an authority on rum," I told him, "and it's an entirely different libation. Coffee stimulates where rum stupefies."

Joel pounded his desk again, sending papers and forms fluttering in all directions.

"No, Gabriel, rum forever! It's not safe to drink these unfermented throat-ticklers! All manner of disease and malady comes from imbibing non-alcoholic beverages. Imagine if peasants started drinking water instead of wine. They'd all get the bloody flux, that's what would happen! Rum is here to stay. It's the perfect byproduct—just process sugar and you're left with molasses and sugarcane juice which you ferment, then distill, and *voila*!"

Joel quaffed the remaining droplets of Madeira and asked, "Why is it called rum anyhow? Rummm, sounds like a dog noise. You colonials ..."

"I don't know. On the sugar casks we sent from Martinique it reads *saccharum* but maybe it stems from *arôme* for the smell...I don't deny that it's a profitable trade, Uncle. But I say that it shall never gain the popularity achievable by a drink that doesn't incite him to public urination. Remember at the Bretonvilliers when you disowned your carriage?"

Joel giggled, "Oh yes, that was funny about the carriage, wasn't it? I really thought the valets had stolen it! God, I was drunk!"

We sat silently reflecting and I got a little melancholy thinking of my father. Joel said wistfully, "Your father would have brutally beaten those valets, you know. Or tried at least. He was a much more spectacular drunk than I. And I mean that in the best sense of the word. He was the kind of drunk that the town refused to arrest for fear of dealing with his singing at the station. *Salut* to him," said Joel, raising a glass.

We downed our glasses and I noticed the low angle and golden tinge of the sun. In a rare moment of genuine affection perhaps induced by Madeira, Joel wiped his eyes and gazed at me.

"Well, nephew, it has been a blessing to have you here. Without your help and diligence, I might not have survived this bank collapse. It would be selfish of me to keep you here when you're unhappy away from the sea. I will be able to take care of my work here without you."

I had rarely noticed actual work occurring in this office. "Say, Uncle, what exactly is your official position here? You've never fully explained it to me."

"I don't really know myself, Gabriel. When positions like mine were hereditary, before Louis XIV mortgaged all France, powers were more clearly defined by the crown. Now every government position from town crier to admiral of the Navy is for sale. When I paid sixty thousand livres for this position to the Duc D'Orleans years ago, I became sword nobility, *noblesse de l'epée.* Like your friend Malon. My duties are very...broadly defined. By me. So as long as I pay my annual *La Paulette,* or one sixtieth of the original 60,000 each year, I can keep my post. I'm sure you've realized that battlefield and merit-based promotions like yours are unheard of here in France. Here we have more than forty-five thousand government officials and I don't know any who didn't pay for the post."

I almost choked at Joel's payment sum. This confirmed my growing sentiment that Paris' foundations were rotten and honest men had no place there.

CHAPTER 26
FRESH-WATERMAN'S DRAWL

Before my departure, I wrote Henriette a note on the inside a paper wrapping for a floral bouquet. Her friend Madame Béjart agreed to deliver it after she spent an hour attempting to pry into our affair. I explained where I had written my note to Henriette inside the wrapping and swore Madame Béjart to secrecy. She vowed not to let another soul know of this. I had spent long enough in Paris to know that my note would be in limited circulation before tea time.

So strong was my belief that Madame Béjart would read my private note, that I had written an introduction to Madame Béjart thanking her. On the day of my departure I received a note in response written on the inside label of a bottle of champagne from Aix and delivered by a very smug Madame Béjart. The bottle wafted Henriette's perfume and the note ended with a rouge imprint of her lips.

June 6th The Year of our Lord 1723 A.D.
To my brave Capitaine De Clieu,

I hope that you will treasure our memories of the opera on your long sea voyage and when you gaze on your coffee plant, think of the pleasure we shared. Things might have been different in another life, but our ways must part. I do hope you will return to Paris some day.

Fondly yours,
Henriette Victoire Collart

June 7th of 1723 was my last day in Joel and Sofia's elegant home; my last morning cup of coffee delivered by a servant. I arose before dawn and ate in the dim aura of candlelight with six sea chests packed and waiting in a wagon outside. The chests burgeoned with the articles that I accumulated in almost three years of Parisian life, plus many gifts for friends in Martinique and provisions for the long journey.

I planned to travel by riverboat from Paris to Nantes near where I was to meet Michel Bégon de la Picardière to whom Dr. Chirac had entrusted my plant. Monsieur Picardière was the intendant of New France and would help me get the plant through the customs inspectors without any mishap—in return for a hefty promissory note from Joel. From Nantes, I was booked to take the merchant vessel *Le Dromedaire* to Martinique.

We clopped through the silent streets to the Siene by the stone arches of Pont-Neuf. Joel and I sat grim as gargoyles inside the carriage. Henry IX's bronze face looked down at me from atop his horse up on the bridge. The first rays of sun glinted across the statue and I fixed this memory of Paris in my mind. The carriage pulled up to the Seine dockside. I paid two stevedores to situate my trunks on the open deck of the *chaland* that bobbed beside the bridge. This *chaland* was a long, narrow open decked barge, some 80 feet in length.

Her obese and unintelligible captain hailed from Burgundy. He grunted at me and gave his name as something like "Auulphaawz." Perhaps he was trying to gather spit, I couldn't discern. It was the same noise that Acadian seals make when clubbed on the rocks. Despite my early arrival, Auulphaawz huffed and puffed at me and I caught words like "is" and "the" in his meaty drawl.

A team of stevedores finished stacking barrels and crates the entire length of the vessel until we rode low in the water. The captain engaged in several arguments with people who came with carts to load and verbally accosted a man loading eight cows onto the front of the boat. I was accustomed to vessels fit for the open ocean and this barge looked about as seaworthy as Auulphaawz. I measured a mere hand's length between the wooden gunwale and the chilly Seine. Should the cattle spook, the whole barge and its contents would become flotsam.

An assistant hooked the heavy leader ropes of the barge to a team of stout horses. The captain sat by the tiller on a tapered seat in the stern like a meatball balanced on a butter knife. One of the crew shouted to the horses and flicked the reins to coax them along the well-trodden path that wound southeast out of Paris. The spires of Notre Dame and the Louvre fortress slipped from view as dawn crept over the roofs.

We gurgled through the calm waters past towns just stirring in the morning with their sinuous blue-grey cook fires curling up through the still air. Barking dogs occasionally rushed out from farmhouses to harass our horses. The muscular Percherons snorted and ignored them. We passed several large barges such as our own headed for Paris along with small boats laden with produce. The captain called out to them in his incomprehensible fresh-waterman's drawl and they shouted back with their own nonsense. By the late afternoon we had changed horses twice and trotted about thirty-five leagues from Paris. At nightfall we tied up in a cluster of chateaus named Saint-Mammès.

Here we entered the new Canal du Loing, built by the Régemortes' father and son company in only three years. For decades, Parisians had complained of onerous travel times, inefficient flood locks, and local officials who made canal traffic unbearable. The Canal du Loing's construction was much accoladed when the Duke of Orleans announced it in 1720, and it exceeded my expectations. Joel had given me a letter of introduction that I presented at the Croix-Blanche Manor in Saint-Mammès where I stayed up late into the night with manor's owner sampling last year's grape harvest. The next morning we pushed off, back onto the river.

The trip up to this point was a gentle decoupling from Paris. Except for the smell of cattle, horses, and captain, the journey was blissful. We often clustered together with other *chalands* navigating water locks and floodgates.

At the final lock of the Canal du Loing near Montargis, Captain Meatball bellowed at a gatekeeper who insisted that the fee had recently increased. The gatekeeper was a shabbily dressed provincial official and Meatball soon brought his two crew members alongside him. I reclined on a sack of grain wondering if weapons would soon be drawn.

Meatball, with the greatest clarity I had yet heard said something resembling, "Joan of Arc didn't piss here for you to charge me fees. Charles VII decreed Montargis not taxed, you dung-eating dog molester."

The two struck a bargain for a fee somewhere below the new one and more than the old one and both sides went away muttering. I got off the barge while the lock was drained and the crew maneuvered our vessel into the ancient Canal de Briare before reboarding.

As we floated close to the village of Montargis, a swarm of children greeted our *chaland.* They shrieked like a pack of coyotes, peddling all manner of food and snacks for us river-goers. A cute boy waded into the canal dangling a bag of fresh-roasted pralines above his head and cajoling in a high-pitched sing-song voice, "Just one *denier,* Master Sir Monsieur, fresh roasted."

I bought it for fear he would otherwise drown, but then this tadpole swam a victory lap around our boat before returning to the shore to be mobbed by the other children. Despite plenty of daylight remaining, Captain Meatball insisted that we tie up for the afternoon and visit Montargis to offload freight and take on more cargo. The cows departed here and were replaced by ten Jesuit priests bound for Nantes.

They wheeled on three carriages which fit end-to-end in the middle of the creaking *chaland.* I got off, wondering if it would sink. By some trick of water displacement, it did not. Captain Auulphaawz, gestured to me and spoke in a friendly tone. I caught words like "here," and "town." He looked up to the heavens and said slowly, "the best honeyed roast ham…"

He wiped a droplet of saliva from the corner of his mouth with his sleeve. I needed no more convincing. I brought my satchel with some valuables that I dared not leave unattended. He led me from the quays into the town, leaving his two crew members to guard the boat for the night.

Montargis crackled with the excitement one expects in a black market town with a three-hundred-year tradition of imposing no taxes on anything. Stalls were bursting with fresh produce of the Loire Valley. My days on the river washed away the stodgy Parisian grime and I bounced past straight stone walls and blooming gardens. The captain waddled to an inn on the main square named The Five Geese.

I spent the afternoon strolling around the town, pondering if villages such as Montargis might someday support coffee shops for their own *petit bourgeois.* The seductive aroma of roasting meat permeated the air and led me back to the Five Geese Inn. I found the rooms very cheaply priced, just eight *sous* per night.

Captain Meatball held court in the cozy dining room surrounded by a feast crowned by a golden honeyed ham, roasted to perfection. He sat with the innkeeper, an old lady who sported a dialect as incomprehensible as the engorged captain's. They motioned me over to the table and said something like, "Front shoe join tree hat?"

I smiled and affirmed with a hearty, *"Oui, oui!"*

The two babbled between bites about a religious matter. Or perhaps they spoke of the weather, or planned to kill me; I couldn't tell. Upon tasting the marvelous roast, no words were needed. The madame filled my glass with a dry white wine of the region called *pouilly fumé* which had a thick, almost-smoky and robust flavor. She passed me a heaping plate of shellfish sautéed in butter with shallots and Meatball shoved a dish of *rillettes paté* with oat crackers at me. A few other locals joined us and a tall gentleman beside me introduced himself as Rene.

Rene was the first man in Montargis that I could understand. After chatting about the weather, he pointed to a platter with three big wedges of cheese. "I am a cheesemaker, you know. Madame Depaul here, she only serves my cheese at The Five Geese. It's the best inn around—some nobles come from Orleans to eat here.

There's one over there," Rene pointed to a party seated by the front windows with an even larger ham than ours.

"They come for the hams mostly, but many buy wheels of my cheese to take back to the city. What you're eating is *Chabichou du Poitou*, a goat cheese aged three weeks…practically fresh out of the goat teat."

I almost spat it out but managed a polite smile. He went on. "The cheese in the salad is my *Crottin de Chavignol*, a more nutty chevre, and the blue wedge is *Valencay*. I coat that cheese with ash and age it from one full moon to another—very fresh."

"You are full of foody lore, Rene. Tell me: is coffee served anywhere in Montargis?"

He said, "Only here in the Five Geese; rich city folks demand it. Madame Depaul serves it after dinner. I drink it with honey; too bitter for me."

Captain Meatball laid waste to such a prodigious quantity as to compare with the infamous eater Louis XIV who they say could eat ten pounds of ham in one sitting. After three hours of stupendous dining, Madame Depaul served a light, sparkling white *vouvray* wine and brought out a delectable *tarte tatin*: a thick, caramelized upside-down apple pie.

Madame Depaul served us freshly brewed coffee in fine china cups with blue dragons flying along the sides. Rene leaned in and whispered, "You know, Madame Guyon was born here."

"Was she that woman Pope?"

Rene scrunched up his face, "No, no, Madame Guyon is the mystic, the holy woman; Quietism!"

He put his finger to his lips and said it again slowly, "Quiii-ett-ishm, she prayed and performed miracles around here. There is a secret shrine to her by the river near your boat. The church declared her a heretic, she was in prison. She brought the Jesuits down on us, they killed whole families of Calvinists here in Montargis. I think she's now out of jail, though. She used to eat my cheese…"

"That's nice," I whispered.

The captain let out such a belch that scattered applause broke out from different corners of the dining room. I sat back and sipped the invigorating coffee. I drew the aroma up my nose and pondered how popular coffee could become. I retired to my room in a warm, culinary euphoria, wondering if I should abandon my dangerous life and take up residence in the Five Geese of the bountiful Loire Valley.

The next morning I bought cured meat, wheat bread, a case of wine, apples, and more roasted pralines from Madame Depaul. I visited Rene's *fromagerie* and bought wedges of the three cheeses we had eaten the night before. I boarded the *chaland* with armfuls of provisions which the clergymen eyed like holy wolves. I offered the clergymen some bread with the *Chabichou du Poitou* goat cheese.

Our hauling horses left us here and the two crewmen took up the lines and marched swiftly along the river banks as we drifted towards Briare. After more water locks, we escaped the placid canal system and entered the turgid Loire River. Traffic boomed with rowboats, barges, and small sloops. The crewmen got onto the barge and we floated free from the banks and out into the center of the wide channel. Tall trees overhung the banks and berms lined the shores.

I finished half my wine in two days by sitting next to Meatball who gave me great help in my drinking. Our course became increasingly unsteady and we soon ran aground near a ruined stone abbey. The clergymen got out to perform Mass in Latin and I wondered if Meatball had meant to ground us here or not. He didn't seem concerned. Broken foundations lay on all sides of the abbey and ample light bathed us from holes in the roof.

After Mass, the clergymen went back into the comfort of their carriages and I lounged on the back of the boat in the sunshine.

An acne-scarred priest emerged and pointed his boney finger at my clavicle. "You drink constantly, my son. Have you no courtesy?"

I looked at him fearfully and corked our third bottle of the day.

"Now see here, good Capitaine, you must share some with Father Prideaux."

I squinted at him. "Are you Father Prideaux?"

"I am he, my son, and I am terribly thirsty in the heat of the day after such a long Mass."

Much relieved, I brought the bottle out from behind my back and the priest took a merciless pull that sent big air bubbles crashing up into the bottle. He went on for longer than I could hold my breath; the bottle was half gone, then mostly gone, and at last he popped it out of his mouth with a *sploink!* and tossed it casually into the river.

I was awestruck. "That was...unbelievable, Father!"

Meatball had seen the miracle and chimed in. "Sheet Rhesus! Duck Tree!"

Father Prideaux sat on a barrel next to me, and startled birds in the nearby trees with a belch. He admonished us, "Take not the Lord's name in vain, for he is a wrathful God. Now. Let's have another bottle, my sons."

I uncorked a fourth bottle and passed it to Father Prideaux who took a moderate drink before passing it back.

"You were asleep for much of the Mass, Capitaine."

I think I was. "I pray very deeply, Father, and don't follow Latin. Can you give me the most salient points of the Mass?"

"Yes, you saw the ghost town we stopped in I'm sure. Well, it was wiped out in the Flood of 1707."

"I heard something of this, but I was overseas."

Meatball nodded mournfully and slurped wine. "The people of the Loire had been sinful, had disrespected God and the King. They had turned to Protestantism and Calvinism. They listened to the likes of Madame Guyon and the Quakers. God sent a terrible flood in 1707 to cleanse this land and remind all sinners of His Majesty. I lived in Orleans, which we shall approach this afternoon. The flood drowned fifty thousand souls in Orleans alone. Jean-Baptiste Colbert constructed the stone walls and dikes that you see on the sides of the Loire but they were engulfed and over-topped."

Father Prideaux leaned in and continued in his raspy voice, "Dark clouds approached from the west and it began to rain on a Sunday. Day after day it rained. It rained ceaselessly for six days. Everywhere, God gave us signs: a man was struck blind on the fourth day, and a cow gave birth to a two-headed calf on the sixth. The river rose to the very top of the dikes. Ominous signs came from upstream. Trees floated by, then dead cattle, then pieces of houses, but the people of Orleans continued their lascivious festivities. The intendant had ordered the city evacuated three days prior but everyone ignored this orders. On the seventh day, a storm of hellish proportions doomed us all!"

Father Prideaux leapt to his feet, waved his arms, and pounded his fists on a barrel. "Late that night, when the rains reached a thunderous peak and lightning rent the skies like sparks from a forge—the levies smashed asunder! They exploded like a child kicks blocks across a room. From the bell tower I saw mighty black waters boil and crash into Orleans. Waves higher than a man surged through her streets. Whole buildings were swept for leagues downstream, trees and boulders shot through the city streets like African spears! Babes, women, and men alike were carried off in the waters.

"The only walls that held were the outer walls of the city on the high ground, away from the river. People ran towards them to escape but those walls meant to hold invaders out now trapped thousands inside the flooded city. Waves with the force of one thousand horses swept the confused masses away downstream towards Nantes. It was the most humbling fury of God I have ever beheld and shall forever haunt me." We sat in silence for a long while until Prideaux went on.

"The next day, the waters subsided and the skies cleared. Red mud and twisted debris covered the city. Stiff arms and legs poked up from the mire at odd angles. An oak tree was lodged inside the cathedral along with hundreds of corpses of those who had sought refuge inside only to be trapped and drowned. The stench of rotting sinners sickened my very soul. Dogs and carrion birds came from far outside Orleans to feast on the dead flesh of my sister, her family, and tens of thousands more. Hell had opened her floodgates, my son..."

He paused a long while, drank more, then continued. "They say it was worse in some towns outside Orleans. The one we stopped in today was entirely wiped out. We hold Mass there each time we pass to ease the departed souls. God only knows how many thousands died in towns such as that with the abandoned abbey. Fishermen at sea were hauling in dead bodies for weeks after the storm."

I looked back and Meatball was crying. He muttered something which Father Prideaux translated to mean that he had lost family in the floods.

I asked the Jesuit, "Surely now they've built the walls higher and the flooding won't return?"

Father Prideaux shook his head, "What wall of man can contain God's wrath? What dike can stop Noah's flood? Only by confession, prayer, and good works can the people of the Loire escape a repetition of their fate."

The powerful current took us from Orleans to Nantes in eight days. We met more and more traffic on the river, to the point where navigating drunk was no longer practical. Meatball suffered through long periods of sobriety at the tiller as smaller vessels weaved around us.

Barges burgeoned with the produce from the fruitful Loire Valley like aquatic caravans. We gurgled past sumptuous *chateaus* with fine gardens abutting the river and slipped by filthy work gangs of peasants building ditches, roads, and tilling fields. By the time we arrived in Nantes, the Loire felt almost like the sea, navigated by large oceanic vessels, fishing boats, and merchant craft from many nations.

Father Prideaux accompanied me for much of this final leg of the voyage, lecturing me on history, local lore, and how not to go to Hell. He explained that Nantes got its name from the Gualish Namnetes tribe that lived there before the Romans came in 56 BC. Nantes had a long and bloody history because of its maritime wealth. Prideaux asserted that the Normans destroyed Nantes so utterly in 843 AD that only plants and wild animals lived in the ruins for many years. I remained skeptical of him and the musty tomes that fed him such tales. But the stories helped me pass the time as I lounged on sacks of grain, staring at the clouds, imagining days gone by.

CHAPTER 27

THE SLAVE PORT

Goods from all over Europe, Asia, Africa, and the Americas surged into the crowded quays of Nantes. We joined a queue of barges waiting to unload. Meatball slapped his thighs angrily and set one of his crew off to see what the holdup was. The crewman returned to report that a large slave ship, the *Mars*, had just arrived from Africa and was unloading her cargo amidst a throng of eager *Nantais* buyers and onlookers. Finally, after two hours waiting in the hot sun, we arrived at a wharf to begin unloading.

Our quay lay opposite to the larger vessels and the *Mars* bounced at the dock as a long line of black girls of about twelve years of age marched out of her hold in clanking chains. Next, a group of shackled Nubian men emerged. They stood like giants compared those gawking at them. Father Prideaux got into an argument with one of the other Jesuits. Prideaux grew red in the face and pointed at the nearby slaves.

"No, Father Lamoreaux. With all due respect, you've misquoted it! In Peter 2:18 the Greek *and* Latin clearly state: 'Slaves, submit yourselves to your masters with all respect, not only to those who are good and considerate, but also to those who are harsh.'"

The Jesuit Lamoreaux grimaced in his plain brown habit and retorted, "Father Prideaux, I must humbly inquire: do not the Hebrew texts all exalt the story of the Exodus? We celebrate the Jews escaping the wickedness of slavery, their flight fueled by God's divine favor! Surely God opposes slavery by this example in His Holy Scripture!"

Prideaux's face grew red as a raspberry but he kept his voice calm. He recited both Latin and French verses like an angry parrot: "'Slaves, obey your earthly masters with fear and trembling, with a sincere heart, as you would Christ.' Ephesians 6:5-6! The Exodus involved the Chosen People, not these African savages fit only for slavery! The two races cannot be compared!" Prideaux stepped closer to Father Lamoreaux's face and menaced him.

Lamoreaux stood aghast at this insult and let fire a long string of Latin which I did not understand, then transitioned into French, "—and finally, if that isn't enough for you, how about Exodus 21:16: 'He who kidnaps a man, whether he sells him or he is found in his possession, shall surely be put to death!' And how about Timothy 1:10: 'for men-stealers, for slave traders, for liars, for perjured persons, and whatever other thing is contrary to sound doctrine!'"

At these shouts, the other Jesuits tumbled out of their carriages to take sides in the Biblical battle. The Jesuits pulled out their Bibles and shouted parables to Lamoreaux.

An ancient priest ran to Father Prideaux and threw up his arms, shouting "Please, stop this bickering at once! I implore you! Christ loveth all!"

Prideaux folded his arms and grunted, "Fine."

Father Lamoreaux calmly walked back into the frantic group of Jesuits who looked him over to see if he was all right. Meatball made some kind of joke and laughed, drawing glares from the Jesuits.

I was only too glad to bid the holy men *adieu* and paid for a servant to load my trunks onto a cart. Two burly black men hauled the cart. We trudged by the island Ile de Nantes to the north bank of the Loire.

I grew nervous as we approached the destination where sweet Henriette had sent the coffee plant for which I had sacrificed so much but had not yet seen. At the Chateau de Ducs de Bretagne I presented my letter of introduction and military paperwork. The gate guards debated it amongst themselves and asked me a long and pointless series of questions before a liveried guard at last showed me into the courtyard. They took my cart to the stables and escorted me into a small building attached to the grand residency of the Dukes of Brittany.

We came to a carved door and knocked twice. "Monsieur Picardière, a Capitaine De Clieu is here to see you with a letter of introduction from His Majesty King Louis's XV's personal doctor, the Monsieur Chirac."

I heard a muffled voice reply, "Oh yes, old Chirac. Tell him to wait. I'm busy."

I waited outside for an interminably long time until the door opened and a white-gloved hand snatched my letter of introduction. After another hour passed, my legs grew tired, and the servant was nodding asleep with his chin on his chest. At last the door swung open and the servant pointed me inside a finely-appointed office with a guard at the door. I saluted the guard and bowed before the man I presumed to be Michel Bégon de la Picardière. He did not acknowledge my presence.

He wore a lavish coat and a wide sash sprouting every possible medal save those involving combat and heroism. He sported a white wig far too large for his skeletal head. His pasty white skin was overpowdered and a strange perfume hung in the air. He sat reading a report at his black cherry desk, which was carved with the *fleur-de-lis*.

Finally, he looked up and spoke to me of the glory of Nantes. He wasted a considerable amount of time rambling about the important matters that prevented him from being able to attend trifling diversions such as mine. Picardière then regaled me with his marvelous works as intendant in New France as I stood waiting for the invitation to sit. Greatly as I wished to admit I had never heard of him, I decided to remain obsequious until the plant was in my clutches.

Finally I caught an opening to speak. "Oh, yes, I heard that it was you who reduced the sugar tariff in the Antilles from six to five *ecus* per ton. My whole barracks celebrated the event."

Picardière flashed a toothy grin. "Yes, that was me, all right. Well, let's have the money, shall we, Monsieur De Clieu? I believe it's seven thousand livres." I almost vomited inside my throat.

My heart fluttered. "Of course, good, sir. However, I'm afraid that the terms of the bank letter state that the plant must be cleared of duties and loaded in its special container first. Banks and their rules, you know…Oh, and the amount is five thousand as agreed to by Doctor Chirac. It says quite clearly after the fourth—"

He snarled, "Give me that!" He snatched the elegant letter of credit from my hands and rummaged through its clauses, mumbling angrily to himself.

"Oh yes, of course," he said after skimming a section about the bank's hours of attention in Paris. I did not have enough to pay this difference and I stood in fearful silence.

He licked his lips. "Well, it makes no difference, of course; your plant is in the botanical garden listed as a dwarf oak. I'm too busy to disburse it today. Come back tomorrow."

"But my vessel is soon to de—"

"Thank you, that is all. Good day, Monsieur De Pieu."

I returned to the courtyard and inquired about my wagon and trunks. "Of course, sir, can I have your receipt?"

"They didn't give me one—they just took it back to the stable."

"Then you'd need a letter of permission."

"You didn't give me one of those, either!"

This flummoxed the two young soldiers who said it should have been issued. The duo informed me that if I didn't have a receipt or a letter of permission I could not get my belongings back. I politely informed them of who I was and how many battles I had fought while they were still learning to pee standing up. The two shrugged and repeated themselves.

"And how do I get a letter of permission for my own personal trunks, which I left in your keeping not three hours ago?"

"The comptroller issues letters releasing items in storage, but he left this afternoon to visit family in Cugand. He'll return next week."

I clenched and unclenched my fists. I drew myself up and tried to conceal the murderous tone in my voice, "I will come for my possessions tomorrow. They had best be ready, boys."

I turned on my heel and left the towering white Chateau de Ducs de Bretagne. I checked into the poorly named Paris Inn by the waterfront and rolled listlessly on a straw cot as the raucous sounds of a nearby slave auction echoed through the thin walls.

I awoke itching all over and found both ankles covered in flea bites. It appeared like I had sprouted ankle pox. I ate a breakfast of three fried duck eggs and walked back to the Chateau de Ducs de Bretagne in the same clothes as the day before. I went to see the comptroller's deputy supervisor first about my belongings. This gibbon informed me that the stables were closed today due to a military exercise and that I would need a stamp from the clerk's office in any case. I curtly thanked the deputy supervisor and went to call on Picardière, hoping that he could put an end to this madness.

The guard at Picardière's door informed me that His Excellency would be gone for the next two days, taking part in the military exercises. I pressed him for a solution and he said that since Picardière never worked on weekends, I should come back four days from now and His Lordship might be able to attend me.

I marched out of the castle's gates and over the drawbridge, my hopes slipping down into moat's algae. Treasonous urges boiled inside me. I stormed around the city square and paced down of side streets and avenues. I walked by the docks, observing merchants and sailors from all corners of the earth scurrying about their business. Their excitement and hustle stood in marked contrast to the bureaucratic malaise surrounding the intendant's lair which had devoured my belongings and dreams. Exhausted, I sat on the end of a long dock where two ships tied to either end were loading cargo. I kicked my legs in the air, pondering what to do.

On the wide transom of the ship nearest was painted *Le Dromedaire*. I jumped up and strode over to inquire of my passage with the quartermaster. He was a dour man, a Quaker from England, and he spoke a ponderous French, "Good day to ye, friend."

It was not a good day. "My name is Capitaine Gabriel Mathieu de Clieu, I am to be a passenger on this vessel to the port of Saint-Pierre."

The quartermaster squinted at me. "I am Joseph Nobletree, but call me Joseph. May I have your papers of passage?"

Luckily, I had kept these in my breast pocket since Paris, knowing their importance. I handed Joseph my documents and letter of safe passage. As he inspected them, I sized up *Le Dromedaire*.

Her spars and rigging were in good order, her decks clean and her cargo properly stowed. No amount of scrubbing and refitting can hide an old ship, and she looked like the kind of India vessel made in my father's youth. I counted twenty-six cannon on her—not a bad armament for a merchant vessel her size.

Joseph ducked aboard and came back leafing through a shipping manifest. "Here ye are, Capitaine De Clieu, paid for a private berth in full."

"Thank you, Monsieur Nobletree. I say, *Le Dromedaire* has sailed on many a voyage, has she not?" Asking any sailor about his ship's history is like inquiring of a mother about her children—the sun may set before he finishes talking.

"Please, call me Joseph. Aye, she's a sturdy old lady, *Le Dromedaire* is, eight hundred ton, draws sixteen foot, one hundred and fifty crew and twenty-six gun. I judge ye to be salty enough to see that she's weathered many a crossing. She has a good luck to her, though, not many like her still afloat. She's a hefty galleon—captured from the Spanish in 1694, I think. We careened her on Guadaloupe last passage to scrub off her barnacles, and the carpenters just finished caulking and replacing her sheathing. With the Divine Spirit's help we shall see through many more journeys yet. On our way back from Guadaloupe we were on a westerly tack at half sail and ..."

I let my imagination drift as Joseph told about profitable journeys, narrow escapes, frightening storms, and far eastern ports. When he mentioned stopping in Mocha, I recalled my task and asked him about my berth.

"Where be your items to load?"

"The primates inhabiting the Chateau de Ducs de Bretagne have stolen my worldly goods, I'm afraid."

Joseph furrowed his brow, "I beg your pardon, sir?"

"Yes, stolen. I shan't belabor the details, but fear that I shall not recover them before we set sail. The only item of value I must recover is a plant entrusted to me from the Royal Botanical Garden in Paris. The plant must be handled with the utmost care. I will be able to load in four days, most likely."

Joseph combed his beard, "I'm sorry, my friend, but we set sail this very afternoon."

"Thundering typhoons! Don't set sail without me, that's an order! I shall return forthwith, plant in hand or shall have murdered an intendant!"

I departed running as Joseph shouted something. I dashed past crews hoisting big crates and barrels aboard with the block and tackle. I struggled through a crowd gathered around a man offering work to able-bodied sailors on a slave brig.

I arrived panting at the Chateau de Ducs de Bretagne and the liveried guards stopped me at the gate. "Papers, please."

I stopped dead. I had left them with Joseph back at the harbor. "I'm Capitaine De Clieu. You know me. I was here yesterday to see Michel Bégon de la Picardière."

They looked at each other, "Yes, we recognize you Capitaine De Clieu, but we must see your papers."

"I left them back on my ship *Le Dromedaire*. She sets sail this very afternoon. I must see Monsieur Picardière this instant—it's a matter of royal exigency."

The taller guard looked at his companion, "Didn't *Le Dromedaire* already leave?"

His comrade scratched his rump and speculated, "No, that was the *Mars*, the slave ship. I think *Le Dromedaire* is the merchant galley that sails today if the wind picks up."

They began to talk about which were rumored to be arriving soon until I interrupted, "Please! Please, I must speak with Monsieur Picardière regarding my possessions and a very valuable royal gift he is helping me with. I have a five-thousand livre note for him. If you don't help me there may be woeful consequences."

One of them finally ambled inside to inquire. He came back

half an hour later to inform me that Monsieur Picardière was busy and had said to come back tomorrow.

"Busy? But my ship is to set sail! I must have my six sea chests and the King's plant at once!"

"King's plant? What kind of plant is this?"

I wondered what these men's heads would look like several yards distant from their necks.

"Sorry, we'd have to see your papers and you'd need a letter from the supervisor stamped by the clerk. But he's not here today—he went to Basse Goulaine on business."

"I thought you said he went to Cugand yesterday?" I felt in free fall, seeing my entire enterprise crumbling before my eyes.

"Oh yes, he did go to Cugand!"

The other disagreed, "No, that's where his son lives, he want to Basse—"

"He can go to Hades! Now, if I go get my papers, will you let me in?"

"Of course, Capitaine, but we're only open for another hour."

I dashed off like a ball fired from a six pounder. In my pell-mell haste I lost my bearings. I tore down the Rue de Marne, passed an ornate theater, and barreled up the Alée d'Orléans. I darted through streets, looking for masts and rigging poking up above the slate roofs of the city, and became increasingly lost. I turned around and ran down the Rue Paré where the tops of flowering trees poked up above the roofs and little blue birds flitted about, chirping. A faded wooden sign half-obscured by white bird droppings read *Jardin des Plantes de Nantes*.

My skin tingled. I darted through the open iron gates like a fox and saw nobody inside. The fragrance of lilacs swam up my nostrils and I peered around blooming shrubbery for anything resembling my coffee plant. Several bushes looked familiar from the botany books I had read but none matched the drawings.

An ancient stone wall overgrown with vines surrounded the garden and I followed a narrow path towards a willow tree. The path led me to a glass hothouse with three broken windows. I darted into the hothouse but found only a few withered tropical flowers sitting on tables among piles of clay pots. I ran out and almost tripped over what I had thought was a broken window frame at first glance.

Sitting next to the door of the hothouse in the dappled sunlight stood my small coffee sprig planted in the De Clieu Portable Hothouse!

I bent over her, swooning in heavenly pleasure like a father first meeting his newborn baby.

I burst out in rapture, "There you are, my darling! I was so worried about you! God be praised!"

A voice froze me like a dunking in the North Seas. "Sir, who are you talking to?"

I whirled around and drew my sword in one motion. A stooped old man wearing spectacles thicker than crepes balanced himself between the willow tree and his knotted cane.

"I've come for my plant. Don't try to stop me!"

The old man squinted and replied in a grandfatherly voice, "Well, see here now, young man, what's your hurry? Which plant have you come for?"

I paused with my sword still leveled at the old gardener, "The coffee plant, of course."

He hooted, "Oh, you must be Capitaine De Clieu from Martinique! However, I'm very sorry, but I'm afraid the plant is under arrest."

He hobbled closer and parried my sword out of the way with his cane. "Have at ye," he chuckled.

He hunched even lower in front of the little plant and held up a leaf. "I was instructed to give it to you but until a bureaucratic issue is resolved, the plant is impounded."

I kept my sword up, "You cannot possibly imagine how unwelcome another bureaucratic issue would be right now."

He knocked my blade away again with his cane and straightened up from his stooped posture, his white hair and beard trembling with indignation.

"The issue is back taxes! The local Parliament voted to maintain beautification funding in the last session but has not paid their outstanding municipal budgetary contribution!"

I paused and then brought my sword up again leveled at his chest, "What in the hell does that mean and why can't I have my plant? The accursed intendant already has my five thousand livre note."

His cane whipped around my blade and smacked me right on my manly block and tackle! I blew out air like a humpback and doubled over.

"It *means,* young man, that I haven't been paid my wages since January. It means I've been eating a steady diet of moldy bean sprouts and prunes. It means that until I get my salary, all botanical transactions are frozen, unless you really want to murder an old man!"

I slid my hand inside my coat's secret pocket and fetched my last golden *Louis d'or.* "Might this cover your expenses?" I wheezed.

His eyes widened at the gold coin sitting in his wrinkled hand and he chirped like a happy bird. "Oh, yes, very good, take good care of the plant! She needs a cup of fresh water and eight hours of sun every day. I made this glass box for her based on the designs that were sent from Paris. Didn't have all the right materials, sadly. Very interesting idea. Pinch these little buds off to produce better rooting. *Bon voyage!"*

He scampered off swinging his cane between two jasmine bushes and left me alone with my waxy-leafed wonder. The dark green leaves had a lustrous coating and came to a fine point at each end. The tiny little trunk of the shrub twisted up from the soil where it was firmly rooted. The ribbing on each leaf reminded me of a fish skeleton.

I covered the glass box with a burlap sack from the hothouse and found my way to *Le Dromedaire's* dock. The wind had picked up and grey clouds came in from the west. I arrived in a joyous mood, humming sea shanties. I forgot entirely about my possessions held hostage in the fortress. I came to the quay and stood stock still. Dragons of fear roared up from my guts. The ship's berth was empty. She was gone. I scanned around and grabbed a nearby sailor, shouting, "Where is she?"

He gasped in surprise and stuttered, "Who, sir? The brothels are right over there."

I wanted to slap him (and every other denizen of Nantes) but held the plant tightly. "*Le Dromedaire!*"

The man's face shone in recognition, "Oh, that old tub? She sailed about an hour ago. Moved over to the customs wharf, she did. That's Captain Neville's ship. Old India trader he is. You know, they say he made a deal with the devil so he can't be killed, and—"

A mixture of fear and relief flooded into me, "Where's the customs wharf?"

He pointed to a dock across the river and sure enough, there was *Le Dromedaire* between two taller India traders. I dashed across the wooden trusses of Pont Haudaudine bridge and wove through a line of ships and stacked cargo to where *Le Dromedaire* bobbed beside a warehouse.

I arrived huffing and puffing like the old botanist who had bruised my bollards. Two customs officials walked off her and Joseph spotted me approaching. "There is he. Come hither, Capitaine De Clieu, we are setting off. Ye must forgive us for leaving thou. I tried to explain earlier, but our owners obliged us to set sail."

My arms and legs burned with acid from the long run and the plant weighed fifty stone in my arms. Joseph called for a young sailor to show me to my quarters. I followed him up the wide gangplank, happy as if walking up the stairs to heaven. I tottered down into my tiny quarters, still panting from my chase. I carefully set the plant down. I recognized the familiar nautical smells of brine, unwashed bodies, and bacon. I set the lock and collapsed into the sturdy hammock strung across the confines of my cabin. I shut my eyes as bureaucrats inspected the ship.

CHAPTER 28

WEIGHING ANCHOR

I awoke to a voice thundering, "Mates aloft! Prepare to set sail!" A chorus of "Aye, Skipper!" resounded and footfalls echoed from the wooden planks like drumbeats.

I slithered into my uniform and rushed out on deck to where men scampered up the rigging like spiders in webs. On this beautiful day, for the first time in almost three years, real salt air massaged my face and the fishy sea brine seduced my nose. Eight sailors manned each of the three lower topsail yardarms, six above them and four more on each of the highest topsail yardarms, all clutching the sails, ready to unfurl. Joseph bellowed, "Main mast, let fall! Mizzen boys, let fall! Fore, let fall!"

On these commands, all fifty-four men aloft released their sails in synchronized splendor with a deeply satisfying *thwump* that reverberated in my ribcage. The canvas caught a breeze and a cheer went up among the eager crew. We sailed a reach towards the mouth of the Loire estuary on a falling tide. The hairs of my body stood on end as I watched this well-disciplined crew mastering a fine vessel.

I brought the coffee plant on deck for sunlight. Ships and boats of all shapes and sizes from a dozen nations flowed into and out of the choppy headwaters where the Loire meets the sea. Navigation was quite fickle and we cut sail until we moved at a crawl around rowboats, barques, and fishermen, cursing vilely and hailing merrily. I felt like an outlaw bearing a great secret, a cargo more valuable than all these vessels combined. I then realized that I might well be an outlaw, depending on how closely the boy king inspected his gardens. I rested my right arm on my plant's container as I took in the view.

I soon met Captain Neville, an aging seaman with a no-nonsense demeanor. Neville gave the helm to his first mate and approached me. At first, I thought that moths had eaten half his wig. His hair stuck out at odd angels from under his tricorner captain's hat. On closer inspection I saw it was no wig at all, but genuine hair.

"*Bonjour*, I am Captain Neville, part owner of this vessel. You are Captain De Clieu, I presume?"

I gave him a prompt salute and replied, "Aye, sir, I am Gabriel Mathieu de Clieu, former lieutenant in *La Royale*, now Capitaine in King Louis's infantry to command Martinique, Chevalier of the Order of Saint Louis, at your service, sir."

Neville clapped me on the back. "Ah, I thought I sensed some saltiness in you. Very good, then, Capitaine De Clieu. I'm sure your presence and experience will be most complementary to my crew and our voyage. I think you'll find the old *Dromedaire* quite eager for service. Her hull was laid back in '89 but she's built like a bull. Rounded the Horn ten times she 'as. All I can tell you now is that we are first bound for Madeira and we should have you to the Antilles well before hurricane season. This old girl has been to the colonies many times, she knows them all. We—" The first mate shouted to Neville, who excused himself and stalked off with surprising vigor.

The crew were mostly Frenchmen with a few English, and Spaniards numbering roughly seventy hands in all. They looked, acted, and smelled like seasoned sailors. We had a diverse cargo aboard of manufactured goods bound for the colonies. All was stowed carefully below along with a small menagerie of goats, hogs, and a few cattle for eating along the way.

I had always obeyed the superstition not to bring live hogs on board a vessel, for they are known to bring luck worse than women. Indeed, even uttering the word *hog* was cause for a whipping among other vessels I'd sailed on. A wigless captain transporting hogs made me uneasy. When I asked a deckhand of *Le Dromedaire* about the swine, he shrugged, and insisted that this ill-luck was more than counter-balanced by their polydachtyl—a six-clawed black ship's cat named Balthazar. Balthazar was a fine ratter and laid several big rodants at my feet during our voyage.

I gazed at my plant inside its container. "What's that there?" came a voice.

I looked up to see a stump of an arm pointing at me belonging to the ship's cook. He was bald on top with greasy strands of hair erupting from the sides of his head and spilling down over his shoulders like wet seaweed. His breeches and overcoat were stained with food and grease and he carried a butcher's knife in a leather sheath at his side.

"It's a dwarf oak," I explained, not wanting to draw attention to my theft even now that I was safely aboard and floating away from France.

He shrugged. "Another passenger said that it's a coffee plant and that you stole it."

Lightning struck my guts and I rose to my feet, "Slander and infamy! Why, anyone can see that it's a simple dwarf oak, *tinyensis smallus oakinisis*. It's a gift for the governor of Martinique. Who had the gall to besmirch my good name? I hope he's a good dueler!"

The cook rubbed his good hand on his stump and shrugged, "Sorry, sir. 'Twas another passenger. He's not on deck now. He was inquiring about you last night after the mess; said his name was Gotthard Vos de Groot, he did."

I peered at the cook, "So he's Dutch, eh? Tell me, my good man, why are you informing me of this?"

The cook smiled, "Oh just thought you might be interested to know who was inquiring after you. Thought you might appreciate it...that it might be valuable information to you...and I hate the damned Dutch."

I reached inside my coat to slip him a copper *sou* and squinted up at him. "I do indeed appreciate your help, and I'm sure I'll value any further information you may obtain."

The cook bounced the coin off his stump and deposited it somewhere in the greasy folds of his overcoat. "Name's Fiver—Fiver

Martin. Hope your dwarf oak survives. Must be very valuable."

I didn't entirely trust him but smiled back with a *"Merci beaucoup, mon chef."*

Around noon we cleared Saint-Nazaire and Captain Neville steered us into open water and unfurled topsails. Joseph was busy blinding himself with the backstaff pointing directly at the sun to measure our latitude. We cruised out into the Bay of Biscay with a light breeze, passing a few small fishing boats and a large inbound slave ship that we saluted with a cannon shot. The boom of the cannon, the snap of the shrouds, and the moist tang of the salt air made me relive a hundred voyages of my youth.

CHAPTER 29

A NEW CAPTAIN

On the twenty-third of June, we rounded Cape Finisterre off of Spain and began a southwesterly course towards Madeira. Captain Neville invited me to dine with him and I humbly obliged. I told him of my troubles in Nantes and of how my trunks had been left at the Chateau de Ducs de Bretagne thanks to Michel Bégon de la Picardière.

"Well, why didn't you just bribe him? I bribe that man more often than I see my wife. You should have told me. I could have gotten your things without any trouble."

I smiled weakly. Neville frowned and confirmed my suspicions about Picardière's character. He was involved in a smuggling ring and earned outsized profits on invented fees and commissions from the rum and sugar traders coming from New France.

I confided the true nature of my plant to Neville and he solemnly swore my secret to silence. I asked after the Dutch passenger and Neville replied that he knew little about him, only that he seemed to be a wealthy cacao planter who was journeying to inspect his holdings in Surinam.

Neville took a swallow of sherry and leaned in to me. "They say the Dutch have a secret coffee plantation in Surinam. Nobody is allowed in to see, but these are things we hear in the ports. I think they had some kind of blight, though, and their plantation is not yet producing well. I'll order that you be granted an extra ration of water from the ship's casks for your plant so that we French can have coffee plantations of our own."

Neville refilled his sherry before continuing in a softer voice, "I heard that in Guyana we've just acquired the coffee plant. I stopped at Cayenne Island to pick up sugar before returning to Nantes and met with a warehouse owner who told me this most strange tale. A clerk in a Guyana shipping office killed the owner, raped his wife, and made off with a sizeable amount of money. He was caught the next day trying to flee and imprisoned in Fort Cépérou, but he escaped and fled to Surinam where the shameless Dutch welcomed him. Being a tricky man, he stole coffee seeds from a Surinam plantation and bartered them to the prefect in Cayenne for his freedom. Since the prefect had not liked the dead shipper and coveted the coffee seeds, he agreed to the deal and has now sprouted a small plantation." I gargled slightly on my wine.

Neville looked concerned. "Capitaine, you have a nosebleed."

"No no, just snorted sherry, that's all. Your news gives me great anxiety. I fear that I shall be late to the coffee scene."

Neville chuckled, throwing me an extra napkin, "Oh not at all. I know of not one shipment of even a cupful of the beans from the Americas. Men are trying to plant it in secret, yes, but none are yet exporting." I sat back, relieved. Our further conversation turned to weather, nautical gossip, and the women of Marseilles.

The air blew warmer over my face as we made good progress towards Africa. A pod of spermaceti whales met *Le Dromedaire*, spouting and blowing in all directions. We counted over one hundred as they breeched, dove, and cavorted in the foaming seas. The towering spermacetis danced along with us for most of the morning, splashing dangerously close to the ship as our vessel rocked in their wake. The lads harpooned one for sport and reddened the water as the creature thrashed beside us. One big bull came shooting out of the water in front of us so high that his ponderous eyeball came on level with our decks. His big fins flapped the air before he plunged back down with a monstrous burst of spray erupting in all directions.

I cannot imagine the bravery or lunacy of the whalers in their tiny wooden shells who seek out these leviathans, pierce them with harpoons, and go surfing for leagues tied to the giants' backs. A whaleboat could be smashed to slivers and even a vessel of our size might be badly damaged by a bull like the one that breached. In the afternoon, we spotted a flock of petrels and then later saw terns and an albatross. We cruised on a hollow southerly swell.

By evening, we spotted long strands of seaweed and kelp, alerting us of land nearby.

Chapter 30
Attempted Murder

On the 29th of June, we arrived in Madeira—a viticultural island with dour Jesuit owners. We eased up to the main commercial wharf in Funchal, the capital. Funchal's ten thousand inhabitants bustled with activity, giving it every appearance of a mainland Spanish or Portuguese city complete with a fine cathedral, sturdy dockside edifices, and ramshackle bars and brothels. The lush slopes of Madeira were zigzags of grapevines that the locals fermented into their famous Madeira wine, similar to a white sherry. Madeira's sweet wine somehow improved with heat and was highly prized by vessels sailing for the tropics.

Smaller vessels bobbed by the wharf and gulls drifted overhead. The tight-lipped Catholic customs officials told us that an English squadron bound for the Indian Ocean had left two days ago. Neville informed us that we would pass three days in Funchal, topping off our water casks and loading one hundred and twenty-five gallon pipes of Madeira wine.

Neville invited me to the cathedral. I locked my Arabica infant in my berth and made for shore. I was eager to buy a few changes of clothes. Neville knew half the islanders, saluting his many acquaintances in the street.

He whispered of one baker, "I first met that man's grandfather here as a cabin boy in 1665. His ship was lost to pirates. They used to be nobles but the mother was reduced to baking mutton pies to survive. Her son, Jean, makes the best *bolo do caco* on the island." I asked Neville what that was and he described it as a wheat flour bread dripping with butter and garlic.

He introduced me to officials and wine merchants who spoke with silly accents and referenced God every fourth word, much as we sailors reference the Devil every sixth. As in Nantes, African slaves abounded here. Madeira lay close to the African coast and bartering humans for pipes of wine was *de rigueur.*

Neville led me to the Cathedral of Our Lady of the Assumption. After a brutal Portuguese Mass lasting several years, I staggered back out into daylight, blinking. Neville said he was greatly relieved and felt sure that *Le Dromedaire* would meet with good fortune. He departed to meet with a *hacienda* owner friend of his and I strode to the garment district. Here a few small shops sold used, ready-made, and custom tailored clothes of all sorts. Expensive silks and Asian wares sold for a fifth of the Parisian prices—evidence of both the India traders and pirates who frequented Funchal trading for wine and provisions.

After ravishing a buttery *bolo de caco,* I strolled back to *Le Dromedaire* with two sets of new clothes. Joseph sat on a stool by the plank and bid me good evening, not removing his hat. Because Neville strictly forbade any women on board, half the crew lingered in Funchal. The other half received little shore leave as they were new sailors and not yet trusted by Neville. Amidst the creaking planks and spars, I strode aft towards the hatch.

A thump came from roughly where my cabin lay below decks. My heart skipped a beat and I hustled to the hatch, darkness enveloping me below.

A great wrenching screech of metal and shattering glass rang out. The passageway was deserted and I charged towards the glimmer of one tiny oil lamp hung from a thwart. In the gloom, I saw my door ajar! I shouted and rushed headlong into the room, colliding with a dark figure, glass shattering all around me. I lashed out and landed a terrific blow on the wall as the figure ducked down. The shadowy man smashed two fists into my head and shoulders, knocking me back into my hammock.

I heard the metallic ring of a dirk drawn from its scabbard, and I lunged out of the hammock like a charging bull to grapple the figure. My rebound knocked my assailant backwards, out the door, and into the bulkhead of the narrow corridor. The force knocked us both to the ground as something metallic went clattering to the deck.

A boot smashed my ribs and I howled in pain. Shouts rose as men dashed from their quarters, stampeding to watch a good fight. Sailors young and old gathered around me in the gloom.

Yet no fight was to be had. I whirled in each direction looking for my assailant but saw only curious faces clamoring to see what was going on.

Suddenly remembering my plant, I shouted an oath and ran, panicked, into my cabin as confusion and shouts reigned in the darkness. I slipped on broken glass as I entered. In the container where my beautiful coffee plant had once been was now left only darkness!

I squinted and saw the outline of my invaluable shrub lying on the floor next to the container. I let out a long sigh on seeing the delicate trunk still firmly connected to the rootball.

I nicked my finger on a sharp edge and gingerly inspected the glass. The top was smashed and one of the sprig's three branches lay severed on the floor, its leaves scattered around the cabin.

"Sabotage and murder!" I yelled, emerging once again to confront the crowd.

Someone jabbed my chest with the butt of an oar. I looked down and realized that it was no oar, but the stump of Fiver's arm.

"What happened, De Clieu? Who was ye fighting? Or was ye having a go at the cabin boy?"

Laughter echoed around, and I yelled above the din, "Let it be known that I have in my cabin France's only coffee plant outside the King's garden! 'Twas entrusted to me by his grace King Louis XV and woe to the knave who has attacked it! I did not make out the assailant's face. He ran off in the dark, but he must still be on board! Fifty livres to the man who finds the villain!" I did not have fifty livres but only remembered this later.

For many on board, this was more than a month's pay and a manhunt was set loose. I was presented with six guilty men, most of whom had been playing cards in the cargo hold at the time of the attack. I declined paying the reward to their captors, as not one of the six could come up with any motive or showed signs of a scuffle.

On deck, the big Quaker quartermaster blocked the gangplank unarmed and two midshipmen next to him carried muskets.

"Who's been brawling down below decks? Or was it manly frolicking? Mr. De Clieu, we'll have none of that on this ship."

"No, I was jumped! Someone tried to murder my plant! Did the Dutchman leave the ship just now?"

Joseph scratched his head, "Murder thy plant? Capitaine De Clieu, as I said, if ye choose to talk in riddles about manly frolicking, Christ knoweth it's none of my concern but—"

"No—someone broke into my cabin, attacked my plant, and came at me with a dagger."

"There be three Dutchmen in this crew and one paying passenger, Mr. Vos de Groot. He just left to escape the racket, said he couldn't sleep. But he's a wealthy planter, not the brawling type."

"Joseph, the plant I carry is a priceless sprig of Arabica coffee that I am entrusted to plant in Martinique. This de Groot is a Dutch spy and fauna-assassin sent to wrest the coffee plant from France!"

Joseph glowered at me with a slight twinkle in his eye from the moonlight, "The proper term be flora, not fauna. De Groot is a paying passenger, paying more than yourself, I may add. Yet, something didn't seem on the level—beyond his Dutchness, that is. The fact that you've been assailed and he has abandoned ship lends credence to ye, so let us detain him and make an inquiry."

I pointed to the docks of Funchal, illuminated by hanging oil lamps. "If he just left we can still find him!"

Joseph eyed the two men at his sides. "If ye wish to go ashore looking for violence, I cannot in good conscience permit it. We are guests here at the good graces of the Portuguese. The captain has left me in command and I shall not have vengeful men roving around Funchal at night. If de Groot returns tomorrow we'll settle this matter. If he does not return...then we shall see that you're telling the truth. Until then, ought ye not be below guarding your priceless Arabica plant?"

I saw the quartermaster's reason and realized that de Groot might already be holed up in a safe house. I thanked Joseph and hurried below where I found a curious crowd of men inspecting my plant and licking the leaves to taste coffee.

"Avast, you seagulls!" I hurriedly went about repotting the plant and patching up the container as best I could. The crowd dispersed and I stood talking with several curious men, explaining coffee's nature and why I was carrying it to Martinique.

At last things settled down on board and the men went back to playing dice games. I closed my damaged door and cleaned up the shards of broken glass. I could not sleep. I shifted from one side to another, worrying about if the plant would survive losing a limb and if more accomplices might still be aboard.

The Dutchman did not return to the ship that night. The next morning, Joseph agreed to escort me through the crowded docks. We navigated tangled stalls of flower sellers, wine merchants, and food vendors. We passed through the old town center to the big yellow stone Fortaleza São Tiago where one hundred and sixty cannon menaced the sea. I was surprised when Joseph spoke to the guards in Portuguese. After some in-depth questioning during which I heard my name a few times, the guards opened a small black door near the big iron gates to let us inside.

After passing through the yellow stone walls, we met with an inspector who took my deposition with Joseph translating. I didn't mention the fifty livre reward. The inspector nodded, scribbling in a ledger, and Joseph told me the guards would search Funchal for de Groot.

Joseph leaned in to translate for me, "The inspector thanks you for the generous fifty livre reward you've offered. He says he knows everyone here and he'll find de Groot before dinner time."

My stomach churned at Nobletree's liberal translation, "I didn't, eh—" The inspector was already ordering men around in stacatto yelps. Guards ran into the big courtyard and struck out on patrols, teasing each other about who would get the reward first.

"I didn't...I mean, in that moment..." The inspector paused and looked at me. Men ran with clanking weapons and doors slammed as the search began. It was all or nothing.

"I didn't expect such professional and prompt assistance, may God protect Funchal and its ever-watchful guardians."

The inspector smiled back at me and said in broken French, "Oh yes! We help gud Frenches cat-tall-licks find deer-tea Holland man."

After paper signing, copying, and stamping, two brightly-dressed soldiers escorted us out of the fort and we saw the masts of three new ships approaching the harbor. Joseph studied them from a vantage point above the fort with his spyglass. He shook his head.

"We have loaded enough wine. I'll go get Neville at once. De Clieu, please stop by the Rosa and hasten our men on board ship at once."

Joseph passed me the spyglass. I peered at the approaching ships, now less than a half league distant. The lead ship looked to be a ninety gun Dutch man-o-war of over one thousand tons escorted by two sixty gun vessels.

"Capitaine De Clieu, do these vessels come for you and this strange plant? I sense matters afoot of which perhaps ye have not enlightened us, begging your pardon."

"In God's truth I know not, Master Nobletree."

I squinted through the spyglass. "They could returning from the India route or they could have followed us here from Holland, after my coffee plant. Look there, the lead vessel has her cannon ports open!"

Jospeh grabbed the spyglass. "How is it that you truly have this Arabian plant? Why didn't the King offer you protection? With the Dutch plantations on Java, they'll not let you escape with this plant. Quickly now, or we'll be sunk on the pier! Run to the Rosa for the crew. We may have time to cast off and at least not be caught on the docks like a seal on the beach."

Joseph raced off to the docks faster than I thought Quakers could go. I sprinted to the Rosa tavern. I brushed by a cart hauling a single enormous barrel almost as large as the cart itself. I ran up a steep winding cobblestoned street towards the Rosa where the noise of a blacksmith's shop created a muffled concussive din. I burst in the entrance and halted, gasping for air.

The Rosa's few customers slumped over ceramic wine pitchers and sailors relaxed on wooden benches inside. I recognized only one of our crew, a gunner named Pitri. He blinked at me in the tropical afternoon heat and waved.

"Pitri, Joseph sent me to retrieve the crew from here—we are to sail at once! Where are the others?"

"What's the hurry? Old Joseph won't mind if you be seated and help me finish this cantankerous pitcher of Madeira. It keeps getting refilled."

"Avast the Madeira! We weigh anchor at once, anyone here is left on this rock without pay and passage!"

I grabbed his jug from the cradle of his arms, took a mighty gulp and slammed it down on the greasy table behind me where four Portuguese seaman thanked me for the gift.

"There, I've drunk with you, now where are the others?" Pitri blinked and pointed to the ceiling. I realized that the pounding noise I had heard from outside came not only from the smithy but from another activity popular among mariners. I ran upstairs and hauled twelve crewmen away from scenes I yearned to forget, yelling of the impending attack.

We flew over Madeira's broad flagstones to the dock as the Dutch squadron drew nearer. Sailors dashed to their stations, flying up into the rigging like spider monkeys. We pushed off the dock, cast off the lines and unfurled our sails to the westerly breeze. A wake began to bubble out from under our hull and our sails caught the gentle breeze. I gazed back at the dock and noticed a flower vending lady gazing at our ship.

Suddenly, she threw off her blond curls and cloak. It was Gotthard Vos de Groot beaming at me in triumph as his countrymen dominated the harbor. Neville boomed a cannon in salute to the Dutch man-o-war that drew close to us. Sailers leaping around in her rigging came into view, furiously cutting sail to slow their advance. She cast a shadow upon the light waters of the harbor and drew alongside Le Dromedaire. The two frigates, both larger than us, followed behind her.

I put down the spyglass and stared up in awe of this juggernaut, bristling with cannons. Memories of sea battles welled up inside me as each cannon slipped by us, almost near to touch with a gaff hook. The ships were too close and moving fast enough to smash us. Men shouted and Neville spun the wheel as our crew and that of the man-o-war scrambled for poles to fend off. I watched as her massive oak sides overshadowed us. I braced for the tremendous impact that never came. Peals of harsh laughter and insults rang from above us. A chamberpot was emptied onto our foredeck. They made no moves to intercept us, but instead slipped by with hundreds of dirty faces peering down on us.

Through the spyglass, I stared at de Groot's receding figure with the spyglass. I longed to have another chance at him, wishing my pistols and musket were not back in Nantes. I realized in this moment that I was not just on a merry adventure to introduce a profitable new crop. I was embroiled in a global trade war, every bit as fierce as the War of Spanish Succession from which we had so recently emerged in a blood-stained truce.

The Dutch squadron went about the cumbersome task of docking and we passed from the calm waters of the harbor to the windy sea beyond.

We made quick progress south from Madeira. The stone cathedral's tower receded from view and the rugged mountain peaks faded to a dim silhouette. I stood rooted to the poop deck, scanning the seas for signs of pursuit. Surely de Groot had by now informed the squadron of our cargo. Perhaps they were low enough on fresh water or had important officers sick enough that she could not give chase. Once we had put thirty leagues between us, we changed course to hug the African shore closer than might be expected near Marrakesh. Our lookouts scoured for signs of pursuit from the crow's nest.

Neville called me into his cabin. The old owl sat dining on *espetada*, a Madeiran specialty which consists of a big chunk of beef with salt and garlic rubbed into it roasted on an open flame. He invited me to sit and the cabin boy brought me a portion. "Well,

Capitaine De Clieu, it seems that we've escaped with our coffee plant intact!"

I didn't like his use of the first person plural in reference to my plant. "Mostly intact, sir. She was wounded but I pray she'll survive."

I thanked Neville for making such a hasty departure to avoid the Dutch. He shifted in his seat and dabbed his napkin to his face.

"Not to belittle the coffee conundrum at all, but *Le Dromedaire* has a history with the Dutch. So we had two accords on which to depart. I'm afraid Joseph knew about your coffee plant since before departure. A good captain trusts entirely in his quartermaster, for if I should die, he must be ready to complete the voyage as captain. I'm sure you understand, Capitaine."

"Indeed I do. Your crew has acquitted themselves admirably in this affair, sir. You have my undying thanks."

Neville took a big bite. "Handpicked, they are. I expect you'll have a chance to repay us before the voyage is out. Until then, rest easy and enjoy the passage."

CHAPTER 31

BROADSIDES

No sooner had I crumpled into my hammock when shouts of "All hands on deck!" rousted me. Planks above me squealed and thudded with pounding feet. I poured myself into my uniform and locked the door behind me. Pitri jostled by me in the gangway and I pressed him for information.

"Sail's been spotted bearing down on us from the north!"

I emerged into the strong night breeze amidst a scuffle of sailors wrestling extra sail aloft. Whitecapped waves the height of horses blasted us on a confused coastal sea.

Neville gestured me over. "If captured, I will present the Dutch with our letter of safe passage in which the cargo is listed differently than what they may find if they board us. We may have to surrender your plant. I am known to the Dutch. In my days, I've helped send four of their ships to the bottom of the Indian Ocean. So ours shall be a merry meeting indeed!" Neville's white hair blew behind him and his eyes burned with fiendish intensity.

Crewmen raced around the deck and through the rigging like airborne crabs, piling on more sail to escape. I helped haul a heavy line to the forecastle. In so doing, I overheard two men's harried exchange.

"Dutch is after Neville, mark my words. Him's a dead man if they catch him."

"And what of you, Garson? You were with him out privateering the Indies seven years back, weren't you? Think they'll forget a pretty face?"

I passed the line through a new set of blocks and another man ran it aloft to raise yet another sail meant only for calm waters. *Le Dromedaire* crashed angrily through waves, lunging ahead and bounding down into the troughs. We pushed our fully-laden vessel too hard into the surging seas.

Despite our frantic efforts, we could not widen the gap. The extra sail gave us a rakish heel to port and sent spray everywhere. Grinding sounds and cracks reported as *Le Dromedaire* protested against this abuse. I caught a shout of, "Will she hold?"

As the white speck drew closer to us, the lookouts in the crow's nest yelled down, "Tunisian rig!"

Shrieks of dismay went around as all souls on board imagined themselves under Muslim whips, rowing in slave galleys. A hoarse midshipman shouted, "De Clieu to the helm!"

I ran to the stern and found Neville clutching the wheel. He grimaced at me as I approached. "De Clieu, take command of the defenses. Joseph's a pacifist and my second mate has seen as many battles as that bucket over there."

A vein protruded prominently from Neville's forehead, "I need a man who'll fight to the death and your reputation will now be put to the test. Take command of our defenses for the glory of France."

He reached inside his shirt and slammed his key to the ship's magazine into my hand.

I felt alive. "I'll muster our fight men, sir. Pirates have no stomach for a real battle. They are all roar and no teeth."

A rough wave smacked into our side, showering our faces with cold spray. I looked down at the key in my hand—no longer the hand of a passenger. I staggered below and distributed *Le Dromedaire's* outdated stock of flintlock muskets, pistols, and sabres. I assembled the twenty men not occupied in the rigging and called them to muster.

"Who here has seen combat or killed a man at close range?" All hands went up.

"Excluding bar fights, murder, and domestic affairs?" I lost ten hands.

Vexed, I rallied them. "I've fought off pirates more times than I have hairs on my arse and these Barbary bastards have large reputations and small hearts for bloodshed. I have known many merchant ships to surrender immediately to pirates and later find that the marauders had not even possessed gunpowder for their cannons nor shot for their muskets. The key is to wait for my command to fire and that we cut them down at once as they board, understood?"

With all agreeing I set the most experienced man to drill the others in musketry while I spoke with the canoneers. In less than an hour, the approaching white sails closed most of the gap. I gazed at the broad red "take no prisoners" flag flapping from her mast like a dark smear against the moonlit sky.

I turned to Neville. "Sir, she rides high in the water. I don't think she can have more than twenty guns. She thinks we'll keep running scared until she's upon us; she won't expect an attack. If we jibe now and double back, perhaps we can surprise her with our broadside. I believe a few cannons of grapeshot might greatly cure her crew's desire to board us."

Neville grabbed my lapel hissed into the wind, "De Clieu, we're loaded with three hundred barrels of gunpowder bound for the forts of New France! We cannot risk a single cannon shot or we'll die as shark bait rather than slaves!"

"Sir, you put me in charge of our defenses and I tell you the best defense is to fire first, and hard!"

Neville stood at the helm unmoving with his hair flying behind him. His gaunt old face tightened and he narrowed his salt-encrusted eyes.

"Joseph, Pitri, Master Berget to the helm! Prepare to wear ship!" he bellowed. His order was repeated along down the deck. Neville then ordered every available hand to the cannons and, after ten minutes of stoking, packing, and preparation, we were ready.

I went below to assist in firing a cannon by the swinging light of oil lamps. Such was the heat and sweat below that we cannoneers could hardly distinguish our pounding hearts from the footfalls on deck. I ordered the port cannon loaded with grapeshot consisting of jagged pieces of iron, bent nails, rocks, and any other metal debris found on board loaded into cloth bags. I had the fuses cut extra short. The spotter reported that the gap between our ships had closed to less than two hundred yards.

From above came the order: "Drop sail, wear away!" *Le Dromedaire* surged hard to starboard, and I grasped the cannon before me to avoid falling onto the thwart. Crashes and bangs burst throughout the ship. The cannons reared like angry stallions against their hawsers. The pressure on the ship's oak planks felt like pain in my own body as she heeled violently. Men grabbed whatever they could and several were thrown head over heels.

As we rocked back upright, the spotter yelled, "We're even with her!"

I gave the command: "Fire all guns!" Now, heeling hard to starboard, we lit the short fuses and unloaded our twenty port guns into the dark void where we prayed the Tunisian pirates were still on deck preparing to board us. Our heel would create a horribly high shot unless we were within spitting distance of the enemy.

Our cannons heaved *Le Dromedaire* over with a thunderous cacophony, slamming the iron beasts back on their rails. I heard wood splinter and felt concussive vibrations through my ribcage. Pops, cracks, gunshots, and booms sounded at once. We were so close to the pirates that I knew not which ship had been hit nor who was screaming.

Acrid smoke filled the gun deck and a horrible ringing clanged in my ears as always when below decks in battle. The hogs on board stampeded in their pens and shrieked. All at once our heel greatly decreased and we swung back to an almost even keel; Neville must have ordered many of the sheets cut to trim our forward velocity.

"Reload!" I shouted as the thunder subsided. I wiped a sheet of sweat out of my eyes and gripped another big iron cannonball from the rack with a gunner and we heaved it into the muzzle after more powder had been applied. Pitri emerged from the smoke with a midshipman, both caked in soot, to grab a round of chain shot from the rack.

Pitri strained under the weight of the ball, connected by an iron chain to its wicked sister. He loaded one ball first, then the chain, then the second ball. We prepared to fire this iron *bolas*, to send it whirling faster than the eye can follow with the idea of clearing the pirates' mast and deck. I shouted for the spotter but no word came as we stood desperately yearning to touch off the next round of powder. So we waited for something to happen, wondering if we were about to be boarded, fired upon, or if Neville had been hit with grapeshot. Slow minutes passed, feet trampled up on deck, and our hearts below sought to escape from our chests.

At last, Joseph called us to our stations on deck. I grabbed my musket from the bulkhead and rushed up out of the sweltering chaos into the fresh air. All that remained of the pirate ship was a white sail receding into the night. Neville ripped off his captain's hat in front of the sweaty crew.

He shouted, "They're running with their tails between their legs! They're off to lick their wounds. *Vive la France! Vive le roi!*"

The crew rushed to join in this shout and sang three cheers to Neville's audacity. Despite our mixed origins, the same Gallic euphoria for victory coursed through our arteries.

I asked a midshipman who had been in the rigging to recount what had happened and he confirmed that our jibe had taken the pirates by surprise. They had massed on deck for boarding. We unloaded on them as we passed and they were unprepared to return our cannon fire, sending only scattered shots our way. Joseph affirmed that the two ships had passed so close that several cowled Tunisians had jumped for our decks. The boarders had misjudged the distance and speed of the two passing ships in the windy night and caught only air before splashing into the whitecaps.

Several men said they thought we'd damaged their mizzenmast and shredded their sails. Pitri swore we'd hit them below the waterline, but I argued that was impossible given our heel at the time. The boswain said three of our cannon that fired grapeshot had cleared their decks like a scythe through wheat. He repeated the phrase until everyone remembered it that way, even those that had been below decks.

The truth mattered little as the white shrouds of the Barbary vessel disappeared into the night. For whatever reason, we were temporarily spared and all rejoiced as Neville ordered a pipe of the Madeira wine opened in celebration. Joseph stood calmly by, the only hand on board not to partake of the wine. After my third cup, I escaped the raucous celebration and inquired of Joseph his version of the events. He scratched his head and squinted up into the rigging.

"I do not rightly know what we hit but I think we scared them. They are gone for the moment. Our course is still close to the Barbary Coast and they may have only fallen off by night to await daybreak and size us up for the capture. What they don't know is that all it takes is one shot to make us crab bait. The hold is packed tighter with powder than an opium den, so let us pray they look for easier victims."

CHAPTER 32
DELICIOUS DOLPHINS

In a few short days we passed between the Canary Islands and the great Sahara Desert, our hairs combed by persistent winds. Neville continued hugging the coast and the crew began muttering of ill omens. I feared the men chose some albatross, some scapegoat to blame. Once fixated on such an idea, a crew cannot shake this premonition and it sprouts like an evil seed into a conspiracy to destroy the cursed person or object. I kept my plant under my constant vigilance, and locking my cabin when I stepped out even to smoke a quick pipe.

Each day I took my coffee plant up for air and sunlight, taking care to avoid the jagged broken edges of the glass top. The sailors grew accustomed to my curious behavior, and came by to inquire on my plant's health as they changed their shifts. The men took pride in aiding the king and France by the plant's passage, though I feared some might grow jealous of her infinite value. I covered the wound where de Groot had ripped off one of her branches with a bit of the ship carpenter's pitch and she grew a thumb's height since the incident.

After three days of easy sailing, the crew relaxed by the sport of fishing for dolphins. These stupid animals came close enough to harpoon and followed alongside us for hours, as if offering themselves up for the next meal. Their meat was delicious and tasted much better than whale or manta ray. An inexhaustible supply of dolphins abounded in this area and they jumped, dazzling in the sunlight before our bow. The night skies were clear and full of shooting stars streaking across the unfathomable depths of the heavens.

After a week, many of the crew's urine burned and it was discovered that they had a venereal disease. There was great debate as to its origin. After much conjecture, consensus formed that they must have picked it up at Rosie's. Talk of a curse increased.

Three more days hence, the lookout spotted the Cape Verde Islands and we changed course to avoid the nearby reefs. The crew grumbled and minor squabbles broke out. Some wanted to cut across the Atlantic with all due haste while a small group of gunners adamantly insisted on the wisdom of stopping in these islands that frequently shelter pirates and slavers. Neville remained below decks.

We cruised near the north tip of the first island called Sal or Salt Island. Two fair-sized mountains loomed up from either end of the northern point and the land seemed quite barren, without any large trees or lush growth like Madeira.

We tacked down to the west side of Sal and anchored in Murdeira Bay. Neville ordered two longboats and our larger pinnace ashore and offered that I join their crew. I declined, politely insisting that no quantity of dry land could tear me from my coffee plant's side.

He gave me a queer look, shrugged, and asked if I would do him the honor of inspecting his pistols before he went ashore. I hefted his two flintlocks and inspected their charge and state of repair. One was an aging silver plated Queen Ann's pistol with a gold butt cap showing heavy wear. The other was a long, brass-barreled dragoon's pistol much like the one I had owned until I was ravaged by Nantes. Neville looked on in fatherly satisfaction as if these were his twin daughters.

"The dragoon looks fine, much like the weapons I've used and very well balanced. It seems properly loaded but the barrel could use a cleaning and the gears should be oiled inside here."

Neville looked to where I pointed at the pivot screws. I then hefted the Queen Ann, adding "This is a beautiful weapon, clearly very valuable, but it has one major flaw. It's British, so it would likely blow up in your face were it loaded."

Neville blanched and chuckled nervously, "Oh no, I've fired it many times, of course. It's not loaded, you say?"

I half cocked the Queen Ann and showed him the empty ammunition space. "No ball and no primer in the pan, sir. But a very lovely specimen, I must say. May I ask where you got it?"

I handed him back the pistols and glanced at the boats being lowered. "Twas my uncle's," he answered. "We must be going, De Clieu. Lower the boats!"

He turned to go and I asked, "May I ask what we're doing here in Cape Verde, sir?" Neville turned around again and gestured at the deck with the Queen Ann. "The cargo got mixed up in Nantes and we loaded extra flour but only a small sack of salt, so we need to collect more. The Portuguese won't mind, I'm sure," he smiled.

Neville left with all the gunners and martial men, leaving the midshipmen, mates, and other crew on board. They hoisted a small sail above the pinnace and the two longboats bounced through the breakers towards the white sandy beach.

I felt something like a seal fin slap me on the back and I whirled to see Fiver sporting a toothless smile. "You snuck up on me, good chef."

Fiver pointed at the men drawing the boats up onto the beach with his stump. "I heard your talk with Captain Neville."

I glowered at him. "Eavesdropping would not be tolerated on a military vessel, you rascal."

Fiver grinned, his rotten teeth dangling like stalactites at the mouth of a cave. "Then I'm sure ye won't be interested to know that we have four big barrels of salt below, enough to sail to the Indies eating salt pork, salted cod, and salty, salty dolphin the whole way!"

He burst into the kind of nasty laughter that is unique to wizened mariners and shoved his flipper into me again.

"So why are they ashore?"

Fiver's cackling subsided and he pulled closer to me looking genuinely concerned. "Mister De Clieu, it don't make no sense to none of us boys. I haven't sailed with Neville before; they say he used to be a slaver who turned privateer and now takes on dangerous cargo. Makes it especially queer that we're stopping in these isles, after old Jacques Cassard raped and pillaged Ribeira

Grande to a smoldering rubble. Portuguese didn't appreciate that none too much."

"I was just a greenhorn then...was that 1713?"

"Nay. 1712, it was. I know because I was cooking for an India spice vessel. We came to Saint Lago to go whoring one last time before returning to France with a hold full of cinnamon. But all we found were vultures picking over dead bodies and a few miserable freed slaves who told us about Cassard's attack. You know, Cassard's from Nantes like me. I saw him in the market not a week before we sailed. He's pissing and haggling with the admirality in Nantes over his pay. Some bureaucratic issue with back taxes and commissions."

"I cannot imagine."

I had heard direct accounts from members of Cassard's fleet who went on his twenty-seven month rampage against the English and the Dutch.

I leveled with Fiver. "Yes, I am aware of Capitaine Cassard's heroic exploits. I embarked on similar adventures with Capitaine Pierre Le Moyne d'Iberville leading up to our capture of Nevis and D'Iberville's feverish diarrhea that slew him in Havana. Cassard rampaged in Dutch Surinam that very same year as his attack here. Gave them hell, freed thousands of the Dutchs' slaves and got paid a king's ransom just to leave them in peace."

Fiver scratched his waterworks and shrugged.

I tried to pry some speculation out of Fiver. "Regardless, our Captain has made an...interesting choice by stopping here with pirates, Dutch, and angry Portuguese about."

Quartermaster Nobletree came up on deck and Fiver straightened up and spoke louder to me, "Very good, sir, I'll grill your dolphin extra dark tonight! Pure dorsal flesh!"

He poked me again with his stump and made a theatrical exit, whistling as Joseph beheld him. From my seat with the coffee plant on the stern, I observed Captain Neville haul the boat up onto the beach above the green seaweed that marked high tide. He then divided the party into two groups and they struck out towards the island's interior.

After many hours of absence, they returned at dusk and lit a bonfire on the beach. The men aboard surmised that they were cooking some of the wild sheep that grazed Sal's scrubby slopes. After a few hours of fire, they returned to *Le Dromedaire* well after dark. I sat drinking Madeira wine and swapping stories with two midshipmen. Neville's party came aboard with four big barrels that all eighteen men and the captain hoisted up with difficulty. They asked for no help and stowed them below under lock and key.

CHAPTER 33

MAN THE PUMPS

On the 16th of July, about one hundred leagues south the Cape Verde islands, Neville ordered the crossing. We changed tack and pointed *Le Dromedaire* towards the open ocean to head for Guyana and the Antilles. Soon, we saw fewer signs of land, just the occasional bit of seaweed. No more birds swung gracefully over our heads. After many years at sea, one feels the difference between hugging the coast and open ocean, even when no land is ever in sight. We became just a fragile wooden speck on the vast sea.

When the breeze quit early on our second day, we laid in irons all afternoon. Men loaded their pipes and lounged about. I spoke at great length with a salty midshipman named Patrice who, for lack of teeth, called me "Cap" and my plant "Cappy." My nickname did not stick, but soon the whole crew asked after Cappy's health and inquired as to her growth and leaf luster.

Patrice and I smoked pipes and watched a majestic pink, yellow, and purple sunset. The sky faded into a deep, passionate red and then slowly sunk into to a peaceful sublime black. Never in all my years at sea had I seen such deep colors painted on such an infinite palette.

I awoke that night because my hammock was swinging more than usual, almost looping the loop, but I grunted and fell back asleep. I came on deck the next morning to find Neville and Joseph puzzling over maps and backstaff readings. The wind had changed from south to southeast, to west, to northwest, and then north. This dizzying spin produced a confused and chaotic sea with waves meeting at odd angles. Big rollers met short series' of little slappers that exploded in spray at strange moments on all sides. The breeze steadily picked up throughout the day until the officer on duty ordered the sails reefed.

The next night, I awoke to the rumble of thunder in the distance. I lashed Cappy down in case of heavy seas. The breeze kept increasing and *Le Dromedaire* groaned as she began charging ahead in the blackness on the front of a good strong blow. The moans and shrieks of the wind through the lines and shrouds increased throughout the night as I lost hope of sleeping. I recognized the strength of the wind by the sound it made through the rigging and prepared for a good gale.

Suddenly, in the dead of night, the storm hit with a terror and violence that words can ill describe. The rigging moaned and shrieked like the strings of a violin being played with a knife. One moment I lay in my hammock, swinging hard in the tossing sea, and the next I lay on the wall of my berth which had suddenly become the floor. All was black. Up was down and down was up, everything falling and tumbling. Acidic fear lanced through my heart. Screams, both human and animal, resounded throughout the ship. We had gone too far.

Then came the impossible—the words a mariner expect to be his last: "Knock down! Knock down! Abandon ship!"

Despite our precautions, the sudden gust of storm wind had slammed our reefed sails and hull so hard that we were pushed over onto our side. Our sails and masts were in the tossing water and we'd quickly founder in the waves, ushered to the bottom as the hatches exploded with brine. I stood up on the wall and braced myself against what had been the ceiling of my berth, looking up at Cappy lashed to what had become the wall. In the cacophony, my only thought was that mariners say drowning can be pleasant. I waited a few interminable seconds for African seawater to smash my hatch open.

Instead, a sickening crack catapulted *Le Dromedaire* back upright, and I tumbled from the wall to the floor like a ragdoll. We reached the correct vertical position and see-sawed far over to the other side, almost capsizing in the other direction. We jolted violently back and forth, up and down, like a bottle of champagne shaken by a drunk wedding guest.

I dashed half dressed from my quarters and ran into someone in the dark gangway: Pitri, who let out a frightened scream. I asked him to go on deck with me to take down the sails but the wind had increased to such a primordial roar that cannonshots would have blended in with the fury.

I dragged him behind me to the deck where the wind's full force hit us. We clasped the rail with both hands lest we be blown off the ship like leaves. Visibility was two feet as the wind atomized rain and spray into a blinding aquatic inferno. A bolt of lightning struck the sea not two hundred yards to port and an instant clap of thunder felt like a physical blow. All color had been bled out of the world, leaving just white and black.

The deck pitched as we were struck prone by an enormous wave and I grabbed onto the hatch cover with white-knuckled determination. A loose line snapped over my head like a whip and reminded me of what had to be done. I crawled, gripping the cap rail, towards the mainmast and looked up but couldn't make out any sails in the pounding fury. I heard them, though, thundering like a thousand galloping horses, threatening to knock us over and send us down for good. Lightning and thunder mixed into a drumroll more ferocious than any enemy battle line. Lighting bolts came so often that reality flickered between high noon and midnight.

If I had let go of the rail, I would have flown away like a delicate dandelion seed. As our deck pitched dangerously low to port, a mighty concussive wave slammed into our side and deck, engulfing all before it. I held my breath and wrapped my arms around the iron rail as a thousands pounds of liquid fury surged over me.

The whole ship was under water, aquatic forces threatening to rip my shoulders from their sockets. Again I felt the assurance of death, regardless of whether this particular wave took me or the next. No vessel could survive such a storm. We pitched to starboard and I emerged from the unstoppable violence of the wave, clinging like a rat to a piece of cheese inside a barrel half full of beer being rolled down a hill. As we lurched, I dove for the mainmast and collided with both the mast and Joseph who clenched a big knife in his teeth. He yelled something to me that I could not hear despite my ear being an arm's length from his shout.

Our wild eyes met and Joseph lifted his chin and eyes skyward, indicating what had to be done to save the ship. No time to cut the mast; we had to cut loose the sails in any way possible. He clamped his knarled hands on the first rung of the trembling mast and pulled himself upward as the wind hauled on every stitch of clothing and every loose hair on our heads. I started up the other side of the mast, and found a line to cut, clinging to the timber like an ant on a swaying piece of prairie grass. I severed any line in my path.

Suddenly, all the hair on my body stood on end and the mast began to glow with an eerie blue fairy flame. It was St. Elmo's fire—a terrible omen. An arcane buzzing sounded in my ears and then a titanic blast of lighting slammed a boiling hole in the sea not ten yards to starboard and my whole body jolted with pain as if I'd been whipped. The buzzing and blue flame disappeared. I was blind for many long seconds. Inexplicably still alive, I inched upwards to where the mainsails should have been; I found them long gone. Above me Joseph's feet receded into the maelstrom though he was still close enough to reach out and touch. I grew dizzy as we lurched and yawed in directions that I didn't know existed.

Joseph's stoic determination inspired my fearful heart upwards and after an endless torture I reached the top yardarm where the topsails lashed and raged like demons. These were destabilizing *Le Dromedaire*, catching blasts of wind and knocking the ship around like a toy. I hugged the mast with one arm and reached out with the other to cut the topsail free. My knife found its target and though the topsail began to flap, it remained dangerously full. Deciding that dying on a yardarm was as good a place as any, I wrapped my legs and arms around the yard and clenched the knife in my teeth so hard I tasted blood. I inched my way out onto this toothpick in the tempest. Black and white flashed alternately.

The sea had no direction, but was like the water in a bathtub in which an angry child flails wildly. In the trough of each wave the wind subsided, cutting our momentum suddenly, only to have it redoubled as we climbed each towering new height.

We pitched down and the yard went hurtling into a void from which a towering wave many times larger than the ship emerged from the blackness in the flash of lightning. It was a pitiless wall of water and I knew we were done for. I clung to the yard with all my strength as we ploughed heavily in the heart of this oceanic landslide.

God wasn't done taunting us before sending us down, and *Le Dromedaire* rose to a sickening height on the crest of this behemoth. Amazingly, she didn't flip or roll as the wind pushed us up her greasy, mountainous slope. With a vicious roll, we gained the frothing crest and fell down its backside, pushed faster than we could've sailed.

I added my vomit to the wave as she passed and inched further to where I could see the top line holding the topsail knotted a few feet ahead. I struggled to find a stable moment in which to reach out and cut the line, fearing that letting go, even for a second, would be my doom. I became dizzier and feared that any movement would be my last so I clung to the mast, certain that a panicked drowning awaited me. I gave no more heed to cutting shrouds free or slashing lines—indeed, I could hardly see beyond my own hands and everything whipped and cracked around me in such a confusion that I lost all hope of aiding the situation.

All at once the spray and rain went from a blinding horizontal inferno to a gentle drizzle and the wind entirely stopped. Nothing.

My hair went from violently airborne to matted. The air cleared and I looked up to see the stars twinkling down at me. All the snapping and thunder stopped, and we gently rocked back and forth. From far below me I heard Neville bellow out a chain of commands, "We're in the eye! All hands on deck! Reef the foremast! Seal the hatches! Clear the decks! Move, you sea cows, move, lest ye dine with Lucifer tonight!"

Whisps of haze resembling smoke drifted around us and an unearthly pinkish glow lit the sky. I finished slashing the topsail lines and slithered down the mast. I planted myself on the foamy decks and looked up for Joseph. There was nothing. He was gone. The mizzenmast was already snapped in half and badly entangled with the main mast. That must have been the crack we heard in the initial knock down. All of our top gallants and sails were a broken mess and impossible to get down by normal means. With that much sail aloft, any further gales would be sure to knock us down and overpower us.

Neville gave orders that few sailors ever live to hear: "Cut her! Cut the main and the mizzen, boys! To the axes, clear the decks! Clear the damn decks!"

Men moved like mountain cats, summoning their final reserves of energy. A team of twenty men took any available blades and attacked our own ship.

For a mariner, there is no more desperate and gut-wrenching duty than this. It feels not dissimilar from the lumberjack, pinned by a tree and alone in the woods, who must hack off his own leg in the vain hope of dragging himself back home.

As panicked men made splinters fly from the base of the mizzenmast, I took a turn slamming an axe-head into the poor trunk of the main mast. Three other men heedlessly slammed axe blades into this once majestic timber in the dim pink glow. Heed should have been paid. The men next to me suddenly screamed in animalistic pain and fell, his neighbor's axe lodged in his leg.

The surgeon rushed forward to help the man whose leg became a hemorrhaging red spout and the panicked cutting resumed with hardly a break as blood soaked the decks. The man died before the storm resumed.

A few sails still fluttered above and a dull whirling sound began to approach. I took big desperate bites into the thick base of the main, not stopping to wipe away sweat and ignoring the powerful blisters forming on my hands. A steady breeze kicked up across the gently rocking sea.

"Hurry! Gale approaching!" shouted Neville. The remains of the mizzen began snapping.

"Look out below!" yelled a gunner.

The mizzen had been cut on the wrong side and fell backwards into the main, becoming fouled in the main's loose lines and tattering sails. Neville threw off his hat and grabbed my axe, his long white hair now flapping in the increasing wind. I stepped back and peered around at the disaster around us in the pink haze. Blood soaked the deck around the mast and the wounded man lay flopping like a fish and screaming. If all hands were on deck then we'd lost at least ten men already.

"Look out below!" With a series of cracks and one big sickening snap, the main mast toppled to port as men dove out of the way, dragging the mizzen with it into the black seas. Two midshipmen got caught in the Medusa's hair of lines and were swept overboard as the broken masts pivoted over the side rail. *Le Dromedaire* rolled to port, threatening to drown herself at the loss of her limbs. Bittersweet success flowed through our hearts as we sacrificed most of our sailing capacity to decrease our odds of sinking.

"Open the fore hatch!" roared Neville. "Dump the cargo, clear the hold. Keep only ballast and two weeks' rations!"

We rushed to dump barrels, crates, and boxes overboard. We gutted the hold, desperately sacrificing all the voyage's profits to the deep in hopes of making her lighter. As men went further into the hold, tearing all things loose, a shout went up, "Water in the hold!"

The hold had accumulated over a foot of seawater. I prayed it was from the hatches, and not a leak. The bowswain shouted, "Man the pumps!"

But Neville's furious voice countermanded him, "Never mind the pumps—dump the hogs, jettison the cargo!" The animals in our hold panicked in their pens and the hogs screamed like children. Fiver slaughtered each hog with a hammer blow to the head and teams of men hoisted their pink bodies up out of the hold and into the churning equatorial seas. We sprinted, trembling with intensity, knowing each minute of calm could be the last.

With the hold cleared and the hogs gone I rushed up on deck to see all hands riveted to their places and staring off to port. "Mother of God, look at that!"

Starlight twinkled on the gently tossing seas. I turned to the east where Neville pointed and beheld an endless black wall, blacker than night itself, bearing down on us.

Neville remained at the helm along with the second mate and a midshipman to guide us up and down the deadly seas with only the foremast and storm jibs reefed back. The wind had been such that even our transom had provided enough flat surface for the wind to push us faster than the old *Dromedaire* wanted to go.

The wall of black cloud pushed a mighty wave in front of it, cresting with white foam as tall as our main mast had been.

"Seal the hatches, seal the hatches! All hands below decks!"

Cries went up and men dove towards the hatches. I was the last one in the aft hatch and saw the fore hatch sealed. The force of the wind slammed the aft hatch down on my head, knocking me down the steps on top of two men below.

The raging black wall hit us at once, knocking us hard to port and burying the bow. I heard shouts from the helm and groans from the oaken bones of the ship as the storm wall picked us up and heaved us like a child kicking a ball. We rose, hung precariously on the crest of a mighty wave, and then ploughed down the back side. I lunged upwards and made the hatch fast before tons of seawater punctured our wooden skin.

We rolled sideways, *Le Dromedaire* again getting knocked down by the hurricane's headwall. This time we didn't stay down but slopped around to begin a deathly sleigh ride up and down waves the size of tall pines trees with fiendishly short intervals between their cresting tops. Nobody could hear anything as men jumbled into each other but soon we were all down in the hold pumping by the flickering light of a whale oil lamp. The water had indeed been from the hatches and we soon pumped the hold dry.

All night we ran with the storm, surging, rolling, breaking, crashing, every instant fearing that we'd roll and sink. Many times we heard sickening cracks of wood, and feared with each one that our seams had split asunder. We waited each time for water to gush into some ghastly wound in our hull.

I sat huddled with the crew, praying, when a gunner shouted six inches from my ear with all his might, "Water rising! We've sprung a leak! Man the pumps!"

We began shifts at the pumps to halt the seawater sloshing into our hold. We began losing the battle and the water rose from one foot to two, then to three, then to four, leaving only our heads free of the water. Panic sizzled through the men and wet sailors shouted their memorized Bible verses. The more water we took on, the more sluggishly we moved in the waves. We became increasingly crippled, like a dying man whose body no longer responds to his commands. Strong stoic sailors cried and wailed at their early deaths foreseen.

I kept waiting to hear that death sentence—*Abandon ship!*—but it never came. Instead came, "Fiver's found the leak!"

We quickly discovered that the leak was not in the hull but at the spot where we had cut away the mizzenmast. A long section of decking had ripped out and each wave that pounded over the decks sloshed into what had been Joseph's berth below. The hole should have been obvious, yet neither captain nor crew had thought of it.

Neville ordered half the men to assist the ship's carpenter in patching the hole with any available timber. Waves swamped the decks and knocked the men back from the hole but at last we tacked up two layers of wood and covered these in fresh pitch. All night we battled against the storm, pumping, patching, and praying in the blackness as we rolled and slammed.

Morning's light never came and day stayed so dark that it could've been an eclipse. We made headway against the water in the hold, pumping it down to one foot. At one foot the hold kept refilling, though. Our battered hull had sprung leaks somewhere and we had to pump constantly.

The rage of the first night settled into a strong gale which allowed some limited movement on deck, but little else. For the next two days we ate only a few pieces of soggy bread and drank water as furious elements abused us at all hours. Men vomited on me thrice. As the storm moved west so did we, surfing precariously on waves larger than *Le Dromedaire* and skimming down into troughs so deep our foremast did not reach their tops. Cappy stayed lashed to the bulkhead and no saltwater entered my berth, thus saving my journal and meager belongings.

The rest of the crew was not so lucky. The crew's quarters were utterly destroyed by the water we'd taken on and the constant pounding. We lost three more men overboard in the ensuing days, and never once saw true daylight. We transitioned from dark, hopeless night to a nasal grey twilight smothered by black clouds, howling winds, and rain that stung like a hard spanking.

With a more fully-pumped hold and no cargo, the old *Dromedaire* changed her lumbering habits into those of a remarkably able vessel. We could once more steer our own course despite the missing sail power from the toppled mizzen and main masts. One hundred incidents had put us within spitting distance of disaster, but each time we emerged afloat and alive. Were I to gamble on a similar escape occurring from such a storm I would not wager one time in a hundred. Several men experienced religious conversions and swore off a host of the destructive pasttimes which we mariners so enjoy.

Three days after the storm hit us, I woke to overcast skies and a steady tossing. The crew could safely move about the deck and begin to wonder about the wisdom of cutting two of our three masts in the mid-Atlantic. Captain Neville called all hands on deck in the early hours. I rushed up to see what new calamity awaited us but instead found Neville holding a Bible to the sky and clutching his hat in the other hand. His long white hair blew gently in the breeze like seaweed in the waves. An unspoken sadness swept over the crew and we all knelt before him around the stump of the main mast.

"Praise be to Almighty God, who hath seen it in his mercy to spare *Le Dromedaire*. We know not why, for we are all cursed sinners. Except my first mate Joseph Nobletree; he was not a cursed sinner, even though he was English. Ye, oh Lord, guided us through a storm no ship was meant to survive and yet our hearts bleed in pain for our lost brothers. We beseech You to take up our departed companions who You took in the storm and bestow on them the lights of your glory in heaven."

Neville named the nineteen hands lost in the storm and the men bowed their heads. Neville then began a series of readings from the Bible in Latin and a few in French from the New Testament. We all knelt, crossed ourselves after each verse, and clenched our hands in silent prayer. Many wept like babes. Neville's fervor grew like a disciple of Jesus bursting to tell his story.

He spoke with great passion and inspiration for the better part of an hour until a gust fluttered the pages and sent his hair charging off to starboard.

He didn't notice and continued on a different page, *"And he found a new jawbone of an ass, and put forth his hand, and took it, and slew a thousand men therewith.* Judges 15:15?...No, no, hold on, I've lost ..."

Neville flipped through a few pages, muttering, "I've always suspicioned that verse. One thousand men with a jawbone?" Loud sobs came from the gunners.

He scanned for his former place, muttering verses he came across, *"For a whore is a deep ditch; and a strange woman is a narrow pit...* No, not Proverbs, where are we?...*And he took the fat, and the rump, and all the fat that was upon the inwards, and the caul above the liver, and the two kidneys, and their fat, and the right shoulder...* Ah! Here it is: *The Lord is slow to anger, and great in power, and will not at all acquit the wicked the Lord hath his way in the whirlwind and in the storm, and the clouds are the dust of his feet. March all we sinners down the narrow path of righteousness, sailors obey ye captains, and ye shall be delivered into the fruitful kingdom of heaven surrounded by virgins, and copious feasting, amen."*

We gave an amen as a few shafts of actual sunlight peeked through the slate gray skies.

Suddenly, cries rose up and the crew shook off their brief religious devotion as we realized that nobody had been manning the pumps during Neville's lengthy diatribe. The waterline had risen some five or six feet on *Le Dromedaire* and we wallowed drunkenly at each wave. All hands rushed below. After several hours of furious work, we again regained our buoyancy and made headway.

CHAPTER 34
ACHING GUMS

On July the 21ˢᵗ, a strange, yellowish light shone down upon us. Sunshine seemed almost foreign after such a dark and terrible ordeal. The storm sped our crossing but we became utterly lost and unable to take our bearings for many days.

Captain Neville squinted into his Davis quadrant at high noon to measure the angle of the sun and thus our latitude. He announced that we'd made six days' progress in three and that we were already halfway across the Atlantic. The surgeon asked about our longitude and Neville changed the subject.

The surgeon persisted and Neville snapped, "All the hourglasses were destroyed in the storm so I cannot keep longitude any more successfully than you cured Mr. Stéphane's leg. You leave worrying of our route to me. One more question and you'll be doctoring fifty lashes on your arse."

The doctor turned red and pressed, "Well, Captain, Mr. Stéphane received a deep slash to his femoral artery because too many men were ordered to wield—"

Neville threw his hat to the deck and stepped close to the surgeon, their chins almost touching. "Belay that talk! Your doctoring failed, so he's dead! Now, in reference to your longitudinal inquiry, we're definitely somewhere between Portuguese Brazil and the Massachusetts Colony. Occupy thyself with blisters and bunions but leave navigation to me!"

The surgeon grimaced and bid Neville a curt *adieu*. As he passed me, I heard him mutter something that would be punishable by at least fifty lashings.

I took my turn once again at the pumps, my muscles already burning and broken. By nightfall the water rose to our knees. The man to my left struck up a sea shanty and we sang in the salty hold. Neville ordered groups of men to search for the leak and these unfortunates dove and searched in the cold water of the hold but none could find it in our multilayered hull.

At the end of my shift I staggered like a dying beaver, and collapsed into my hammock next to Cappy. Cappy's leaves looked less waxy green than before and a bit yellow. Several had turned brown and shriveled.

The sun cooked us on an endless sea. We moved sluggishly with one mast and water up to our waists in the hold. We had little left to eat: just one barrel of biscuits and three boxes of hardtack. We had no luck fishing with lines off the stern. Neville halved our water and biscuit ration and apologetically halted Cappy's extra ration of water. I began sharing my meager ration with my friend's thirsty little roots, leaving myself in a parched state. I brought Cappy up on deck for a day of sunshine and she regained some of her green luster in the gentle breeze as we cruised slowly and unsteadily westwards.

The pumping continued but *Le Dromedaire* wallowed ever lower in the water. Everyone knew what was happening but nobody dared talk of it. The ship's carpenter and his crew spent the entire afternoon repairing the longboats and caulking the little pinnace.

On July 23rd, I ran up on deck early in the morning to furious shouts and found much of the crew ringing around the ship's carpenter who landed blow after blow on Fiver. The cook recoiled from his beating and then caught the carpenter in an upper cut, sending his head snapping backwards and his weight crashing to the deck. The crew broke up the fight with both men bleeding and upset. Neville didn't even come up on deck. Discipline had all but broken down on board.

Le Dromedaire foundered in the calm seas. I brought Cappy up on deck and watched the crew attend their duties with tight-strung nerves. Several men had lost teeth—an early sign of the dreaded scurvy caused by the bad ocean airs. The battered carpenter came up on deck around noon and spoke with Captain Neville, who nodded gravely. They gazed at our puny longboats.

Neville assembled our ragged crew and gave a peculiar order. He decreed that all hands on board cut off all their hair and give it to him. I blinked at him like a child, wondering if I was hallucinating.

"By Jove, cut me your hair and give it here at once! And you three midshipmen, bring up all the dung from the animals' old pens! We'll need that too. Step lively!"

Men muttered and looked at each other. The boswain at last cried, "What's all this, captain? We want to die with our hair or else Saint Peter might not recognize us."

The carpenter responded, "Old Petey knows you well enough by yer smell to send you down wer ye belong thar, bowswain. Obey yer captain like a good lad." This brought on the first laughter I'd heard in over a week.

Neville thundered, "Twenty lashes to the man who will not cut his hair! You greenhorn land-lubbering babies, none of ye would be interviewing with Saint Peter anyhow. Now shave, damn you!"

We looked from one to another, fearful that our captain was going mad. The carpenter explained, "It's to try to patch the hull. We mix the manure, hair and caulk onto a sail and then drop it with lines to rub along the bottom of the hull so as to fill any aperture there…It's an old carpenters' trick from the India route, but it often does not work, so don't ye boys blame me if it don't plug us up."

The gunners spread an extra mainsail on the open deck. We took boat knives to our heads and cut off great shanks of hair, beards, and mustaches. Long scraggly curls fell to the sail, mingling with buckets of caulk and rank pig excrement. A few men were not too parched to vomit. We mixed this putrid putty and slopped it onto the top side of the sail. This we secured with five lines on each side and all hands lifted this heavily crapped canvas and lowered it down the port bow. We brought the lines up under the starboard side also and began hauling it along the keel. We strained upward against the lines to smear the hull as forcefully as possible.

Neville ordered all hands to haul for the stern and we carefully smeared our hull in hairy feces. Not wanting to waste a perfectly good mainsail, Neville ordered this wretched nautical rag hauled back up, scrubbed for half a day, and then hung to dry. That evening the crew lay listlessly in their hammocks, utterly worn from such exertion fueled merely by water and biscuits.

I awoke the next day to a new motion, one that filled me with joy and a tinge of apprehension. We now bobbed light as a cork upon a glittering sea. The carpenter's plan had worked! The leaks sprung in our hull from the storm's battering were temporarily sealed with our repulsive remedy. Baldness was a small price to pay and *Le Dromedaire* went from looking like a tattered pirate ship to a floating monastery full of bald, fasting monks. The sky brought not a puff of wind and we bounced lightly in irons, the foresails gently luffing with each bounce.

More men joined the sick list and began dying of scurvy, and mutterings of a curse arose. I overheard a rumor that some even suspected Cappy to be the cause of our misfortunes. I guarded her on deck all day, flintlocks loaded, and slept with the door locked and barred.

After escaping maelstrom, we now bobbed on a motionless sea. Sadness and desperation clawed at my heart. The storm's fury had brought a disciplined urgency to our crew, but the doldrums took a heavier toll on men's minds. In three days, half of our remaining crew joined the sick list and our water supplies grew so low that we set out containers by night to collect the morning dew.

A man died on the next day from the effects of scurvy and dehydration. Those few of us still fit to stand heaved his body overboard in an empty flour sack and watched his dark form slip underneath the waves. The next day three more died. The fourth one that we tossed began to sink when suddenly the body was hit by something underneath the water and a red cloud erupted beneath the waves.

"Sharks!" Pitri yelled, "Grab the fishing tackle!"

The deck became a chaos of shouts and motion. We ran with reanimated vigor to cast lines baited with moldy biscuits. Soon the water churned with sharks, fins, and teeth ripping our deceased friends apart. All we saw was food. One of those big monsters could feed every man for a day. We had only three lines but the sharks took none of them and the frenzy began to subside. Suddenly the line held by the surgeon went taut and jerked him overboard.

"Man overboard!"

I grabbed a line that snapped in front of my face. The wet rope wrapped around my wrist and I lurched towards the gunwale, hauled by a wrenching force towards the churning seas. The sharks had become the fishermen and we the fish. The surgeon hit the water screaming and I wavered on the edge with the line wrapped around my wrists.

Then hands grabbed me, arresting my fall. Three midshipmen grappled me around the waist and together we heaved on the surgeon's line. Our combined strength popped the healer out of the sea and slammed him into the port hull.

We hauled him in, landing his soaking form as we would a dolphin. His hands were swollen, red as cherries from the ropes constricting them. The crew paid him little heed as we heaved to bring in our nutritious quarry.

Someone yelled, "Fetch the harpoons, get the gaff hook!"

The strength of hungry French sailors is unmatched and, when we heaved together, we pulled so hard that a shark shot out of the water, thumping into the port side. This was a true sea monster, easily twenty feet long, a big, grey body thicker than a biscuit barrel with dark, malicious eyes and teeth streaming with the blood of our dead comrades. It was a moment frozen in time as the mighty animal crashed into our hull, sharky surprise on its face, its thrashing tail catching air instead of water. Fiver lept towards it with a gaff hook in his one arm and impaled the monster through the flank.

Our great strength and desperation was our own undoing. We hauled again and up whipped a severed line with two wet strands at the ends. The gaff hook snapped and the shark escaped. Away swam enough meat to feed the entire crew with a big gaff hook sticking from its side like a porcupine quill. Other sharks turned on it, creating a great churning maelstrom. Men hurled the harpoons at the dark shapes flashing through the reddened waters, but to no avail. We quickly affixed a new hook and sacrificed another precious biscuit but we caught nothing else. The thrashing fins soon receded into the inky depths, the remains of our friends picked clean. Like demons, they descended into their watery hell.

Le Dromedaire's crew sunk into a deep depression, palpable in the motionless air. Captain Neville ordered the water ration halved again and with slumped shoulders invited me into his cabin. With the door shut and locked behind him he turned to me in the elegant quarters and asked, "Want an apple, De Clieu?"

I looked up like a curious woodchuck, but Neville chuckled. "I jest. There's no more food. But let us share the last of the Madeira."

He poured two glasses and cut thin slices out of a sickly, brownish-green lime, plopping them into our drinks.

"Here's to the endless seas, De Clieu, as fine a resting place as any sailor can desire. I'm afraid these rotten airs will do to us what the storm could not. I'd like you to help me draw up a will. You know how write these sort of contracts from your work in Paris, yes?"

I had no idea how to write a will but hated seeing the old man so sad. "Yes, sir, more or less."

Neville heaved into his chair with a sigh. "Good. Then, De Clieu, we can write it out and seal it up in a wine bottle so that it may float if the caulk in our hull fails or I perish before we drift to land."

After seven more glasses, we finished the will, which became less and less coherent as he dictated its provisions. I divvyed up

Neville's slaves and possessions among his legitimate family in Nantes and his mistress' family in Saint Domingue. Then the will digressed into a recitation of his favorite poem. It ended with some scattered notes about the process of fermentation scribbled in the left margin.

Neville slumped forward as I penned the document. "How does it look, De Clieu?"

I put down the pen and slurred, "Very fine, sir. Very fine. A formal last testament if ever there was one. King Louis should be jealous of such a document."

Neville raised a hand, "Good, De Clieu. Leave me now; I'm too fatigued." I left the white-haired captain slumped forward in his chair and quietly shut his door to check on Cappy.

CHAPTER 36
SKELETON CREW

By July 28th, the stench of death filled *Le Dromedaire*. Two more men had died of scurvy the night before. I felt weak and dizzy. For the past three days I stepped on teeth that fell from the rotting gums of the scorbutic sufferers.

Neville called me into his cabin once again that night. He looked like a pale ghost inside his dark quarters and his hands shook as he poured Madeira. The place reeked of alcohol, which perhaps Neville had resorted to drinking for lack of water. He thudded into his chair and gestured for me to sit.

"I am dying, De Clieu...I left something out of the will that I need you to add. Six of the twenty men who went ashore with me on Sal are still alive and I need you to kill them."

I squeezed another rotten lime slice into my glass of precious liquid. He looked up at me with sickly yellow eyes.

I told him the obvious. "Sir...I cannot kill six French sailors. Nor have I the strength. I fear that these trials have made you—"

Neville pounded his white hand onto the table which shook even though it was bolted to the floor. "One is Welch! One is Welch and five are French!"

He slurped from his glass and continued, "They are pirates, De Clieu! Buccaneers! Thugs and corsairs!" He panted for a few moments, his chest heaving. "You must kill them because we have something aboard that does not belong to them and they want it... Concealed in the hold are four barrels disguised as ballast."

I waited for him to continue but he just stared blankly until I asked, "What is in them, sir?"

Neville whispered, "Treasure!"

He leaned so close to me that his cracked lips tickled my earlobe. "It's a portion of Cassard's treasure that he buried on Sal before he left Cape Verde. Most of the gunners were buccaneers who sailed with Cassard and signed up with me because I offered to pick up their loot…for five shares, of course."

I could not believe this. Neville repeated himself: "De Clieu, I said that the barrels are full of Cassard's treasure!"

"Yes, I heard that part. But sir, in good conscience I cannot kill six of the men who have taken *Le Dromedaire* so far, regardless of how Welsh or piratical they are."

Neville got up abruptly and took the seat cushion off his captain's chair. He produced a big black bottle of sherry from Jerez and poured himself a glass. He slid the bottle towards me on the table.

"Kill them, De Clieu, and I'll give you an entire barrel for yourself. We counted 14,234 Portuguese *reales*, and 513 silver bars. Of course, most of the buccaneers count with their fingers so there may be a deviation. And I'm almost positive that Pitri siphoned some off before we nailed the barrels shut. Regardless, we have enough treasure to make you one of the richest men on the Spanish Main!"

His babbling scared me and I knew better than to get between pirates and their treasure, "Captain Neville, sir, I'm sure you'll make it through this journey, but as a staunch admirer of Cassard's, all I could rightly do with this treasure is return it to him in Nantes so I must respectfully decline any involvement in this affair. My foremost concern on this voyage is taking my coffee plant to Martinique."

Neville was already pouring another glass of sherry, his red eyes watering and hands shaking. "Very well, De Clieu, how about this? You give my share to my widow if I die. You don't have to kill anyone unless they break the pirate's code and refuse to give up my fair share. I'll carry your plant to Martinique should you precede me in death. Considering that we're dying, it little matters. What say ye?"

For this I needed another glass of sherry. "With all due respect, captain, which widow are we talking about?"

A smile traced across Neville's broken face, "It shall go to my petite Adélaïde in New Orleans—oh, sweet little Adélaïde."

This was the last coherent thing to leave Neville's lips and marked the existence of yet another mistress or wife of whom I had been unaware. After wresting the glass from his slumped hand, I took my leave and returned to the listless decks.

By the first of August, dehydrated and desperate men struggled to survive. Instead of the unity I saw during the storm, the disparate nationalities and allegiances on board *Le Dromedaire* combined with Neville's increasingly rare presence on deck created a barbarian state. Our water supplies were twice as low as they ought to be, indicating that someone or ones were stealing this precious exilir of life. Accusations and rumors flew back and forth. Twice, men drew lots to shoot and eat someone, but both times Fiver dispersed this macabre ritual.

Poor Fiver. The skin of his arms hung in loose flaps, like that of a flying squirrel. His eyes were sunk back into his head and his gums were black with scurvy. We buried six more sailors at sea, lacking even decent cloth to wrap them in. Where last time we had yearned to eat the sharks for food, this time we yearned to eat the men and only the most tenuous threads of decency held us back. They were not to last.

That night I awoke to the sound of tinkering with my lock. I bolted upright in my hammock and my skull slammed into the low ceiling. An axe blow fell on my door and I leapt out of bed, shouting, "I've four loaded pistols for the first men through the door!" Nobody acknowledged the incident and none professed any interest in pursuing it the next day.

I continued giving half of my water ration to Cappy each day. My tongue was so dry that it bled when it moved and Cappy looked like a oak tree in late autumn with all her leaves beginning to turn brown and fall to the deck. I thought that most likely, *Le Dromedaire* would eventually be found floating with all crew perished of famine and thirst with only little Cappy clinging to life.

We swung in slow circles with whatever deep water current drove us, without a breath of wind in the scorching equatorial air.

By the third of August, I decided that I would die up on deck with Cappy. That way she might benefit from the first rains and have enough sun as I rotted away beneath her.

I carried her once more up on deck. This time I brought my diary, cleaned out my cabin, and locked the door. My throat was so parched that it hurt to talk, hurt to swallow, and the air felt like sand passing in and out of my desiccated lungs. I was weary of the fight to survive and willing to finally greet oblivion as a respite from the tortures of starvation. I watched the blurry events on deck with glazed eyes.

The crew were well along the final descent into the utmost depravity and madness. Pitri thought a particular oar was edible and Fiver just sat against the foremast rolling his head in circles and groaning from time to time. Neville had not been seen on deck in two days and rumors passed between chapped lips that he had died in his cabin. This may have been just as well, because were Neville to have appeared on deck, I think that Pitri and others might have eaten him.

Patrice the toothless midshipman died that night. His body remained by the stump of the main mast, the symbol of all our despair, and a small cluster of men surrounded him quarrelling over what to do. Some wanted to cut him up to use for shark bait while others want to drink his blood, and still more wanted to cook and eat him or some combination of those three options.

I kept my pistols in hand to avoid any premature feasting on myself or Cappy. The argument over Patrice's corpse grew worse, and I heard curses spat with the last drops of moisture on men's tongues. We had become ravenous hyenas, gnashing our teeth in eagerness to eat one of our fallen brothers. I sat baking with Cappy in the sun, my mouth ajar and eyes closed. Life consisted entirely of waiting for the daily ration of one cup of water to be announced. That's when it hit.

A great sound kicked up like one thousand chambermaids ruffling a field of bedsheets, then died. I blinked. Again, the maids began rustling bedsheets and my bloodshot eyes looked up to see the foremast's topgallant sail luffing and flapping violently in a strong new breeze. The sluggish sea turned to whitecaps and the air on my skin was as pleasurable as Henriette's caress.

As if on cue, Neville burst out on deck. "Avast, you cannibals! Up the shrouds, hoist the foresails, trim that topgallant sail! You, Mr. Poisson, hard to port. Move, ye dirty cannibals, before the wind dies again!"

The men forgot their misery and rushed up into the foremast rigging. Joyous shouts rang out and men fell to their knees as our sails unfurled and *Le Dromedaire* made headway. I got up from my deathbed with Cappy and looked over the poop deck to see the beautiful white bubbles of our foaming wake. God, what a sublime and marvelous sight! We began a westerly tack, making the best progress we could with one mast and a skeleton crew.

Despite our progress, the situation on *Le Dromedaire* remained critical. The joy of wind gave way to thirst and desperation. Two more men died of scurvy and all but a handful showed terrible scorbutic symptoms. Keeping the rudder pointed west was all our dying crew could muster.

The difference between gunners, midshipmen, and passengers disappeared. I took my turn at the wheel, assuming the duties of the dead. My throat burned and I developed a fever. That morning I gave half my water ration to Cappy. She looked on the verge of death, starving for moisture, her soil cracked and leaves brittle.

Pitri, in a hallucination of his own, drank a big swallow from an imaginary tankard of rum, wiped his blood-cracked lips and then passed it to me. He growled and stared for an uncomfortably long time at my neck. I cannot recall how long I stood riveted to the helm for lack of anyone else interested in steering...it may have been a day and a night.

Chapter 37
Mount Hillabee

Neville's voice ended my swooning. "Land Ho!"

I jumped up and saw Neville lying slumped on the stump of the main mast pointing at a cloud that looked like France. My arms remained locked in the position they had held for so long, gripping the wheel. Fiver took over, though nobody knew or cared if he actually knew how to hold a course. We sailed briskly in a heavy turquoise swell from the northeast that pitched us up and down.

Twice more that day, lunatics sighted land. The first time it was a log floating by, and the second time it was a skinny seagull that had landed on the poopdeck. I drew a bead on it and murdered the gull with my flintlock. We each got a sip of its blood and a bite of raw flesh. We had a quarter cask of water left and the ration was to be cut the next day from one cup per day to just half. A cat would die of dehydration on such a ration. I curled into a ball alongside a barrel with Cappy and went to sleep, not knowing or caring if I should ever wake again.

Another tentative "Land Ho?" woke me from a dream about waterfalls.

Through the slits of my eyes I saw only open ocean. The shout echoed again. Nobody moved and several sincere curses went up to the watchman—but he persisted. "Land ho, I tell you!"

The few men who could still speak described some very unnatural things they had recently done with the watchman's mother. I joined the chorus of abuse and put my head in my hands, croaking, "Shut up!"

I finally clawed myself upright, preparing to kill the watchman—and saw four men gathered by the bowsprit peering at a green dot on the horizon.

I shouted to the beleaguered men below, "'Tis true—land is in sight!"

Ghastly men rose up on deck, teeth and hair falling out in clumps. The green dot bounced on the horizon. It was either a mass delusion or a sweet, savory, blessed island. As the afternoon came on, the breeze held firm and we sailed closer to the dot, which grew in size. Two solitary tears slid down from my sunken eyes and dripped from my protruding cheek bones. These tears represented a significant portion of that day's water ration and I licked them back in.

So I stood—lashing my dry, cracked tongue about, trying to drink my own tears as individual palm trees slowly distinguished themselves from the larger green mass of the approaching island. Nobody felt brave enough to climb the tattered foremast shrouds to get a better look, so we gazed like dogs at a banquet. A cry went up from the third mate, "It's Martinique, God be praised! There's Mount Pelée, bless her bald slopes!"

Scratchy dry eyes squinted in the bright sun towards simmering silhouettes emerging from the distance. Fiver peered from under his stump and then swung it up and down onto Bucy's cap.

"No, Bucy you fungus, that's not Mount Pelée. That be Barbados' Mount Hillabee. Much too rounded to be the Pelée volcano...Just like yer momma's teat, and I would know!"

The surviving men enjoyed their first smiles in days. The crew heartily agreed that the mountain resembled Bucy's mother's teat. The gunner Chirac, who I had deemed on the verge of death yesterday, emerged from the hold, coughed, spat blood, and cackled, "Nay, 'tis not near craggy enough to be that of Bucy's mother. Looks more like Fiver's daughter's to me!"

We all laughed and gazed lovingly at the approaching green bosom.

Fiver scratched himself. "Barbados is English, I reckon..."

Chirac croaked, "Is we at war with the English at present?"

Fiver rasped, "Aye, that we is."

Several men dissented and called him a fool. Fiver defended himself by saying, "I was just saying we's probably at war with them, but I still say we land. They can't do any worse to us than we've done to ourselves, can they?"

I pondered for a moment, "We weren't very much at war with them when we left. But I can't recall being at peace with them either ..."

A gravelly voice barked from the poop deck, "I am at war with the English. Prepare to come about."

A gaunt Captain Neville braced himself against the aft rail. He was cursed down by mutinous croaks. Chirac hobbled towards him, brushing me aside. "Not land? Are you mad, old man? Half the crew's dead and the other half be dying before our very eyes. I'll be damned to the very fires of hell if we don't beach this vessel on the nearest shore and drink from the first puddle we find on that island! English can't do us more ill than you's done!"

Neville drew his heavy Queen Ann pistol and pointed it with both hands at Chirac's chest. "Who saved you from the Dutch man-o-war? Who scared off the Barbary pirates and guided you through a storm the likes of which would've sunk the Spanish Armada? You stand one word away from mutiny, Chirac."

Chirac, who had spent most of the last few days splayed in the hold, brushed past me and took another step towards Neville. "Nobletree and De Clieu's done most of that, you maggot. Go ahead, you worm of a captain, fire away, you coward. After all, ye don't want the rest of these boys to find what's in the hold. It's only me and six more of the boys now, captain. You's outlived us, so why not make it five and pull the—"

Boom! Chirac screamed and plunged down onto the deck. It was odd that he did this, since Neville's shot sliced through my right arm and hit someone behind me.

I toppled down to the deck. The men surged onto Neville. A leather-booted foot kicked my head as they ran towards Neville and I blacked out.

I awoke groggily to the sound of the capstan cranking the anchor chain down. My first thought was for Cappy. I listed over to see where I was and tumbled out of my hammock onto the raspy wooden deck and passed out again. I opened my eyes to see that I had either gone blind or it was night. The former seemed more likely as I rehashed the skirmish that had knocked me out. I slowly felt around me and realized that I was on the floor in my berth. In a miasma of pain, I sat up and leaned my back against the bulkhead.

We were under sail. I recognized every creak and groan, every wave and roll of a ship's proper momentum. I let out a long slow curse and held my head. The hot smell of rotting flesh permeated everything around me and I tried to vomit but had nothing inside me. I gingerly pushed a hand through my hair and encountered a wetness I knew was blood. This movement caused a very sharp pain in my right arm and I reached over with my left to feel an improvised bandage wrapping my arm. At this moment, I began suspecting I had died and was soon to meet Satan, Peter, or whatever deity awaited me.

In the blackness I heard footsteps and saw a light approaching me.

"Mango, sir?"

In my pain I didn't understand, "What…the…Devil?"

The dim light swung closer and Fiver's pockmarked face appeared, looking like a curious badger. Relief flooded me, briefly overpowering my throbbing pains.

"Will you have a slice of mango, Capitaine De Clieu, sir?"

I coughed up a ball of phlegm that tasted like biting an iron bar, fearing my head would split open like an old gourd. "I am unwell, Fiver…what's happened to us? Who is this Mango? A pirate?"

Fiver knelt down and placed a cutting board next to me; six yellow mango slices glimmered with moisture in the lamplight. I greedily pushed one into my mouth. The taste was beyond description. I groaned in ecstasy and Fiver smiled and ambled off with his light to let me eat in the dark. I forgot entirely about Cappy until I was done ravaging the mango slices and licking the cutting board like a tiger cub to get every particle of moisture and fiber into me.

Fiver returned with a bucket full of water. "They say not to drink it too fast, sir, many's the boys been regur—" I could no longer hear him as I submerged my head in the bucket and began sucking it up like the Paris fire brigade.

When I finally came up for air, Fiver was long gone and I lay back dripping and panting. Water surged through my body like a runaway team of horses; waves of fresh water breaking over my every muscle and fiber with refreshment and relief.

I licked mango juice from my fingers for the better part of five minutes and then slowly stood up, my headache much diminished. I followed the rough wooden bulwarks to the passageway and up the narrow ladder to the main deck. As I emerged, the wind whooshed across my scruffy head. I stood for a minute leaning on the hatchway, savoring the joy of nourishment and navigation.

Above, a universe of stars blazed magestically and I inspected their position for the first time in many weeks. By the moon's transit, I judged us to be north of the Equator. I peered up at the magnificent heavens and found old Polaris, the North Star, and measured the old man's distance from Cassiopeia's breasts and back down to the Seven Sisters of the Pleiades. Then I went up to Menkar, the whale's nose, and back down to Ursa Major and then measured over to Deneb, the hen's tail. Yes, we were near the Antilles, I was sure of it! Without an octant and star chart I could not place our latitude more precisely.

I gazed longingly at the virgin Adhara, then the mango slices hit my shriveled stomach like a match to a powder keg. A long low seismic tremor shook my guts. All my intestines spasmed and contracted.

As the intensity of the mango storm increased, I doubled over and a voice called out, "No vomiting in the hatch! Get ye to the rail, that's an order!"

I blew out a fine mist of mango onto the steps. "Fire and brimstone!" I heard. "Is that De Clieu?"

I felt much better and hauled myself fully up on deck. I stood up, recognizing the dark shape that emerged from the stern. "Ah, Chirac," I called. "Ce va?"

Chirac's face pressed close to me and I noticed two pistols at his waist. "That's Captain Chirac to you, passenger."

I had the terrible notion that he was not joking. Suddenly, the events leading up to my blackout rushed back to me and I recalled falling to the deck in the midst of the crew's rage at Neville. A knot twisted in my stomach that had nothing to do with the mango.

"Where is my plant, Chirac? Where is Captain Neville?"

Chirac took a step closer, "Neville had an accident, De Clieu. I'm captain now. As for your plant, it's in my quarters and if you wants it back then ye must make a choice now. I 'as spoke with the boys and we's got no quarrel with you. Indeed, you's done this voyage a load more good than our blighted captain. But you was mighty friendly with the old devil, so if you want your tree back, I'm sure you'll agree that Neville's departure was a very unfortunate accident and swear yer oath of loyalty to me."

"Oh, I see," I said in a low voice. "Well, did you know that sea turtle meat is better grilled than fried?"

Chirac squinted and leaned forward. "What?"

I slammed my elbow into his face and kneed him in the groin. I whipped him around by his left wrist and put my right arm around his neck from behind and pressed hard against his Adam's apple.

"Shall we go get my plant, *Captain* Chirac?" I said, with clenched teeth. Chirac gurgled and I pressed him harder. "Was that a yes?"

He tried to nod, though my arm blocked his head from moving. I walked him forward to the rail and bent him over it to gaze at the dark foam below.

"Yes, you will give me my plant back and not bother me? Or, yes, you like swimming with the sharks at night?" I released my arm from his neck and ripped his pistols out of his belt and thrust them into my own.

I released my arm from his throat. Chirac gasped and expelled air, "You can have your goddamn plant, De Clieu! We've no quarrel with you or that stupid shrub. It's yours if you swear your allegiance to me."

I jerked his left arm upwards until the sinew wouldn't let me pull it any higher behind his back, "Verily?"

Chirac expelled air. *"Oui, oui!"*

"Very well, then. And I hope for your sake that the plant is as I left it yesterday because if any leaves are missing, I'll take your toes to replace them."

I released Chirac and stepped back. I misjudged how far he was leaning forward and he fell head first into the black waters below with a mighty splash. My eyes widened and I shouted, *"Merde!"*

I raced to the stern, uncoiled a docking line and threw it over the port side where Chirac had splashed into the water. Below, I saw only smooth swells, darker than octopus ink and no sign of Chirac. *"Merde, merde, merde!* Man overboard!" I yelled.

On the back of a swell just off the stern, Chirac's head burst up from the water and his arms flailed about. "Help!"

I yelled to him, "Line in the water three strokes to your starboard!"

Chirac pounded and flailed at the water as if he was trying to fly. I wrenched the hemp line up and to the right with all my strength. This sent a spiraling surge down the line and it curled towards him. The heavy cord whapped him in the face. He let out a hoot and grabbed it. I hauled on the heavy line, but with so little nourishment for so long, I had hardly the ability to hold it steady, much less pull it in. I heard running footsteps and shouts behind me and I nudged my overcoat out to cover the two pistols in my belt.

Confused sailors barreled to my side and helped haul in the line. Chirac clung shivering on the end. Five men helped me flip him up over the rail and onto the poop deck where he lay on his back, gasping and sputtering.

"What the devil happened?" Bucy demanded.

I knelt beside Chirac with a cold smile. "I came upon *Capitaine* Chirac trying to fix our position by the stars and…just at the moment a counter-swell tripped him up and he fell overboard like a log off a lumber cart. The captain was all alone on deck and 'twas lucky I came up or we would've left him in our wake. Good to have you back, Cap, how are you?"

He coughed and shuddered like a catfish at the bottom of a rowboat. I and three other men lifted him up and bore him to the captain's quarters where we laid him out on the captain's berth. Cappy stood beneath a painting of Louis XIV behind which I knew Neville hid his stash of fine cognac. As the men ministered to their new captain I rushed to Cappy and hefted her up.

Her leaves tickled my face. I yanked three bottles of cognac out from the cavity behind the painting and presented two of them to Chirac and the assembled crew. Chirac remained speechless and fear bubbled in me. My fate hung on his word.

I knelt beside him and whispered, "You shan't believe me, but I didn't intend for you to swim. I'll take my plant back and vouch for whatever account of Neville you give on our arrival, Chirac. You have my word as a gentleman."

His chest rose, his eyes shut, and he nodded. This did little to assuage my fears but I hefted up Cappy and made my retreat.

In the gathering dawn, I strode to my little cabin. I sat Cappy down and gently poured the remainder of my water bucket into her parched soil. I could almost see all her leaves perk up as the water sealed dry cracks and connected with her famished roots. I moved to pour some cognac into her, too, but thought better of it and uncorked the bottle for myself. I lit a candle and peered at the bottles.

I recognized their vintage and muttered, "Neville, you sneaky old swordfish…"

I had in my hands a bottle of Frapin's "Rabelais" Gran Cru de Cognac from 1665. Joel had fantasized about possessing these as if they were wealthy and lonely widows. I kissed the bottle and swished some of the deep magma-colored cognac in my mouth.

Ohhh. The sturdy taste of oak, mixed with a shot of smoke, curl of chocolate, and a little nip of coffee coursed through me.

A knock at my door raised me out of my cognac ecstasy. "De Clieu!" I lunged to make sure I had set the bolt and grasped the pistols. "Who is it?"

A grunt. "Fiver it is. Got a coconut for you."

I threw back the bolt and opened the door with one hand on the big Queen Anne. Fiver balanced four coconuts in his arm and barged through the door without any further words. I shut it behind him.

"Fiver, where did we land? How long was I unconscious? What happened to Neville?" Fiver peered at me with a lusty gleam in his eye that I had only seen when we slaughtered fresh hogs and turtles.

Suddenly, he dropped the coconuts on the floor and whipped out a long dagger from behind his apron. He raised it over his head and plunged it down as I tried to wrench the Queen Anne out of my belt and shoot him. I was too slow! His eyes glistened in the flickering candlelight as I stumbled backwards and his blade came down with perfect precision.

The knife found its target with a solid *thunk* and Fiver raised up a coconut on the end of his dirk. His head bumped into the shaking pistol I had finally drawn.

He looked up, surprised, "De Clieu?"

We beheld each other for an instant, me with the pistol and Fiver with a skewered coconut. "Christ in a rowboat, De Clieu!... I's just offering." He gulped. "Want a coconut?"

I breathed deeply, "Err, yes, that would be lovely. *Merci beaucoup*... Sorry, I have been on edge."

I lowered the pistol and hefted the scratchy shell up to my lips. Fiver grunted and shrugged. Soft coconut milk cascaded over my parched palate. My stomach was quite empty after regurgitating all the mango. We spoke no words until I drained my first coconut and was halfway through the second.

"De Clieu, ye can see the truth plainly enough, so I'll tell it straight. Right after ye went down, I kicked your noggin, I did.

Totally by accident it was, sir, there was a terrible confusion when Neville shot you and Bucy. When old Neville shot you in the shoulder without any recourse to proper sanctions, we half-dead blighters rose up and mutinied."

I let a long silence pass as Fiver waited for my reaction. I sucked the coconut. He continued nervously, "We wanted to land, we had to land, everyone knew that except Neville. 'Twasn't right of him to draw his pistols and shoot for insubordination. Not even that mule molester, Chirac, who's wearing the Captain's hat now.

"We had a fierce meeting after we'd put Neville down. Neville confessed that he'd been pirating with the gunners before this voyage and stopped in Cape Verde to dig up treasure they had buried with the pirate Cassard. He'd told us we were loaded with foodstuffs but it was gunpower. If we'd just crossed earlier in the season we would not have lost a man. Many's a good matey of mine we've dumped to the sharks thanks to that old pirate Neville. What's more, even with every man gnawing leather and drinking piss, he wouldn't share a brass doorknob of Cassard's treasure with us, no. 'Twas down in the ballast hold gathering dust, his share growing with every new death. Him having his own store of food. Scurvy taking to us all, we was such a sorry bunch—"

I gestured in circles with my pistol and rolled my eyes as I slurped coconut juice. "I recall all too well our recent misfortunes, my friend. Please, what did you do to Neville?"

Fiver shifted and harrumphed, "So anyway, we clapped him in chains, we did and, err...got rid of him."

I stopped and looked at Fiver for a long moment. "How did you get rid of him and how did you get mangoes, coconuts, and buckets of water?"

Fiver smiled, "We got cassava, too, and breadfruit; we got some onions, a whole pile of mutton, and parsley, and—"

"Where, man? What happened after you booted me senseless?"

Fiver looked away and scratched his rump with his stump. "On Barbados... We just anchored off Bardados and rowed in when you was out cold. 'Course all the boys was mighty concerned for you and yer little coffee tea plant so we putcha in yer cabin here below, tending and ministering to you, we were. Bandaged you up good, we boys did. 'Twas just with Neville with whom we had a quarrel, not with you, Sir Dee Cloo. I knows you liked 'im, you did. Hell, back in Nantes, I loved him like a new puppy, heard good tales of his shipping. A wolf in in disguise he was, eating us all up 'til there was none left and when he wouldn't let this dying ship land even to steal stores from the blasted English—well, that's just beyond what a man can endure."

I stabbed a third coconut and nodded at Fiver to continue. "So, you rowed ashore to Barbados at night?"

Fiver cracked open a coconut with his dagger and began scooping out the sweet white meat inside. "Aye, sir. We saw lights from a village ashore and rowed in on a calm sea. Passed a little island with sheep on it. Two of the gunners is English, so we was led by them and came ashore on a pretty white beach. We marched old Neville up to the village in manacles. 'Twas a sugar estate and the slaves were sleeping in clapboard shacks. They offered to help us if we freed 'em. We came to a building, big stone place, and banged on the door 'til a startled feller came down and we tied him up. We loosed his slaves, ransacked his larders and storehouse. We drank every drop of his well water and then his rum. We just ate and ate, vomiting at turns, for we'd not been used to the stability of the land, you know, after so long at sea. Turned mighty festive it did.

"By morning we started hearing horses and shouts. We spied a troop forming up on a hillside and we dashed off with these foodstuffs. With all the folks cleared out, we set the buildings alight for good measure. Then we's rowed back to the old *Dromedaire*, nabbed some sheep off the rock, and leaned into the capstans to weigh anchor. We was off before the Barbadans knew what had happened."

I glared at Fiver. He swallowed. "And?"

"We's uhh, we's left him there. He's got that deal with the Devil that he can't be killed, everyone knows it. We took a vote and decided not to have his curse fall on us by killing him. We did dishonor him, though. Left him naked as the day he's born. We's told the negros he's a slaver and told the planter that he's an abolitionist. It's better than he deserved."

CHAPTER 38
MARTINIQUE

I awoke the next morning with half a bottle of Frapin cognac underneath my head. My mind thundered like the surf on a reef. I rolled my head off the bottle and curled up into a ball, waiting for the pounding to subside. It didn't.

I staggered to my feet and felt my way along the corridor to the main hatch and emerged into the blinding Caribbean sun like a mole.

It was afternoon. I squinted upwards to see our French colors snapping in the wind. I could see the rainbow of coral through the clear waters some ten fathoms below. I looked again and judged it to be closer to just six fathoms.

All the crew was crowded on the port gunwale, hailing a sturdy stone fort flying the *fleur-de-lis*. Fort de France! I fell to my knees, tears drizzling down my gaunt cheeks.

The fort's cannon boomed a salute that echoed off Mount Pelée. Then another shot boomed. Two shots. A warning. But why?

"Reef!" called the lookout frantically from the crow's nest.

All hands turned to see that we had entered the bay too far to the south and were drifting right into the waves breaking over the Banc de Boucher reef. The Banc was a great fishing spot that I had visited on calm days in small boats during my early time on Martinique.

Chirac threw the wheel hard to port and men streaked up the shrouds to change tack. We drifted closer in a strong southerly wind. Two more booms. I charged back to the wheel where Chirac was barking orders like a flustered poodle.

"Chirac, don't you know how to pilot the harbor? Why didn't you ask for the course?"

He whirled at me. "Thrice, we tried to wake your sorry—"

With a boom, *Le Dromedaire* lurched to a stop and listed violently to port. I grabbed a stay line but was thrown to the deck.

Billowing clouds of mud, sand, and flecks of crushed white coral plumed from our hull. A school of blueheads charged away from the aquatic explosion.

Waves broke in gentle surf all around our bow and Chirac began furiously ordering the foremast sails furled. The grating sounds ceased and we held fast on the sharp coral and rocks of Banc de Boucher.

The crew cast off the anchors and checked the damage below. A man dashed up from the hold, "She's leaking, Chirac—err, Captain, but not too heavy. We can pump her if she don't spring any more holes."

I took a turn at the pumps below and then came back up on deck for a rest.

Two small *pirogues* set out from the docks in the harbor towards us. A short man in a large hat stood in the prow of the closest boat, and I soon made out a grizzled face and bulldog stance. It was Sargeant Fossieu. No sooner had the *pirogue* heaved to below our side than Fossieu climbed onboard and began firing off orders.

Chirac's authority was forgotten and men scurried to obey Fossieu. He was less interested in getting us off the reef than in establishing that all of *Le Dromedaire's* crew's mothers were whores whose mental capacities were outshined by tree frogs.

His litany of abuse reached such a height that he had our famished crew standing stiff as ramrods looking at their boot buckles or cracked toes. Then Fossieu recognized me sitting on the poop deck with Cappy.

"De Clieu? De Clieu—is that you? What are you doing with these inbred sheep and why are you clutching a dead shrub? My God, you are skinnier than a minnow!"

Fossieu inventoried our misfortunes. "Missing the main mast, mizzenmast, and sailing with a scurvy-ridden skeleton crew on an empty ship that's growing plants and soon to be broken apart on the Banc de Boucher, which a drunk sand crab could easily could have avoided!"

I looked over the rail at the aquamarine waters. "I was resting after my turn at the pumps. No one bothered to ask me how to enter the harbor." Charic glared at me and cursed, "Thrice we tried to rouse this alcohol-soaked—"

Fossieu spat something onto Chirac's tunic that looked alive.

"It was low tide two hours ago, so with any luck you can be lifted off if you use the longboats to set those stern lines in the deeper water. If not, I hope you can swim, because we'll be busy in Saint-Pierre."

Fossieu scratched himself and swung over the rail to climb back down to his *pirogue*. "*Bienvenue en Martinique, mon amis!*"

I squinted at the shore and saw a curious crowd gathering by the docks. The arrival of any ship always marked an important event, and we were no doubt already the talk of the island. As the sun's rays deepened to bronze, our hull ground against the coral. Chirac gave the order to man the capstans and attempt to pull us off. I locked Cappy in my cabin and went to the aft capstan where two skinny men pushed, to little effect. Fiver joined me at my side to push on one of the four heavy iron bars. When three more men reached for the bars, she began to turn.

We rocked twice and then came off the shoal. It was a blissful feeling to have *Le Dromedaire* back afloat in deeper water. Over this arduous journey, our bodies melded into one, hers of stout oak and pine, mine of Frenchman, such that every cruel misfortune to befall *Le Dromedaire* felt like a wound to me. Men let fall the foremast sails, and the clanking of the anchor chain and creaking of the hulking iron capstan marked our departure from the reef. Another cloud of white dust spread out into the azure waters as we shoved off into the delightful bounce of the waves.

The ship responded slowly. Chirac squawked that we were taking on more water. Fiver grunted, "Just point this damn raft at the pier."

We sailed clumsily for the last time before reefing the sails as we lumbered up alongside the long wooden pier. We threw the heavy hawsers over to the bare-chested slaves waiting to wrap them around the barnacled pilings.

Hundreds of curious faces gawked at our half-wrecked ghost ship. Chirac drew me aside as I waved to several acquaintances below. "De Clieu, listen closely here. With Neville gone and our hold full of treasure, you owe us our dues."

I glared at him. "You stole my plant for which I've endlessly toiled."

Chirac shurgged, "You did assault me and throw me overboard."

We looked at each other for a long moment. "Well, let's call it even," I finally replied. "What's the favor you seek?"

Chirac paused a moment. "Me and the boys voted and we're for going privateering if we can get a commission from the governor here. We could pay a dite of our riches to him to overlook Capt'n Neville's little misfortune and a dite more for new masts and we'd be jolly ready to go! Given that you know the governor and is starting a high commission here, we reckon you can—"

I raised my voice for the crew's benefit. "It's none of my concern what *Le Dromedaire* does after this, so I won't hinder you if this has been the vote. Nor is her cargo my concern; I want no part of it. I do recommend that she find a captain capable of keeping her off the reefs!"

Chirac pursed his lips, then wheeled around to go below. The rest of the crew hastened to lash the gangplank into place and touch French soil for the first time in many terrible weeks. A few fishermen bounced around us in their small boats, peering at the battered hulk of *Le Dromedaire*.

Muttering crowds of onlookers swarmed the dock and called out to us, "Hurricane? Clash with the Spanish? Pirates? Sea monsters?"

A few in the crowd recognized me and called out as I carried Cappy down the gangplank. Two customs inspectors hustled up, readying scrolls and forms. I recognized one of the two as Monsieur Ebert.

Ebert jabbed his finger into my chest. "Now, hold on, Monsieur De Clieu! Welcome back and all, but where are the ship's papers?

Who's the supercargo to represent the owners' interests? Were you aware of the new tax on finished goods? What's her cargo?"

I waved to a sugar planter whose daughter I found quite appealing. "My good Ebert, I'm just a passenger. The supercargo succumbed to scurvy, then sharks ate him. We threw our cargo of gunpowder overboard in a storm. The ship's papers might still exist. Her new captain, the one who landed us on the shoals, is still aboard. Now, if you'll excuse me, I must go assume command of this island."

I moved to push by them but Ebert held me up. "What's this plant you've got, then? Let me get my flora registry forms. We'll have to assess import taxes and quarantine it."

Murder welled up in my shriveled belly. "Oh, this plant? It belongs to the navy, to the King—"

A scream rose above the din. "She's sinking! To the pumps!"

This drew their attention for a moment and I slipped past them into the crowd. The two officials made their way eagerly towards *Le Dromedaire* which could be fined for incurring two rescue boats, and improperly documenting her cargo. I could only imagine the flurry of taxation that would transpire if the officials discovered the Cape Verde treasure in the hold.

I tried to slip past a huddle of rum magnates and planters. I had been on bad terms with this lot, owing to my style of interpreting and enforcing the slave codes. I knew something was wrong when they all smiled and greeted me as if I were a first cousin of marriageable age. Monsiuer Girard, a distillery owner, drew me aside.

"Monsieur Capitaine De Clieu, what a pleasure to have you back! My God, you look like a castaway and smell worse than a field slave!"

I ran a hand through my scraggly beard. "Monsieur Girard, how are you?"

"Oh, Sir Capitaine De Clieu, my liege, orders arrived for you six weeks ago. We've all been expecting your arrival and worried for you."

I straightened up and felt like smacking him. "I assume you've read my orders, then. Does the rank of rum baron now confer this privilege to read royal edicts?"

Unfazed, Girard continued. "Of course not, sir, of course not, but they say you're to take command of the island's defenses here and in Saint-Pierre. Why, you've been the talk of Martinique! Welcome home, sir!"

His group of sycophants blurted out their agreement and expressed boundless joy at my return, pledging their respect and loyalty. Another land baron named Plissonneau stepped forward.

"Good God, Capitaine, you look a mess. What has happened to the poor *Dromedaire*? She's stove in and half-sunk! What has become of her crew?"

Before I could answer, Girard peered at my plant. "I say, Capitaine, what is that shrub you cradle?"

How simple a question. But to answer it would have been to recount three years of trials. I opened my mouth, searching for words. Eyes and faces peered at me.

At last the words came, and I announced to the crowd, "My dear Martiniquen friends, this shrub is *coffea arabica!* A gift to me from the King's botanical garden."

Girard gasped, "Coffee? How can that be? I thought the Mohammedans would behead anyone trying to traffick these trees!"

The mass of curious people began repeating my declaration and crowding closer. I proclaimed, "It is a coffee plant, my dear *habitants*! It was entrusted to me directly from King Louis XV's private botanical garden to be planted and cultivated here on our island for the benefit of all."

Girard, my new suitor, pushed the gawkers back. "Give our good Capitaine space, give him air! The plant must breathe, and so must he!"

The mosquitoes of swampy Fort de France began greeting the flustered onlookers with buzzes and bites. Plissoneau pushed several children out from under me and clapped his weighty arm around my shoulders, "Why, the poor Capitaine has lost his wig in the hard journey. Here—let him have mine."

What felt like a steaming clump of hot seaweed enveloped my head, obscuring my vision. It smelled like a mouse that had drowned in a bucket of Parisian perfume. Curious children gleefully screamed at "Baldy," who I presumed to be Plissonneau. Arms jostled with my hot headgear and daylight flashed into my eyes. I saw the white curls of Plissonneau's wig cascading luxuriantly around me.

Girard popped up in front of me. "Capitaine De Clieu, I humbly offer you my personal garden and three gardeners to give your plant hourly attention. You remember my townhouse in Fonds Coré with the pink bougainvillea?"

I struggled to make progress down the dock towards the fort as questions assailed my ears from all flanks.

"De Clieu, can I touch the plant? How does it taste? Is coffee like rum? What can you sell it for?"

I swayed through the throng, still accustomed to the rocking of *Le Dromedaire* beneath my boots. The dock vibrated with the tramp of soldiers and a group of the *gendarmes'* black hats with their gold rims bounced forward. As their gray and blue *justaucorps* coats came into view, I saw their leader was none other than my former private, Marcel. I realized that I would be dressed like that in short order and sweating as profusely as these French farm boys.

"*Boules de singe fumeur!* Monsieur De Clieu! What took you so long? We'd thought you were dead or had married!"

I embraced Marcel, kissing his cheeks. "I had a touch of scurvy and a productive affair with a married woman and her servant—nothing more!"

A few of the other soldiers in Marcel's troop recognized me and they quickly forgot whatever duty brought them to the docks and begged information.

Marcel gazed on *Le Dromedaire's* devastated decks. "What the hell happened to that ship? My God, look at her! She's about as bad as the wreck that washed up last October."

To these men, now my men, I related the tale of our crossing. I accidentally hit a woman with a parasol as I demonstrated how we had desperately cut away the main mast. She let out a yelp, but continued listening. I apologized and continued to the end of the story.

Marcel scratched his head and lowered his voice, "Surely there was a Jonas aboard. Something wicked that turned the tempest against the vessel. Such a string of ill-luck comes not by chance."

I retold my story faster and faster. A flock of bright, green parakeets flew overhead with chirps and squawks. A group of barking dogs zipped around us and raced off. Firm earth never felt more sacred or joyous.

As I described the eye of the storm and headwall that raced towards us, I grew disoriented and nauseous. My blood refused to make the arduous climb to my brain and I took only shallow breaths. Marcel saw me tottering and caught me as I almost dumped Cappy off the dock and into the water. The once-timid, superstitious, and innocent Marcel barked confident orders to his men.

"Take the Capitaine to Fort Royal and bring Dr. Scie to inspect him. You there, take his little bush, and for each leaf that falls off, I'll have one of your fingers. De Clieu says this plant is a gift from the King himself."

I groggily watched a young private take Cappy out of my grasp as two others took my arms around their shoulders.

CHAPTER 39
PAPERWORK AND MOSQUITOES

I awoke when a manservant brought me breakfast in my quarters. This was not the breakfast of an enlisted man but the kind of breakfast the commander of six hundred troops on an important slave island eats. I feasted on bacon, buttered rolls, and fresh fruit.

My gut was still accustomed to a diet of boiled leather and nothing, so this delicious breakfast spent only a brief time inside me.

I ordered Cappy to be watered and put under a heavier guard than the Fort's vault. I summoned Marcel and Fossieu and made my first order as commander: that the Le Dromedaire's crew be ministered to, fed, and treated as honored guests on Martinique.

I spent five days recovering my strength in Fort de France; a fort which I slowly realized was mine to command. My head adjusted to the stillness of solid ground and I regained my land legs. Solid food began to digest normally inside my gut instead of launching back out of me.

I took advantage of my repose to write a full account of the voyage's events in my journal. I felt immeasurably recovered from the journey and its hardships after these days of relaxation.

Old Fossieu had been in command after Francois's transfer. He had brought good order and drill to the men here and had kept them on their toes. This alone was a towering achievement in the ill-disciplined garrisons of the West Indies.

However, he had in fact induced such a state of fear and alertness that men tripped over each other to keep in line. This was the inevitable result of removing a commander like Francois and installing the man who had most yearned for the rigid discipline of the old days when corporal punishment outpaced yellow fever as a cause of death among our troops.

Rumor soon reached me that Fossieu had snapped eleven switches in the past weeks over the backs of the troops. Two men came to me, whispering that morale was so low that certain grenadiers openly discussed desertion in the taverns. Men grumbled that the slaves were better treated than they, and seethed with resentment.

After convalescing, I made my entry into society. I laced up my boots, donned a new wig, petticoat, splendid leather and silver belt, new sword, and a most triumphant hat. Soldiers in the fort looked up and snapped to attention like startled squirrels. The light blinded me upon leaving my cave-like quarters in the fort.

A light rain sizzled all around, hitting the coco fronds above the red tile roofs of the barracks. I took stock of my surroundings anew. Tall palms with clusters of coconuts swayed in the drizzle and a breeze cooled the steamy air. Mosquitoes welcomed me back by searching for exposed flesh. Beyond the stone battlements and grass-covered earthworks, whitecaps kicked up the turquoise waters of the bay.

Five merchant ships were tied to the docks. I spotted *Le Dromedaire* careened on the beach for repairs. I passed the stone mess hall and saluted soldiers lounging by a cannon emplacement before arriving at the squat stone armory where I saluted again.

I had forgotten the excessive formalities required just to walk from one place to another in the army. I made my way north from the tip of the Fort Royal peninsula towards the interior of the island and came to the series of embankments guarding our rear. This twelve-foot-high wall separated the fort from the town and was built by the industrious Comte de Blénac, who had governed for over twenty years until he was ousted.

Up above, the two jungled humps of Morne Garnier and Morne Tartenson loomed over the village's red roofs. Beyond them, the spires of the Pitons du Carbet sliced into the sky, their rocky slopes repelling the jungle to expose jagged rock. Another flight of green parakeets chirped overhead in the rain.

I walked past the main battery and came upon two grenadiers standing back to back about five feet apart around a small wooden fence. Without saluting, I hurried up and peered over the fence.

There was Cappy. She looked immeasurably greener, her leaves waxier; fluttering and dipping with each rain drop that her roots then thirstily drank from the black soil.

"Good morning, gentlemen, how is your charge? Have anyone attempted to bother her? What of her watering schedule? You haven't shaded her, have you?" The grenadiers turned to look first at each other and then at me.

Finally, the shorter of the two uttered, "Well. It goes well, sir. The plant is planted...and seems to be growing."

"Has anyone attempted to seize the plant by force or by trickery?"

They again exchanged looks and reported back, "No, Monsieur Capitaine, no one has yet attempted to seize the plant from us."

I narrowed my eyes. "Good. And you have my permission to kill anyone who tries."

The short one scratched his bulbous nose and nodded. "Of course, sir."

I saluted and marched toward the gates. The two wet and bedraggled sentries at the broad wooden doors jumped up and put out their pipes. They cranked the winches, and Fort de France's iron-clad gates swung open, revealing two sandy ruts leading into the village.

A narrow spit of land joined the Fort Royal peninsula with mainland Martinique. The village outside the fort huddled around the fort's walls in fear after a century of raids by Caribs, pirates, the English, the Spanish, and others. The masts of the five ships bristled by quays. I exchanged my former cloud of mosquitoes for a new one as I strolled into town through Savane Park.

The smell of bougainvillas preceded their sight. Their fantastic red, orange, and pink flowers came bursting over the walls of the one- and two-story homes on the main street and flowed down onto the thoroughfare. Bees and insects buzzed around thousands of wet flowers. Vegetation sprang from every direction like a slow green tidal wave. Grass and vines required trimming by slaves almost daily. If Fort de France's inhabitants were to take a two-week cruise, they would come back to find that the island had swallowed the village whole and converted cow pasture to monkey jungle.

If not for sugarcane and its marvelous derivatives, molasses and rum, this island would long ago have shrugged humanity off her back. Four slaves heaved a wagon full of sugarcane past me, yammering away in their Creole dialect as they strained. The cart wheels squirted mud as they reluctantly bumped along a stream masquerading as a street.

I turned north towards the prefecture. The gentle rain let up and steamy palls of mist clung to the jungled tops of Morne Garnier and Morne Tartenson. The clouds swirled and churned before my eyes.

The small stone prefecture sat kitty-corner to the edge of the Savane park and nobody greeted me as I strode up the steps in my full regalia. Amidst the chirps of songbirds in the Savane trees, I heard someone say, "That's him."

I looked up to see two figures emerge onto the balcony of the Prefecture. One hailed me and doffed his cap. I doffed mine and sprang up the steps.

No guards or attendants could be found in the lower lobby. An unseeing leopard's head graced the back wall. The stone exterior gave a stern impression, but all the walls and floors inside were built from rough-hewn wood. I had spent enough time around ship's carpentry to note shoddy work when I saw it. The Prefecture paled in comparison to the *chateaus* of the sugar barons which aspired to those of the Loire valley.

I froze as a strong, musky scent invaded my nostrils and a furtive black shape dashed underneath an empty desk.

"Muskrat!" I yelled, drawing my flintlock and leveling it at the desk. Footsteps thudded on the stairs, "Capitaine!"

Down came the new governor. Bartholomew Roberts had asphyxiated the last governor, poor Jean-Pierre de Charite, while I was in Paris.

"Capitaine De Clieu! Is everything all right? What did you yell?" I peered under the desk but the creature was gone, so I holstered my flintlock.

I bowed to the governor, removing my hat. "I yelled 'jungle cat,' thinking at first glance that your leopard head mounted on the back wall was alive."

More steps on the stairs produced Monsieur Girard and his pointy mustache. He shook my hand. "Yes, I thought it sounded something like cat or rat! So wonderful to see you, *mon Capitaine!*"

The governor bowed and shook my hand. "It is a pleasure to meet our new commander here on Martinique. I am the Honorable Martinique Governor Jacques-Charles de Bochart de Noray de Champigny. Your reputation precedes you, Capitaine De Clieu. I must apologize for not having the proper welcoming celebration in readiness, but we had expected you over a month earlier. I hope to hear all about your arduous journey! Much has happened on the island since you left. Monsieur Girard tells me that you've brought a coffee plant to place in his gardens!"

Girdard's little shark eyes watched me from the side.

"Yes, I have indeed shepherded a delicate coffee plant through an impossible ordeal. It was a gift to me from Louis XV and my dear friend Monsieur Michel Bégon de la Picardière, intendant of New France."

I shuddered at using the words Picardière and friend in the same breath, but knew that it would carry weight with Girard. Picardière was a man with the power to tax planters like Girard out of existence.

I continued, "I'm afraid that the royal botanist made it quite clear to me that the little shrubs cannot grow near the sea in such places as the good Monsieur Girard's garden but must be on sloped volcanic soil such as that of my estate in Prêcheur. The intendant ordered that I personally plant and supervise its growth, so as a humble servant of God and king, I must meekly obey."

The Governor gave a hearty, *"Vive le roi!"* I continued, not wanting to give the old *béké* planter a chance to open his mouth.

"Quite so good, Monsieur Jacques-Charles de Bochart de Noray de Champigny. My forces are at your service and, rest assured, once I have the plant nursed back to health and growing, your wife shall be receiving the first cutting! Now. Did you wish to hear of *Le Dromedaire's* voyage?"

Girard excused himself with the pretense of needing to attend to one of his brigs arriving from Guadeloupe. The governor invited me upstairs and I gave him a censored account of *Le Dromedaire's* horrific ordeal over several glasses of spiced rum. I omitted the pirate treasure and mutiny. I urged him to consider a privateering charter for the vessel once she was shipshape.

The governor coughed into his rum, "Oho, that will be some time yet, then! I've heard that twenty carpenters are employed there and they say it will be like building a new vessel. The next load of mast timbers from Quebec won't arrive for three weeks if all goes well."

"But you would consider such a charter, sir? I vouch for the crew. The surviving men deserve some recompense for their gallant service against the harshest odds. I have seen them in battle and believe they would be a proper scourge to British shipping if given a privateering commission."

The governor gazed into his rum. "We shall see. I have heard that these men have been spending gold coins in the town already. Perhaps they are a more experienced privateering crew than you let on?"

With that, I decided to explain the full truth to him and he took it without comment. I ended with Neville's marooning and Chirac's dubious ascension. He peered deeper into his rum and then quaffed it without warning.

"I sailed two tours as a young lad with Neville, you know. He was a first mate back then. He had me whipped for stealing when another man wouldn't confess. Me! A noble's son! Worry not about your *Dromedaire*, De Clieu. I agree that these boys deserve to sail to whatever point on the compass they desire. I'll help them arrange something with the ship's owners, investors, and insurers back in

Paris. But oh, what I would have given to have seen old Neville naked on Barbados ..." A gloved servant produced more rum.

From his balcony we surveyed the commerce on the streets below. Our conversation turned to Paris and I filled the governor in on the latest gossip. He soaked up my Parisian reminiscences like a damp rag and begged for more until I had told of every single prominent affair, betrayal, and bear-baiting I could recall. I ran out of Parisian news and our discussion sailed across the Atlantic to Martinique.

"Hurricane season was very hard on us last year. Five ships were lost and almost eighty people died from mudslides, roof collapses, and rogue storm waves. Mostly slaves, mind you, but still very valuable property destroyed by the elements. Half the sugar crop lost and most of the best coco trees downed... Frankly, I can't stand visiting this malarial mangrove swamp."

I sipped the spiced rum and inquired on my home, "How are things in Saint-Pierre and the village of Prêcheur?"

The governor adjusted himself and replied, "I mostly stay in Saint-Pierre, as you know. I've only been to Prêcheur twice. It's a charming shire. In Saint-Pierre I've got worries and problems to spare. The planter's guild and Judge Adaire conspire to smuggle to the English colonies and New Spain. Far too openly. Far too openly, and they'll bring Paris' wrath down on us all. They have no concept of subterfuge."

A idea popped into my mind, bounced down into my gut, and then stormed out my mouth.

"Then come with me to Saint-Pierre, my most Honorable Monsieur Jacques-Charles de Bochart de Noray de Champigny! I'll recount more of my journey and you can visit my estate in Prêcheur on the slopes of *La Montagne*. The air is so fresh that mosquitoes are but an occasional nuisance and you can bear witness to the first coffee plant ever rooted in Martinique's soil!"

The bags under his eyes lightened and the corners of his mouth turned up, "I miss the days when I could just set out on a whim. But alas, I've already delayed an important meeting and put aside much paperwork today, so I'm afraid I must forstall my visit."

I bid the governor a friendly *adieu* and hurried back out to meet the cloud of mosquitoes that had waited patiently for me at the front door.

CHAPTER 40

BARGING

I chose to take the freight boat north to Saint-Pierre instead of Girard's brig. She was built like half a rum barrel with with a crew, sails, and several tons of sugarcane piled on the decks, giving the whole affair a sickly-sweet smell. Instead of slicing over waves, the freight boat barged through them. Sweat glistened like black diamonds on muscled African backs as they skirmished with the rigging of this clumsy raft. The young one attending the halyards was bald and his back a crisscrossed mess of red and purple scars. Even the captain's skin was the color of coffee and I wondered whether I had mistakenly booked passage on a ship of Maroons escaping from slavery.

I lit my pipe on the stern and bid the festering heat of Fort de France goodbye. I took off my insufferable wig and exposed my head to the wind. *Le Dromedaire* and her hive of repair workers on the beach faded in the distance as we slipped up the coast past the fort and harbor.

As we barged along, a gurgling leak formed near the main mast. The slave with the mangled back spent the rest of the journey bending over with a bucket, tossing water out. The captain of our floating oxcart pushed the rough wooden tiller to port and asked me about Cappy in Creole French.

"Yuh drink the plant?"

I puffed out a very contented and relaxed smoke ring. "So I do."

He looked at its waxy green leaves closely for the first time, and then up into his sails, "So it's like tea? —Oy merde, Rolly, getcher up over dem bowsprits, bowline'sa draggin!"

Rolly swung gracefully over the bow and snatched a line out of the water. The mulatto captain shook his head and cursed his slaves as fiercely as the stodgiest *béké*. He looked to me for agreement but I just stared at the turquoise waves. He rattled on about selling sugarcane to the British and Dutch to refine, in violation of King Louis's orders, and other such traditions of the West Indies.

I nodded, "Skipper, you're a magicians for steering this bathtub around the reefs in high wind. Oh, I forgot to introduce myself. I'm Capitaine De Clieu, new commander of the island's defenses."

He turned a bit red and straightened his back. "Beggin' your pardons, Master. I'm Jaffe, freeman I am. Saved my coins and bought my freedom three years ago. I didn't know you were De Clieu. The planters said he was likely drowned weeks back, said good riddance to you, they did, if I may say so, sir. They was celebrating mostly."

I blew out another smoke ring. "At ease, Jaffe. My concern is entirely for the island's defenses, though I do have orders to stop smuggling. They're quite explicit, actually...I have them here in my pocket!"

I whipped out a bundle of letters tied and sealed with the intendant's marks. Jaffe's eyes widened, as if I had produced a pit-viper from my pantaloons.

I continued, "You're a freed slave, right? It hardly matters; I should arrest you and confiscate your slaves for smuggling. However, enforcing these scraps of paper would involve arresting and punishing every man, woman, child, and parakeet on this rock. Myself as well. Luckily, the governor and intendant are both avid smugglers, so any enforcement will be selective. Essentially, whoever I dislike ..."

I smiled coldly at Jaffe and he gripped the tiller with both hands as we came around the lee of a reef. For the duration of our journey, only the sound of waves spanking our angular sides interrupted the silence.

Soon the sparkling white beaches of Carbet passed over the starboard rail and small fishing skiffs darted around our ponderous tub.

I counted fifteen masts of ships moored off Saint-Pierre. The town's red tile roofs came into view over the swells and her whitewashed walls glistened like pearls in the midday sun. Gulls squawked in a frenzy until they realized we had only sugarcane, and departed to harass other vessels. The noon church bells gonged as Jaffe broadsided the dock, causing it to shudder and creak in protest.

All along the graceful arc of Saint-Pierre's beach, barrels of rum waited above the high tide mark for loading onto ships. The beaches and hillsides were speckled black with strong slaves working. The whole scene buzzed with mercantile fervor as the colony's harvest flowed towards the docks.

A skinny man I vaguely recognized squealed orders to slaves on the dock who began feverishly loading our mountain of cane onto carts. I ducked a flying bundle of stalks and scampered with Cappy up onto the dock. The skinny fellow peered at me.

Jaffe tugged on my coattail urgently. "Master De Clieu, sir, don't be fogettin' your wig, sir, if you please, sir, many thanks to you, sir." I donned my wavy curls, lest I be seen as anything other than the grand commander I was made out to be.

I struck out for the fort in town. I felt light as a feather to be back in bustling Saint-Pierre, so close to my beloved Prêcheur. All my memories of hurricanes and hardships were erased as birds chirped in the tree-lined streets and negro women sang at their chores. How I missed their songs, which, though tinged with sadness, reflected a certain vivacity that Paris only pretended.

CHAPTER 41

TWO DEATHS

At the fort, I locked Cappy in my office and began proceedings. I assumed command with as much pomp but less ceremony than might be expected. They couldn't find the drummer boy, so they hauled in one of the black ammunition carters. This slave was twice the size of the drummer boy and gave the ceremonial march a fast tempo. The other instruments quickened their pace and the King's March was perhaps never played so exuberantly. The regiment's colors unfurled on the flagpole and my new lieutenant leaned in and whispered to assure me that he should whip the cart hauler after such an un-French drumming performance.

I nodded, saying, "I'll take him to my plantation in Prêcheur for a spell to teach him."

The lieutenant took this for exactly what it wasn't, and nodded in satisfaction. After some further pomp and a big meal of roast pork and pineapple, I requisitioned a carriage team to visit Prêcheur. How I had missed the ability to requisition things! I set out with two gendarmes and the ammo cart slave. We passed the Place Bertin where four men repairing the gallows argued about logistics. We bounced up the cobblestoned lane and over the new wooden bridge across the stream descending from Mount Pelee. We stopped a while to water the horses before wiping our brows and continuing.

Tall coconut trees bowed in all directions until we passed the sprawling Guerin distillery complex. Acrid smoke smudged the otherwise unblemished skies above the refinery and the honeyed smell of molasses permeated the hot air. It smelled like home.

The cart bounced into the crossroads that served as Prêcheur's main street and familiar faces rushed out to say *bonjour*. We took a right turn and began the rutted zigzag trail uphill, slowly scaling the lower flanks of *La Montagne*. Vines, ferns and creepers hung over the road, darkening it with their soft, green fingers. We passed a girl carrying a bunch of bananas and a dead snake crushed beneath a cartwheel.

At last our tired horses came to my turnoff: a wooden sign posted on the side of a flowering tree that read *Chateau De Clieu*.

Memories rushed back as we bounced up the two grassy ruts. I made a mental note to remonstrate Pierre for leaving the entry road overgrown. Weeds were knee high in my sugarcane fields. Clearly, the estate had been farmed during my absence, but it was not up to the standards I expected. No black heads bounced in the fields, no sounds greeted me except for the rustling stalks and twanging insects.

We rounded the final switchback and I looked at my old home and its outbuildings for the first time in three years. All seemed in decent order, but again—no people were anywhere to be seen. We parked the wagon in the broad entryway by the stable and I jumped off.

I rushed inside to the kitchen, expecting to find Teetha or Aimee. Emptiness and the smell of rotting food greeted me. Corn husks lay on a stone countertop and all else seemed in its place.

A knot twisted and grew in my stomach, acid surged in my veins. "Hello?" I called out. Nothing.

"Pierre? Aimee? Teetha?" The dim room was dappled only by shafts of light coming through the windows. Onions hung overhead and I smelled the remnants of the Acadian salt cod that the slaves had to eat. Something rustled in the big washtub and I wondered whether a neighbor's child might be hiding there. I walked across the room to peer in up over the lip of the basin.

A fat, large fer de lance sprang out with a terrific hiss from where it had been coiled in the washtub! It shot through the air towards me. I leapt backwards by reflex, yelling in panic. The viper flew past me and hit the floor. My shouts alerted the two gendarmes and a slave outside; they rushed towards the house.

The serpent coiled itself on the floor, rearing its head up, spitting and hissing with its black eyes narrowed at me. The words of my father somehow echoed in my mind, *Gabriel, if you want to catch the frog, just talk sweet to it and sing it a lullaby.*

I slowly backed against the wall and spoke soothingly to it, "Sorry to interrupt your bath, mama. Didn't mean to bother you. I'll just let you finish your bath time…shhh, shhh." The snake seemed to calm down at these soft words. It lowered its head a bit and moved to one side.

Suddenly, the two gendarmes burst into the room with weapons drawn and screamed on seeing the fer de lance. The snake shook off its stupor and lunged towards me with a snap and a hiss. With a blinding flash and terrific roar, the two guards unloaded their flintlocks. As I tried to jump behind the large kitchen table, agony shot up my leg. The snake's head connected with my boot and its jaws came crushing down on my calf. I yelled like a stuck pig and kicked the snake's head against the table. It released my leg and I fell against the washbasin.

Smoke filled the room and I stumbled blindly, roaring. Everyone was screaming, including the snake, which made a high pitched scream unlike any I had heard. My leg burned and my heart was exploding.

"Get out, men! It's bit me, I'm dying! I'll kill this bastard and we'll die together!"

I heard the hissing and saw the wicked viper at my left. I drew my sword and lunged towards it. Despite its large size, it nimbly jumped to the right. I raised my sword again. My leg began to go numb and a tingling reached my chest, then my arms. I brought the sword down to smite the fer de lance but it again jumped away with unbelievable agility. My blade shattered on the stone floor, sparks shooting in all directions in the smoke. The snake leapt to the right and coiled to spring at one of the gendarmes who clumsily wielded a sword in fear.

Suddenly a big, black body darted from behind the snake and grappled it! For a moment, the two united. Two legs, two arms became entangled in coils, head and tail all thrashing on the floor. From this desperate grapple, the cart driver jumped up triumphant, holding a bulging snake head in his right hand and gripping the body tightly with his left. Its tail thrashed wildly against his back.

He grimaced as the monster squirmed, twisted, and lacerated him with its tail. The slave, after years of hard labor, was stronger than the serpent. His veined arms crushed the snake until its eyes bulged wide out of its head. He ran outside into daylight, squeezing forcefully, screaming as he strained to hold the violently thrashing reptile, "Cut it, masters, cut it, cut it!"

I dashed out, dragging my left leg. I drew my belt knife and slashed the snake in half, screaming, "Die, hell beast! Nobody gets away with killing me!"

The snake's bulging eyes opened even larger as red and green liquid sprayed and squirted out of its severed torso. Its top half screamed and hissed. The cart slave tossed the head over on the dirt and both sections twitched for many long seconds before finally lying still, coated in dust.

As the adrenaline subsided, pain cascaded throughout my body. I sat down in the dirt, looking out to the crystal blue seas below the sugar fields. At least I was dying at home.

A gendarme rushed to my side, "Shall I suck and spit, sir?"

I shook my head, my veins bulging and feeling lightheaded. I wheezed some final words, "No, it's too late. I feel the poison clutching my heart. Listen to me. Find my slaves, find Pierre. Bring them back here. Find my friend Marcel—he will own this place now. Goodbye."

The cart man hadn't heard me and began lifting up my leg to start sucking. I saw blood bubbling up and spilling out of my boot. It was an awful lot of bright red blood. The cart man ripped off the boot, jabbed his hand into my tortured leg, and pulled out a small, black ball. He held it up as the blood dripped off. It was a musket ball.

"Master De Clieu, sir! Why, you's been shot with a musket ball! Look here: these two bite marks in yer boot isn't through the leather!"

The gendarmes looked at the musket wound and the bite marks. They froze, their mouths agape. They then let loose such a string of expletives that I cannot repeat them more for brevity than decency's sake. They wept with apologies so profound that even the Virgin Mary would have told them to shut up. Their apologies and blubbering continued all the way back down to Saint-Pierre in the wagon as one applied pressure to my leg and the other whipped the horses.

My heroic cart man hit every bump and rut at full speed, threatening to pound the carriage and its contents to splinters. Such was our speed that the cart launched into the air several times as we hit ruts, crashing back down and swaying like a ship at sea.

By the time we got to Doctor Scie's home, the gendarmes had consigned their immortal souls to the seventh layer of hell. For a long while I enjoyed their guilt-ridden wailing.

As we neared the doctor's, I grimaced in cruel pain and threatened them, "I'll only consider sparing your worthless lives if Scie saves my leg without amputating ..."

I laid back and wheezed from the effort of speaking. I felt many hands carry me to a bed, and then saw Scie's whiskered face squinting at me. He handed me a cup to drink and muttered, "Laudanum, he'll need that."

Laudanum's blast of pure alcohol and nutmeg roiled down my gullet. My consciousness rushed towards the back of my head, as if being sucked out of existence down a long tunnel. The last thing I saw was Doctor Scie gesturing towards a rack of metal implements that included saws and oddly twisting knives.

I awoke with my neck at a painful angle, staring at the floor. A pool of dark blood lay congealed on the bricks. I looked up to where my left leg had been to find only a jumble of rags and bandages. Behind a tray with several bloody knives stood one of the gendarmes biting his lips. I felt no pain but everything seemed wrong. A slow concern tickled my gut and grew into a firestorm of panic.

I leapt off the table where I lay and assaulted the gendarme, "You maggot! I told you not to let him cut off my leg!"

The guard screamed in shock as I went from motionless to merciless. I grabbed his belt knife out of its sheath and held it to his throat, screaming, "My God, I told you one simple thing and you got it wrong! If I had to die, let me die, but I didn't want to live without my leg! Prepare to die, you—"

"Sir, you're standing up, sir!"

I paused a moment, my knife still at his throat, and looked down. I was indeed standing underneath two legs. I jumped a little and landed far better than would a recent amputee. I let out a long, low laugh. A broad smile spread over my face and I jumped higher and higher until my head hit the wooden ceiling.

"Eureeka, you're right! I have my legs!"

The guard shrieked as I accidentally slashed his chin on my fourth jump. "Oh, *Merde!* I'll get Doctor Scie. That was an accident...but you deserve it."

The guard looked up at me, his white hands clutching his bleeding chin. I scowled at him. "Stop your blubbering. Maybe the Doctor will do us all a favor and amputate your head."

With a crash, the door burst open and the hirsute doctor stormed into his operating room.

"Just what's going on here? Monsiuer De Clieu, you must not walk yet—you'll bleed through the bandages! Oh, my God, what's happened to this man?"

I narrowed my eyes at the trembling gendarme. "He's had several accidents. Birth, to name one."

Scie bent over the man and inspected his gash. "Oh, yes, this will leave quite an ugly scar, I'm afraid. You'll have to wear a beard like me."

I remembered the snake and my missing slaves. "Doctor, I must ask you if you know what's become of my slaves? They were all gone from my plantation."

Scie's eyebrows bunched up to resemble contorted caterpillars. "Have they not told you? They hung that Pierre today at noon shortly. He'd been in the prison with the rest of them. How cowardly of them not to tell you—people must have known you'd be upset. You were known to be too liberal with them. Now, you must sit down and rest."

I hobbled out of the operating room and cast about for some means of escape despite Scie's protests. My leg gave me stabbing pains and I walked with a limp. Outside, the cart driver stood like a statue beside the mud-spackled carriage. The second gendarme sat inside on the black cushions. I ordered him to run behind the carriage and urged the driver to take me to the main plaza as fast as he dared.

Doctor Scie ran out behind me. "Sir, come back! Guards, stop him! The laudanum hasn't worn off—he's insane. I just finished the bandage…he can't walk on it for three weeks!" The driver lashed the reins onto our horses' backs and we jolted off.

We ground into the Place Bertin as shouting masses of people blocked our way. I leaned out of the carriage and inquired of a passing slave, "What's going on here? What's become of my slave, Pierre?"

The slave stopped in her tracks and curtsied, "Master, sir, they's strung up that rebel slave from the gallows, sir."

I bellowed, "They can't, he's mine!"

I cursed and threw open the carriage door into the gendarme's face, who had just caught up. I hobbled and wobbled my way through the jeering crowd towards the empty gallows. I thought perhaps this was a nightmare, or that I had really drowned on *Le Dromedaire* and this was all a hellish dream. Ahead, a group of gendarmes struggled to carry Pierre's body out of the plaza. The crowd booed and hissed. Yelps and mocking shouts cascaded around.

"Too big fer ya?"

"Him's must'a ate rocks all week!"

I swam through a stinking sea of dirty workers and mariners who had come to enjoy a hanging. Finally, I burst through the jeering crowd and pushed through a line of gendarmes protecting the gallow's staging.

I shouted, "I'm Commander De Clieu! What is all this and where is the slave?"

Lacking my wig, uniform, and all else, the guards lowered their muskets at me and shouted, "Back, you rabble! There's no souvenirs yet!"

One of them suddenly shouldered his weapon and straightened, elbowing his fellows. "It's him—that's the new commander back from Paris! That's De Clieu!"

His neighbor laughed at him, "That blood-soaked bastard is our commander? Oh yes, and I'm the Empress of the Orient. Don't let that drunk pass."

I made a note of this man and then spat out questions and orders in a whirlwind to all those who would listen. By way of answering, the guards pointed at the gallows. The top beam had cracked in two and lay splintered on the staging. At last, one gave me some useful information.

"Sir, they hung a slave this afternoon but the rope broke. Then they hung him again but the gallows broke, so now they're getting a sturdier crossbeam, sir…It's that big slave from Prêcheur that's been causing problems. And, sir, your leg is covered in blood… you've been wounded!"

A glimmer of hope raced through my heart. "You four tell the crowd to disperse. The event is canceled."

The guards looked at each other, "Well, sir, Judge Adaire ordered him hung today, sir."

I reached up to grab my hat and throw it down in anger but grabbed only air. I had no hat to throw down, and this made me even angier. "I don't care if The Virgin Mary ordered him hung! I'm your commanding officer! Now, disperse this crowd or we'll hang you today, too!"

I grabbed two gendarms from the line and shouted in their faces. "You! Go get those men carrying the slave and bring them back here. And you, go get that miserable judge!"

The first man ran off at a good clip and the second turned white. "Sir, the judge is right here, sir."

I turned around to see a white wig with a man inside standing behind the scaffolding contemplating me with a stony face. From underneath the wig came a frosty reply.

"If you are indeed the new commander De Clieu and not the blood splattered barfly that you appear, then you've dishonored God and one of His Majesty's royal judges. You've countermanded a royal judge's edicts and interrupted a formal punishment of the court. All of these are crimes are punishable by public whipping, imprisonment, or death regardless of rank."

My eyes widened like saucers and I advanced on Judge Adaire. His two beady eyes glared at me haughtily from beneath his white plumage and his angular cheeks reddened as I got close. He placed his hands on his hips and pursed his thin lips. I said nothing and bent down to his level so that our noses almost touched.

I whispered to him, "I've got fourteen scars from killing enemies of France but I doubt I'd get any from killing you."

Acting on my rising urge to annihilate something, I whipped my arms up and grabbed his wig from both sides. I savagely ripped it into two pieces, throwing the woolly mass off his head as if I were slaughtering a flock of sheep. Judge Adair yelped and grabbed the fragments of his wig. His face and head turned redder than an engorged tick and he furiously marched off to the unrestrained glee of the crowd.

Six gendarmes approached, straining to carry an enormous black body. I leaned over Pierre's corpse and enough wrath to sunder another hundred wigs arose in me. His neck was purple and swollen, his body bruised, and his back shredded from whipping. His eyes were rolled up under his lids, showing only the whites.

Before I could curse, his lips moved and he whispered something, "That you, Master Gabriel? ...Can you do old Pierre one last favor?...Tell that short gendarme to get his hand out of there."

The men carrying Pierre shifted their grips in consternation. I commanded, "You six load Pierre carefully in my carriage over there like he was your goddamn daughter. Take him to Doctor Scie and tell the doctor to save him at all costs."

I climbed aboard the carriage, wincing as my leg began to regain feeling. The pain of the wound was doubled by the fact that it was inflicted by friendly fire.

I leaned out to address the gendarmes. "Where is his family? The other slaves?"

One replied nervously, "At the Clasp and Buckle, sir, I believe they're to be auctioned."

I frowned. "What's your name, soldier?"

"Sargeant Sprague, sir."

I replied, "Very good, Sargeant Sprague, you have my orders to fetch all of my slaves from the Clasp and Buckle and proceed with them to my estate in Prêcheur; they know the way. You are to disregard any counter-orders or monetary complaints, especially if they're from Judge Adaire. Keep your musket handy. Colonial judges have no business meddling with the King's royal infantry!"

I thought ahead drearily about the amount of drilling we'd need once I got my affairs in order. The carter asked in Creole, "Todah morgue, sir?"

I shook my head, "No, back to Dr. Scie's from whence we came. He's not dead."

The carter whistled superstitiously, "But he looks dead."

Pierre muttered without opening his eyes, "I ain't."

The cart slave slapped his thigh, "Well, look at that! You know what they say about a man twice hung dat doesn't die?"

I grew impatient, "No, pray tell, what do they say?"

The carter flicked the reins, "Uh, they don't say nothing, sir, beggin' your pardon."

I grew angrier, "No, verily, what do they say? You've saved my life from the snake, so I won't do you any harm. Now, speak the truth!"

We lurched forward and he shrugged, "I dunno master, sir, maybe that he a warlock or used black magic. But I wouldn't say nothing like that. That's just what other folks' would say."

I closed my eyes and leaned back on the velvet seating, "No, he's just heavy, that's all. They used a worn hemp line to hang him from a half-rate gallows."

A chuckle rasped out of the motionless Pierre and ended in a cough. He whispered, "I feel pretty bad about that damage I done, Monsieur De Clieu, I'll pay to repair their gallows if I make it through." I smiled and bid him rest.

CHAPTER 42

EPILOGUE : COFFEE ABOUNDS

I could tell much more of this story but my liver aches and my bladder is weaker than a British beer. Besides, what follows is well documented for posterity.

Pierre recovered quickly, faster than me, and was back at work in two months' time. Arriving at home, my first care was to plant my coffee tree in the part of my garden most favorable to its growth. Cappy delighted in Mount Pelee's fine soil. Suspecting thieves and planters' agents, I put her under heavy guard by both day and night. I knew two gerdarmes who owed me a significant favor, and I assigned them this duty.

The plant had become as much a part of me as my leg, and both made a full recovery. I ordered a strong stone wall built around my garden and guarded it like a dragon.

After three years of steady growth, in 1726, I collected two pounds of seeds. Holding these beautiful red berries in my hands was as close as a man can come to giving birth.

Offers to buy them surged in, each larger than the last, until the seeds were valued far higher by weight than gold. Hundreds and then thousands of livres were thrust at me just as down payments for these precious seeds. Planters from all over Martinique and even from other islands like Guadaloupe came like suitors asking for my hand. I grew tired of their rapacious appetite for profits and endless entreaties.

After sacrificing so much and coming so near to death on so many occasions for Cappy, I could not sell her children. They say that the more slaves a man owns, the more he himself becomes a slave to his work, and I made a decision with which I have been eternally satisfied.

After more than three years of risk, worry and sacrifice, I gave the coffee plants away to my friends and refused all payment.

I gave some seeds to the governor's wife as promised. Then I gave some to Marcel. Then to a group of lesser planters from the village of Le Robert who were poorly regarded as new immigrants and upstarts. I gave some to the priest on Guadaloupe. I gave the seeds away to people I liked and thought capable of properly cultivating the plants for the greater glory of France. Girard only got some secondhand in 1728 and I admit taking satisfaction in his fury and frustration at seeing common housewives planting coffee seeds before he. The coffee-growing boom was started. First, Martinique blossomed in coffee and then soon all the West Indies began the planting.

I was quickly promoted to a major in 1726, more for my horticultural largess than any military achievements. After two seasons of free giving I became the most popular man on Martinique and was loved by all but a few planters like Girard.

On August 19th of 1728, the day began with a red dawn and ended early with a strange green glow on the horizon. Soon a breeze kicked up and blew into a strong gale. The slaves ran into the stone section of the main house as their thatch roofs flew off. After a night of rampaging wind and terror, Martinique awoke to find all the coco trees and sugar cane fields flattened and shredded. Furthermore, most of the low-lying pastures were very badly flooded and remained quagmires past Christmas.

My coffee trees weathered the storm with their deep roots and preference for high ground. A great wave of coffee planting sprouted on Martinique to replace the lost cane and coco. So much coffee did we have that I soon felt free to give seeds to other islands like Santo Domingo.

And yes, I even gave some to the governor of Cayenne whose ungrateful people have since thanked me by claiming that their coffee arrived by a brave importation from Mocha. In this same year, my beloved coffee fell into the hands of the Englishman Nicholas Lawes who brought it to Jamaica.

Sadly, my time commanding the forces on Martinique was not to last, as the intendant of New France appointed me governor of the island of Gaudaloupe in absentia in 1737. Don't ever let yourself be nominated for anything in absentia; the grander the title, the worse the job.

I didn't last long in politics, due to my disagreements with the slave owners I was supposed to respect. I had spent enough years as a lowly cabin boy to resent being worked like a dog for no pay and whipped without cause. The Guadaloupe plantation owners did not share my sentiments and never was there a more mutual divorce than mine from politics.

I resigned from politics to take a commission back where I wanted to be: as captain of a fine French man-o-war with the wind in my hair.

I retired in 1752 with a pension of six thousand francs. After almost five decades at sea, my fame as a captain was such that many begged me to resume my command. So it was that I answered the call of duty and went to sea once again the next year. I finally retired for good in 1760.

The Parisian politicians whimpered about the economy and reduced my pension to two thousand francs. You can proclaim to divorce politics but politics will never leave you alone. Military men beware—the state shall shower you with honors while you serve and then abandon you like an illegitimate child upon your retirement.

Few now care about my military career or that I was made a Commander of the Order of Saint Louis. My proudest moment came when I met King Louis XV in person in 1746. I trembled, expecting him to berate or punish me for the coffee theft of 1723.

Instead, with a twinkle in his eye, he thanked me for my service to France and referred to the coffee plant as a "gift."

As I write this in 1772, Martinique has over eighteen million coffee trees, all descended from my little Cappy. Places as disparate as Brazil, Mexico, Hispañola, Guatemala, and Peru all acquired my coffee seeds and now boast countless millions of trees. They say that almost all of the coffee drank in Europe comes from Arabica trees descended from my little Cappy. When I left Martinique to captain a ship, I gave Pierre the plantation and freed his family. He insisted on paying me what he was worth, which he judged to be about twenty livres so that he wasn't "'stealing himself," and we haggled for some time before settling on thirty. In the end, he became the coffee farmer and I the Maroon, adrift on the high seas that I so love.

I have the honor of being, DE CLIEU,

THE END

FACT AND FICTION

CHAPTER 1 ✦ DESMAREST'S PILORIE

All the characters except De Clieu are fictional in this chapter. The Girards and Dujons were real plantation owners on Martinique. The giant Antillian Rice Rats, or Desmarest's Pilorie, are real animals that were found only in the Antilles.

Most sources put De Clieu on Martinique prior to 1720 (including De Clieu himself), so the 1719 date is correct. De Clieu had a small plantation in Le Prêcheur, although sources don't indicate one way or another about his owning slaves. He would have lived near the Rivier du Prêcheur. Given that he was also a professional soldier, I believe he would not have had time to farm his plantation without servants.

The descriptions of Martinique's jungle and volcano are accurate, although I must admit the ants incident comes from my own unfortunate experience sitting on a log in Honduras. The references to Mount Pelée's activity allude to its catastrophic eruption in 1902 which killed about 30,000 people and obliterated Saint-Pierre, once known as the Paris of the Antilles. In De Clieu's original letter, he mentions an eruption of Pelee after he planted coffee, so the volcano was definitely active and other sources mentioned sulfurous smells and tremors before the eruptions. Up until 1902, residents did refer to Pelée as Le Volcan Debonaire.

Chapter 2 ✦ Chummy

De Clieu is said to have had a wife who died, although I found no documentation of her life beyond the one line that she existed. So I dutifully gave him a wife and killed her with a snake bite. I think it more likely that any wife he had actually lived in Paris. I came across no mention of him having children, although archival research in France or Martinique might shed some light on his lineage.

My earlier drafts included a recounting of the struggle against the war—like Caribs for control of Martinique in the 1660s, a topic that fascinated me to the point of including a Carib character and original words from the Carib language. Wise editors suggested I get to the point ,so they left the manuscript. Their only remnant left from that draft is that I had one of them kill Dr. Scie's first wife.

Martinique's average people, whom De Clieu calls *Petit Habitants,* did refer to the wealthy planters as Bekes during this era, and continue to use this word today.

Cod were so abundant in the North Atlantic during this time period that salt cod was a common slave food in the West Indies. Many of the islands at this time were dependent on food from France and other colonies.

The Tomb of the Caribs is a real place on the Martinique shoreline where the Caribs were massacred by the French in 1658. Some legends say that they jumped from the high cliffs to kill themselves rather than be captured by the French.

Chapter 3 ✦ A Coffee Trader's Tale

Percy is a fictional character but all of Percy's stories about Kair Bey, the French East India Company, and coffee are documented very similarly in multiple sources. The Martinvalet Raphael was the name of an actual bar in old Saint-Pierre, although that's about all I know about it. The origin of the word "buccanneer" is thought to come from the Arawak Buccans and *poulet boucanier*, or "Chicken on the Boucan," still a popular dish in Martinique to this day. Bastinado was a real form of torture. The Le Robert estate is a real place on Martinique from this era.

CHAPTER 4 ✦ THE SAILING DEAD

The *Liberté* was not a real ship although the slave trade was booming across the New World in this era and many thousands were arriving in Martinique to work on the sugar plantations. The French used slaves from Africa because the indigenous inhabitants of the Caribbean had already suffered a thorough genocide (both biological through disease; and via warfare, rape, slavery, and expulsion) by the 1700s at the hands of Europeans, beginning immediately with Columbus and continuing for centuries.

Oidah (or Whydah) was a major slave port on the so-called Slave Coast of Africa. There was a slave revolt in New York in 1712 in which 23 Africans killed nine whites. News of this had a strong effect on slave owners throughout the New World and led to stricter slave laws on Martinique. I wanted to include an incident in which nuns on Martinique in this era were thought to have been conspiring with the slaves to rebel but it was too far off topic. I include chapters like this to highlight the friendly relationship between De Clieu and his fictional slaves, which is at odds with the murderous reality of the era.

CHAPTER 5 ✦ THE LETTER

Joel and his letter are fictional, based on De Clieu's account that personal affairs called him back to France in 1720. Francois is fictional but he really could have read *La Princesse de Clèves*, a French novel published in 1678.

Chapter 6 ✦ My Second Goodbye

Guanacaste trees grow on Martinique. Many native peoples of the Americas drank out of halved gourds, and most gourds are native to the Americas. With very few exceptions, slaves were not taught to read, and this was prohibited by law, so again De Clieu's slaves are different from the norm. *Looterlu* and *brelan* were popular games in this era and the Pigalle district of Paris was indeed known for its prostitutes.

Chapter 7 ✦ Vigo Bay

De Clieu was born in 1686 and grew up in Angléqueville-sur-Saane near Dieppe and La Havre in the Normandy region of France. Little is known about his family. Some sources state that he came from minor nobility. Peasants were not generally able to join King Louis XIV's professional army and soldiering would have been below someone of noble birth. Sources are spare regarding his life before soldiering on Martinique. De Clieu could have participated in the Battle of Vigo Bay, but I found no evidence to support or refute this.

The incident of D'Iberville's arrival and raid on Nevis is true and it's very likely that De Clieu, if he was in Martinique by this time, would have been involved. The Comte de Chavagnac also participated in this raid and they really did capture most of Nevis' slaves for use on Martinique and Guadaloupe, so it's conceivable (but totally undocumented) that De Clieu could've obtained slaves in this manner as compensation for soldiering. D'Iberville was indeed furious about the raid on St. Christopher giving away his great fleet's intentions and putting the British on guard. D'Iberville did die of some kind of disease, perhaps yellow fever, in Havana in 1706. De Clieu was indeed decorated as a Chevalier of Saint Louis in 1718 and named as a capitaine de campagnie of the Martinique infantry garrison in 1720, although it's not known for what reason he received these promotions. The description of the insignia is accurate from this period of French military attire. Marcel and Judge Adaire are fictional characters.

Chapter 8 ✦ A Swift Affair

This chapter is almost entirely fiction. What is true is that schooners had been invented recently and were considered marvelously fast and sleek. Hammocks were an indigenous invention and Europeans were impressed by them upon coming to the Americas, and quickly adopted their use. The book *Voyage de l'Arabie Heureuse* (Voyage to Arabia the Happy) was published in French in 1716 and documents Jean La Roque's coffee adventures from 1708-1713. No evidence exists about whether De Clieu read this or not, but he certainly was literate and might have heard about it if not read it firsthand.

I think that De Clieu's arrival to Marseilles is extremely unlikely; in fact he would've avoided it like the plague. I took him there because I learned a fascinating fact too coincidental not to be woven into this book: the last major outbreak of the bubonic plague in Europe, The Great Plague of Marseilles, occurred in 1720. So I threw him in. The Great Plague killed an estimated 100,000 people and the population of Marseilles and the surrounding areas took over two generations to recover to pre-1720 levels. De Clieu probably would have made for a port near Paris.

Chapter 9 ✦ Dust and Bones

The forts Saint-Jean and Saint-Nicholas did guard the Marseilles harbor and the plague was brought on the Ottoman merchant ship *Grand-Saint-Antoine* which was placed under quarantine. Madame Dushon is fictional but boarding houses like hers were common, especially in port cities. In this era the plague spread in part because its transmission through fleas and bodily fluids was not well understood. Cats were often regarded with superstition and sometimes blamed for spreading plague, although their effect on the rat and flea population tended to have the opposite effect. Likewise, few physicians had realized the importance of handwashing and cleanliness in preventing the spread of infection.

Olivier "The Buzzard" Levasseur was a real, and fascinating pirate, who at that time was indeed headed towards Wydah (or Ouidah). No ships were allowed in or out of Marseilles, although the sinkings I reference are fictional.

Chapters 10 ✦ Nightmares in Marseilles

As mentioned earlier, there is no evidence that De Clieu ever went to Marseilles during the plague; he probably didn't.

Potatoes are from the Americas (originating in the Andes) and took hold across Eurasia for their hardiness, ease of storage, and nutritional content, but they were still new and interesting to many people at this time.

Chapter 11 ✦ Mur de la Peste

There really was a plague wall, the Mur de la Peste, built around Marseilles to prevent anyone getting in or out; the penalty of crossing was death. Alessandro is named after my delightful Italian friend Alessandro Manno, who is not a brigand.

Chapter 12 ✦ Treasure Hunting in Paris

I chose the historic Rue Du Coca near the Louvre for Joel's home because I chew coca when I'm with my wife's family in Bolivia. So no historic basis there. Tobacco smoking was coming in vogue during this period and Saint-Domingue produced cigars for France. The characters at Joel's are fictional, although the Nicot family was associated with tobacco since Jean Nicot introduced snuff and tobacco to the French court in 1559 and Queen Catherine de' Medici got wildly addicted. From Jean Nicot comes the word nicotine.

Investments in the Mississippi Company had multiplied many times over by this point and were soon to crash later in 1720. King Louis XV did indeed own the only coffee (of the Arabica typica varietal) plant in Paris. It was given to Louis XIV by the Burgomaster of Paris in 1714. Louis planted it initially at the Chateau de Marly and then moved it to the Jardins des Plantes, the Royal Botanical Gardens under the care of chief botanist Antoine de Jussieu.

Many sources say that the Dutch had obtained their coffee plant from India where the Sufi mystic Baba Budan had smuggled it from the port of Mocha, defying a death penalty for such an infraction. Other sources say that the Dutch obtained it more easily through trade. It is from this single plant that the Bourbon and Typica varietals originate (which produced most of the Arabica varietals extant today), giving Arabica coffee its current narrow genetic roots. While it is difficult to know exactly what percentage of coffee comes from King Louis XIV's tree and its ancestors, it's likely a majority with some estimates putting it at 90%.

Chapter 13 ✦ The First Cup

Some coffee in France was coming from Île de Bourbon (renamed Reunion after the French Revolution). The price of six livres per box is fiction. Austrian *kipferl* bread is throught to be the predecessor of the croissant. Pendulum clocks of this period were quite large and valuable, so the Comtoise clock in the De Clieu's residence would have been curved on the sides and looked similar to what we call a grandfather clock.

CHAPTER 14 ✤ SMOKE AND CIGARS

The Wittelsbach breweries produced the now-famous Bavarian beer following the 1487 Reinheisgebot purity law and were a precursor to today's well-known Hofbrauhaus in Munich. John Law oversaw the Mississippi Company's merger and subsequent collapse in 1719-1720, though, in all likelihood, De Clieu and his family were not so closely involved. Law advocated paper money and when the Mississippi Bubble burst, his ideas were temporarily discredited.

The Marquise de Lambert did have a salon in the Hotel de Nevers on Rue de Richelieu; the Cafe Le Procope was among the first and most famous coffee shops in Paris of the time. Le Deux Magots is fictional.

CHAPTER 15 ✤ VERSAILLES

The Duke of Maine is a real figure from this time. While De Clieu did petition many nobles at Versailles for permission to plant coffee in Martinique, we don't know which ones. Versailles boasted about 350 apartments for the Bourbon family, nobles and courtiers who vied for access to the monarch. Lodging assignments and proximity to the royal apartments indicated status.

CHAPTER 16 ✤ ENTREATIES

De Clieu was rejected in all his attempts to petition the King and nobles for a coffee plant. Les Halles was Paris' largest market at this time. Cardinal Fleury and the Duchess of Ventadour were powerful figures of the era who De Clieu might have contacted and would certainly have known about but I didn't find any evidence of who he petitioned for coffee beyond the King.

Chapter 17 ✦ Years Slipping Under the Hull

Welsh pirate Bartholomew Roberts terrorized the French Indies from 1719-1720 and hung Martinique's governor, so De Clieu would surely have despised him. The Mississippi Bubble and its aftermath dominated the economy of this time and Russia's Great Northern War ended. The Tour d'Argent restaurant was founded in 1582 and De Clieu might have dined there.

Chapter 18 ✦ The Gabelle

Sébastien Vaillant was one of the royal botanists of this time working at the Jardin Des Plantes from 1702 onwards. He would certainly have known of him and contacted him regarding obtaining a cutting of coffee but the café meeting is fiction. Vaillant's recounting of coffee's history including the arrival in Amsterdam and Michel Isambert are based on historical fact. Don Manno is fictional.

Chapter 19 ✦ The Botanists Duel

Sébastien Vaillant introduced the use of greenhouses into Paris. When I learned that he had died in 1722 (from an illness) when De Clieu was in Paris, I knew I had to weave his death into the book. The duel never happened, of course. Antoine de Jussieu was one of the royal botanists with whom De Clieu dealt and De Clieu mentions him in his letter.

Dr. Fagon did kill most of the royal family through bleeding. De Clieu is credited for inventing the small portable green house he used for transporting his coffee plant.

CHAPTER 20 ❧ SEDUCING STATUES

Louis XV's coronation happened at this time and the Bretonvilliers mansion was owned by the noble Bretonvilliers family, although there is no evidence De Clieu was connected with them. They probably would not have waltzed, since this was only popular in Austria at this time.

De Clieu did retire from and re-enter military service later in life, but his status during his Parisian interlude is not known. It is often written that he seduced a noble woman with a strange illness who was able to press Doctor Chirac to make a cutting of the plant, so I made Lady Malon into this noble woman. The Malons were a real noble family in Paris at this time, and Henriette Victoire Collart was a member of this family who lived from 1694-1729, though again I have no evidence of a connection to De Clieu. The play *Les Fêtes de l'Amour et de Bacchus* was popular in the 1720s.

CHAPTER 21 ❧ THEATRICS

This chapter is historic fiction except for one important fact: Doctor M. de Chirac was the actual physician whom De Clieu's lady friend seduced or "influenced" to get a coffee cutting. This reference comes from De Clieu's original 1774 letter printed at the end of this book. Phillippe Hecquet was another contemporary royal doctor.

CHAPTER 22 ❧ TWO CHILDREN

This chapter is historical fiction with the exception of the plays and playwrights mentioned: they are true to this time. Claude Balon, from whose name we have the word "ballet," was a real figure who lived in Paris at this time. The part about Crébillon and King Louis is true. Crébillon was a heavy smoker and lived to be 88 like De Clieu. While De Clieu indicates in his letter that he got the plant from Dr. Chirac, other sources indicate that the plant was delivered to him through an intermediary (Monsieur Bégon at Rochefort in Nantes). Given the high treason and secrecy involved, I consider this plausible and probably not something De Clieu would want to boast about in writing.

Chapter 23 ❧ La Paulette

Sources don't agree on the origin of the term "rum" but it may derive from the plant genus *saccharum* to which sugar cane belongs. De Clieu's family was minor nobility and Joel's explanation of La Paulette, and *noblesse de l'epée* are historically accurate. This policy was intended to raise new revenue to reduce the debt incurred by Louis XIV but placed many inept officials in high office and contributed to the unrest that led to the French Revolution.

Chapter 24 ❧ Fresh Waterman's Drawl

Doctor Chirac did apparently entrust his cutting to Michel Bégon de la Picardière for De Clieu to pick up in Nantes. De Clieu did sail in a vessel named *Le Dromedaire*. All of the canal descriptions, names, and dates are true although I found no documentation of how De Clieu traveled from Paris to Nantes. It might have been by coach, horseback, or through the canal system. While barging was a very common and efficient form of transport, the barge trip probably didn't happen as I describe it.

The 1707 Loire Flood drowned thousands of people—50,000 by some estimates. The water rose by nine feet in three hours in Orléans, destroying houses and washing away entire neighborhoods. The Roman origins of Nantes in 56 BC and Norman sacking in 843 AD are true, and at this time few people would have known of them except priests and scholars. Percherons were (and are) strong French draft horses used in this time for hauling carts, wagons and barges.

Chapter 25 ✦ The Slave Port

Nantes was a giant slave port and the *Mars* was a real French slave ship of this time. Ukers writes that De Clieu departed from Nantes in 1723, although the sources don't all agree on this (some have him leaving in 1720 and from another port). Cugand is a nearby town and De Clieu might have met Michel Bégon de la Picardière in the Chateau de Ducs de Bretagne to retrieve the plant Doctor Chirac sent him, although there is no evidence that he had any difficulty in obtaining it.

There really was a Jardin des Plantes de Nantes at this time, and De Clieu's coffee plant might have been cared for there until his arrival, but there are no sources to support this. Jasmine had been introduced to Europe and might have grown there.

All the *Dromedaire* crew are fictional. I could not find any records of the ship's crew beyond mention of her arrival at some ports (like New Orleans) in this era.

Chapter 26 ✦ Weighing Anchor

I tried to make the departure description as accurate as possible for a tall ship of this era. Crews were often international in composition and seventy hands is plausible for a ship of *Le Dromedaire*'s size.

Chapter 27 ✦ A New Captain

Neville's talk about coffee cultivation in Surinam and Guyana are supported by some (but not all) sources and their dates vary. No individual names or locations are well documented, nor did I find documentation of any coffee exportation before De Clieu's in the 1720s. De Clieu himself recounts that people had been trying to introduce coffee to the Americas unsuccessfully for forty years by

1723. What is well known is that Martinique's later production in the 1723-1750 time period dwarfed any other New World planting and most plantings of the era came from the seeds and cuttings that De Clieu gave away to his friends.

Whale pods reached this size in the 1700s before most were hunted almost to extinction by the mid 1800s; such large whale pods were decimated.

Chapter 28 ❦ Attempted Murder

Many ships stopped at Madeira to take on stores of its famous wine and other provisions for long sea voyages ahead. I found no record of *Le Dromedaire* stopping there, although the island would have been near the route. *Bolo de Caco* is one of Funchal's specialties. Someone on board *Le Dromedaire* definitely tried to harm the plant, and some sources attribute this to a Dutch spy, although De Clieu himself implies it was simply a jealous compatriot.

Chapter 29 ❦ Broadsides

Several sources state that Barbary pirates attacked *Le Dromedaire* and were driven off by the merchant vessel's firepower. De Clieu himself does not mention this in his letter, however, so I question the origin of this episode. It makes for a great adventure though. It is true that pirates of the 1700s often used their fearsome reputations to induce merchant vessels to surrender without a fight and many were not interested in pursuing prey willing to fight.

Chapter 30 ❦ Delicious Dolphins

Dolphin was a common food for mariners. Giant turtles were even more highly sought after for their portability and durability—a live turtle could keep in the hold of a ship for over a year.

There is no evidence that De Clieu landed at Cape Verde but the Jacques Cassard stories are true. The Queen Anne style pistol was in common use from the 1680s into the 1720s and beyond. A pinnace was/is a small boat kept on board a larger one, usually powered by oars and sometimes by sail, similar to a longboat or lifeboat.

Chapter 31 ✦ Man the Pumps

Many sources assert that *Le Dromedaire* was hit by a fierce storm before entering the doldrums. De Clieu does not mention this in his letter so I think that this is perhaps more likely than the pirate attack episode, but still unproven. They probably were not knocked down nor did they have to cut a mast because these events would have spelled almost certain disaster. St Elmo's fire is a real electrical phenomenon known to mariners that foreshadows a nearby lightning strike. Pigs are considered bad luck on ships, to the point where many modern mariners refuse to even refer to the animals by name while at sea, although it's unclear to me if this superstition dates as far back as the 1720s.

Chapter 32 ✦ Aching Gums

Le Dromedaire was becalmed during her passage and they began running out of food and water. Rationing was instated and De Clieu famously shared his water ration with his coffee plant. Men might have contracted scurvy from lack of Vitamin C in circumstances like these. The causes were unknown in those days, although many mariners thought it caused by bad airs far out to sea and thought land to be the cure. The Davis quadrant would have been used on the ships that De Clieu sailed on. Smearing a load of hairy feces under a ship's hull was an actual last-ditch method of plugging leaks in this era. I did not find any evidence of shark fishing or crew members' deaths during the voyage.

CHAPTER 33 ❦ SKELETON CREW

The graphic description of scurvy symptoms is based on medical fact. De Clieu and *Le Dromedaire* had no role in Cassard's treasure to my knowledge.

CHAPTER 34 ❦ MOUNT HILLABEE

I found no record of which land *Le Dromedaire* first encountered, but it was surely a joyous sight for the crew and they likely would've made landfall to replenish their exhausted supplies. Given that Britain and France were not at war at this time, they might had even bought supplies from a place like Barbados.

Suddenly rehydrating a severely dehydrated person can cause painful cramps, sickness and even medical complications. Skilled mariners of this era like De Clieu were experts with celestial navigation—finding directions based on the stars. The Frapin family have been expert wine and cognac makers since 1270 and the 1665 Rabelais was one of their finest vintages.

CHAPTER 35 ❦ MARTINIQUE

Martinique and the Antilles have many treacherous reefs around them and the Banc de Boucher reef sits in the bay just off Fort de France. The Plissoneau family were wealthy planters on Martinique at this time.

Chapter 36 ❈ Paperwork and Mosquitoes

Ships were often careened (hauled up on a beach) for repairs and *Le Dromedaire* might well have needed some after her passage with the storms. Both Morne Gernier and Morne Tartenson loom above Fort de France. Comte Blénac governed Martinique for most of the years from 1677 to 1696 and helped develop the island's defenses significantly. Blénac also ruled that male mulattos (mixed race children of white slave masters and African slaves) were to be free upon age 20 and females on age 15. De Clieu would likely have needed some time to recover from his arduous journey. Savane Park existed at this time around Fort de France.

Chapter 37 ❈ Barging

Martinique during this time was not simply an island of rich whites and enslaved blacks, although this was the predominant dynamic. There were also indentured whites. There were free blacks and so-called mulattos of mixed race—both free and enslaved. No free blacks or mixed race individuals were sugar barons to my knowledge, but some might have risen to Jaffe's level and owned their own slaves. Slave culture on Martinique was known to be particularly brutal, where slaves were forced to serve as the executioners of their own friends for petty infractions.

Chapter 38 ❈ Two Deaths

I found no evidence that De Clieu ever owned slaves, although I think it likely given that he had a small plantation, so the scene with Pierre is fiction. Place Bertin was a central square in Saint Pierre. Laudanum is a powerful tincture of alcohol and opium that was beginning to see widespread use in this era.

Chapter 39 ✦ Epilogue : Coffee Abounds

The epilogue is the only chapter that is entirely based on documented sources (minus the part about Pierre). De Clieu gave the coffee seeds away, became a ship's captain, and met King Louis XV. He lived to be 88 years old at a time when average lifespans were below 30, dying shortly after his letter was published in the *Année Literaire*. It felt fitting to end the book with the same line De Clieu uses to end his famous letter to Le Année Literaire, *"I have the honor of being DE CLIEU."*

Author's Note

If you encounter any grammatical, spelling or historical errors in this book that should be corrected in future editions, please email me at dave@coffeesmuggler.com and you have my thanks!

Please visit www.dave-holman.com to join the author's newsletter, read updates, and join the conversation!

ORIGINAL 1774 ARTICLE
PUBLISHED BY DE CLIEU
IN *L'ANNÉE LITERAIRE*

Author's Note: On the following pages are both the English translation and original French of the only primary source I encountered written by Gabriel De Clieu. Ukers used this letter as one of the sources for his account and many subsequent authors seem to summarize Ukers.

In this letter, an old and indignant De Clieu rebuts a published assertion that Coffee came first to Cayenne and tells his story of how it came from the King's garden. Thanks to my French-American friend Emilie Bartels for helping with this translation.

Historians give the possible dates of 1720 and 1723 for De Clieu's introduction of coffee to Martinique. However, because of this letter, I consider it unlikely that De Clieu could have brought coffee to the Americas in 1720. De Clieu says he was an infantry captain on Martinique in 1720. The Atlantic crossing in ships of the day could take anywhere from one to three months, with an average of about two. Once he arrived in France in 1720, De Clieu spent "a long time" trying to get a plant, and then eventually sailed back to Martinique after "18 to 20 months." Therefore I think 1723 is the most likely date.

Letter from Mr de Clieu,
former ship Captain, former Governor of Guadeloupe,
Cross of the Royal Military Order of Saint Louis,
author of these sheets:

I was greatly surprised, sir, to read, in one of this year's sheets (N° 24 or Tome V, page 282, year 1774 tome VI) a letter regarding an article about coffee.

The anonymous author of this letter assures that it is wrong that the coffee we cultivate in the American islands, comes from the trees in the King's Garden. I was in 1720, Captain of Infantry in Martinique. Personal business called me back in France the same year—but, more busy with public wellness rather than my own interests, without being discouraged by the little success of the forty years attempts to introduce and naturalize Coffee on our islands, I took further steps to obtain a foot in the King's garden. They remained unsuccessful for a long time. I kept trying several times without being discouraged—at last success crowned my confidence. I received some [coffee] from Mr. Chirac, first doctor of the King. He could not refuse this shrub to the repeated requests of a Noble Lady, which influence I used with him. It is unnecessary to get into details on the infinite care I had to give this delicate plant during the long sail, and the difficulty of saving it from a man's hands, jealous of the happiness I was going to taste by taking the coffee plant from me, tore a branch. I could not help myself to say that water became rare on the ship I was on and was distributed sparingly to everyone, I shared with my dear plant the little I received.

I had no sooner landed in Martinique, then I planted, in a suitable and prepared land, this precious shrub that became more important to me because of all the dangers that I encountered and by the cares it had cost me: after 18 to 20 months, I distributed/shared to Religious Houses and several inhabitants who knew the price of this production and sensed how much it would increase their wealth. It spread little by little. I kept distributing/sharing the fruits of my young plant which grew under the shadow of the "common father." Guadeloupe and Santo Domingo were soon abundantly filled. As for the island of Cayenne, that the anonymous pretends it has been the warehouse/storage for the Coffee from Moka, which was planted in the French Windward Isles Colonies, is what we should keep in mind. Cayenne's inhabitants were suspected, and maybe we blamed them for no reason (Mr. de Jussieu pretends justifying this reproach to the Cayenne's inhabitants in his Memoirs on Coffee inserted in a collection of the Science Academy, year 1713 and quoted in the COFFEE article of the Encyclopedia. But it does not change the truth about my anecdote and I prevent an objection of the anonymous) to take the jealous precaution of drying their coffee and even put it in an oven, or dip it in boiling water to dry out the germ, so it would prevent the multiplication of this commodity elsewhere, which would denied them a substantial income. Mr. de Chevalier de Feuquières General de Martinique, asked me about two dozen coffee grains, he sent them to Mr d'Orvilliers Governor of Cayenne, and asked him with a laugh, to advise the growers and farmers to spare themselves the unnecessary care, since we had coffee of our own, which was easy to judge from the inspection of the grains we showed him.

This new production multiplied everywhere. But what made it faster in Martinique, is the mortality that struck the cocoa trees with no exception, disaster that some people attributed to the eruption of the island's volcano on which a new mouth opened, the others to the heavy and constant rain that lasted for more than 2 months. Anyway, those we call the Petits Habitans [the little inhabitants], among five to six thousands are definitely deprived of territorial commodity, the only one they had to exchange with France, and found their resources in growing coffee, that they would grow exclusively with success that surpassed their loss. Within three years, the island was covered with as many coffee trees as cocoa trees. There you have it, sir, the real story of the introduction of coffee in the Windward Isles, it is an unlimited source of wealth for four-fifths of their inhabitants. But without success they would have grown this important part of trading without the known protection granted by the Count of Maurepas. I made this enlightened minister, who honored me with his kindness, realize how much the trade would be good for France. Mr de Maurepas, who always had the public best interest, gave it preferential treatment, in spite of the best effort of the Compagnie des Indes, which protested as long as they could, against the introduction of this new production in France; he kept on protecting this branch of trade, which owes him the flourishing state, we are in today. This minister, I dare to say, will if it comes to it, vouch for the veracity of these facts.

Upon my return in France in 1749, I was introduced to the King by Mr Rouillé, then Minister of the Navy, as an Officer to whom the State, the Trade and the Americans owed him the plantation of coffee in the colonies. Every Créol in Paris would testify to the truth of the facts and all the people named in this letter. If it becomes necessary to quote some authority figures to back me up, I will find them. Mister Valmont de Bomare, in his dictionary of Natural History, said that the French islands owed their Coffee to me. Mr le Brun, lawyer, took upon himself to write to the Naturalist, to know who told him that, to what Mr Bomare answered him that he got it from Mr Thibauld de Chavalon, former Intendant of Cayenne, in his book that he published in 1763, entitled "Voyage à la Martinique" [A journey to Martinique, page 122]. If Cayenne were like the anonymous pretends, the Moka coffee stores that were brought to the French Windward Isles, M. de Chavalon would have known and would not recognize me as the one who naturalized in our islands this precious production for the trade and which also fabulously increased the sugar production. Could you please, sir, put this letter on the front page of your next sheets to be published.

I have the honour of being, DE CLIEU.

Lettre de M. de Clieu,
Ancien Capitaine de Vaisseaux, Ancien gouveneur de la Guadeloupe, & Grand'Croix de l'Ordre Royal & Militaire de Saint Louis à l'auteur de ces feuilles:

J'ai été fort furpris, Monfieur, de lire, dans une de vos feuilles des cet année * (N° 24 ou Tome V, pag 282. Anne 1774 tome vi) une lettre fur un article concernant le Café. L'auteur anonym de cette lettre affure qu'il ést faux que les Cafés que l'on cultive dans les isles de l'Amérique, proviennent des arbres qui font au jardin du Roi. J'étois en 1720 Capitaine d'Infanterie à Martinique. Des affaires personnelles me rappellèrent en France dans la même année. Mais, plus occupé du bien public que de mes propres intérêtsm fans être découragé par le peu de succès des tentatives qu'on avoit faites depuis quarante ans pour introduire & naturalifer le Café dans nos isles, je fis de nouvelles démarches pour en obtenir un pied au jardin du Roi: elles furent long-temps infructueuses. Je revins plufieurs fois à la charge fans me rebutér; enfin, la réuffite couronna ma confiance. J'en eus l'oblication à M: de Chirac, premier Médecin du Roi; il ne put refufer cet arbuste aux instances réitérées d'une Dame de Qualité, dont j'employai le crédit auprès de lui. Il est inutile d'entrer dans le détail des foins infinis qu'il me fallut donner à cette plante délicate pendant une longue traverfée, & de la peine que j'eus à la fauver des mains d'un homme, baffement jaloux du bonheur que j'allois goûter d'être utile à m'enlever ce pied de Café, en arracha una branche: je ne puis cependant m'empêcher de dire que l'eau devenant rare dans le vaisseau qui me portoit & n'étant distribuée à chacun qu'avec mefure, je partageai avec ma plante chérie le peu qu'on m'en donna.

Je fus à peine débarqué à la Martinique, que je plantai, dans un terrein convenable & préparé, cet arbuste précieux qui m'étoit devenu encore plus cher par les dangers qu'il avoit courus, & par les foins qu'il m'avoit coûtés: au bout de 18 ou 20 mois, j'eus en furent distribuées aux Maisons Religieuses & à divers habitans qui connoissoient le prix de cette production, & pressentoient combien elle devoit les enrichir; elle s'étendit de proche en proche; je continuai à distribuir les fruits des jeunes plantes qui croissoient à l'ombre de pére commun. La Guadeloupe & Saint Domingue en furent bientôt elles-mêmes abondamment pourvues. Quant à l'isle de Cayenne, que l'anonyme prétend avoir été l'entrepot de Café originaire de Moka, qui a été planté dans les Colonies Francoises le vent, voici à quoi il faut s'en tenir. Les habitans de Cayenne étoient foupçonnés, & on leur reprochoit peut-être fans fondement, * (* M. de Jussieu prétend justifier de ce reproche les habitans de Cayenne dans son Mémoire sur le Café, inséré dans le Recueil de l'Académie des Sciences, année 1713, & cité dans l'Encyclopédie, Article CAFÉ. Mais cela ne fait rien à la vérité de mon anecdote, & je préviens par-là une objection de l'Anonyme.) de prendre la précaution jalouse de passerleur Café à l'étuve & même aufour, ou de le tremper dans l'eau bouillantepour en dessécher le germe, afin d'empêcher qu'en multipliant cette denrée ailleurs, on ne les privât d'un revenu considérable. M de Chevalier de Feuquières Général de la Martinique, m'ayant demandé anviron deux douzaines de grains de Café, il les envoya à M. d'Orvilliers Gouverneur de Cayenne, & le pria, enriant, de confeiller aux cultivateurs de s'épargner déformais un soin inutil, puisque nous avions du Café de notre crû; ce qu'il étoit facile de juger à l'inspection des grains frais qu'il leur presentoit.

Cette nouvelle production se multiplioit par-tout. Mais ce qui rendit ses progrès plus rapides à la Martinique, ce fut la mortalité qui frappa tous les Cacaotiers * (*Je préfere le terme de Cacaotier à celui de Cacoyer qui est difficile à prononcer, & j'aime mieux fuivre l'analogie : Coco, Coco-tier, Bigarreau, Bigarreautier, &c.) fans exception, désastre que les una attribuèrent à l'éruption du volcan de l'Isle oú il s'ouvrit alors une nouvelle bouche, les autres aux pluies abondantes & continuelles qui durèrent plus de deux mois. Quoi qu'il en soit ce qu'on appelle les Petits Habitans, au nombre de cinq à fix mille abfolument dépourvus par-là d'une denrée territoriale, presque la feule qu'ils eussant à échanger contre celles de France, ne trouvèrent de ressource que dans la culture du Café, à laquelle ils fe livrèrent exclusivement avec un fuccès qui passa leurs espérances, & qui répara bientôt leurs partes. L'isle fe trouva couverte en trois ans d'autant de millions de Cafiers qu'elle en avoit eu de Cacaotiers. Voila, Monsieur, la vraie marche de l'introduction du Café dans les isles sous le vent; c'est una source inépuisable de richesse pour les quatre cinquièmes de leurs habitans. Mais inutilment auroiton cultivé cette branche importante de commerce fans la protection signalée que lui accorda M. le Comte de Maurepas. Je sis sentir à ce Ministre éclairé, qui m'honoroit de ses bontés, combien ce commerce seroit avantageux à la France. M. le Comte de Maurepas, toujours occupé du bien public, le favorisa, malgré les efforts de la Compagnie des Indes qui s'opposa, le plus long-temps qu'elle put, à l'introduction de cette production nouvelle en France; il a continué de protéger cette branche de commerce, qui lui doir l'état florissant dont elle jouit aujourd'hui. Ce Ministre, j'ose le dire, seroit, s'il le salloit garant de la vérité de ces faits.

A mon retour en France en 1749, je fus préfenté au Roi par M. Rouillé, alors Ministre de la Marine, comme un Officerà qui l'Etat, le Commerce & les Amériquains étoient redevables de la plantation du Café dans les Colonies. Tout ce qu'il y a de Créoles à Paris attesteront le vérité de ce fait & de tous ceux que j'annonce dans cette Lettre. S'il étoit nécessaire de citer des autorités pour appuyer mon assertion j'en trouverois. M. Valmont de Bomare, dans don Dictionnaire d'Histoire Naturelle, dit que c'est à moi que les Isles Francoises doivent le Café. M. le Brun, Avocat, s'est chargé d'érire à ce scavant Naturaliste, pour scavoir d'aprés qui il avoit cité ce fait. M de Bomare lui a répondu que c'étoit d'après M. Thibauld de Chanvalon, ancien Intendant de Cayenne, dans l'Ouvrage qu'il a donne au public en 1763, intitulé Voyage à la Martinique (page 122). Si Caynne eût été, comme le prétend l'Anonyme, l'entrepôt de Café de Moka qui a été apporté dans les Isles Francoises sous le vent, M. de Chanvalon l'auroit sçu, & ne me reconnoîtroit pas comme celui qui a naturalisé dans nos Isles cette production précieuse pour le Commerce, & qui a augmenté fi prodigieusement le débit du fucre. Je sous prie, Monsieur, d'inférer cette Lettre dans le premier (number) qui patroîta de vos Feuilles.

J'ai l'honneur d'être, &c, DE CLIEU.

BIBLIOGRAPHY

I thought about presenting all the dozens of books, periodicals, papers, and online sources I consulted over five years of research in MLA format and have erred against it. I'll take the liberty entitled to historical fiction authors and only present you with my favorite sources.

I proudly declare that Wikipedia is my favorite starting point for information and research. I consulted hundreds of Wikipedia entries for this book and felt so indebted to this source that I donated to the Wikipedia Foundation and urge you to do the same. Wikipedia's lists of sources provide fantastic links to more specific research and books.

William Ukers' mammoth tome *All About Coffee* formed a pillar for *Coffee Smuggler,* and provided me with more anecdotes and story lines than any other source. Most of the other coffee books I read heap well-deserved praises on Ukers and his exhaustively researched coffee Bible. If you're a bona-fide coffee nut, reading *All About Coffee*'s 817 pages, cover to cover, will be a rare badge of honor. It will enlighten your brewing and sipping ever after.

Many history books I consulted were dry (especially the ones I read about 1700s Paris and France, for some reason), but some brought literary spray bursting over the bow. Here are a few favorites that either provided helpful information about this story or context for the places and time period:

A History of the World in Six Glasses by Tom Standage

Coffee: A Dark History by Antony Wild

Fire Mountain: How one man survived the world's worst volcanic disaster by Peter Morgan

La Catastrophe: The Eruption of Mount Pelée, the Worst Disaster of the 20th Century by Alwyn Scarth

Pirates and Buccaneers by Robert Larranaga

Pirate Hunter by Richard Zacks

The Coffee Trader by David Liss

The Devil's Cup by Stewart Lee Allen

The Explorations of Captain James Cook in the Pacific edited by Grenfell Price

The Sugar Barons: Family, Corruption, Empire, and War in the West Indies by Matthew Parker

Uncommon Grounds by Mark Pendergast

ABOUT THE AUTHOR

Dave Holman lives in Maine with his wife Rommy, cat Patas and four dwarf goats: Whoopie Pie, Aurora, Canela, and Silly Willy. He attended Carleton College and co-founded the Spitting Llama Bookstore and Outfitter while living in Bolivia. Dave co-authored Youth Renewing the Countryside in 2009. He holds an MBA and has worked for non-profit organizations, including Safe Passage. He currently works full time at Bowdoin College and writes most mornings thanks in large part to the plant De Clieu smuggled to Martinique.

Website:
www.dave-holman.com

Join Dave's mailing list for inside updates and offers:
http://eepurl.com/09_ib